WHEN IS A MAN

WHEN IS A MAN

a novel

AARON SHEPARD

BRINDLE
& GLASS

Brindle & Glass Publishing Ltd.
brindleandglass.com

LIBRARY AND ARCHIVES CANADA CATALOGUING IN PUBLICATION
Shepard, Aaron, 1973–, author
When is a man / Aaron Shepard.

Issued in print and electronic formats.
ISBN 978-1-927366-26-4

I. Title.

PS8637.H4875W44 2014   C813'.6   C2013-906015-4

Editor: John Gould
Proofreader: Heather Sangster, Strong Finish
Design and cover illustration: Pete Kohut
Author photo: Alana McArthur

Brindle & Glass is pleased to acknowledge the financial support for its publishing
program from the Government of Canada through the Canada Book Fund, Canada
Council for the Arts, and the Province of British Columbia through the British
Columbia Arts Council and the Book Publishing Tax Credit.

The interior pages of this book have been printed on 30% post-consumer
recycled paper, processed chlorine free, and printed with vegetable-based inks.

1 2 3 4 5 18 17 16 15 14

PRINTED IN CANADA

For Alana

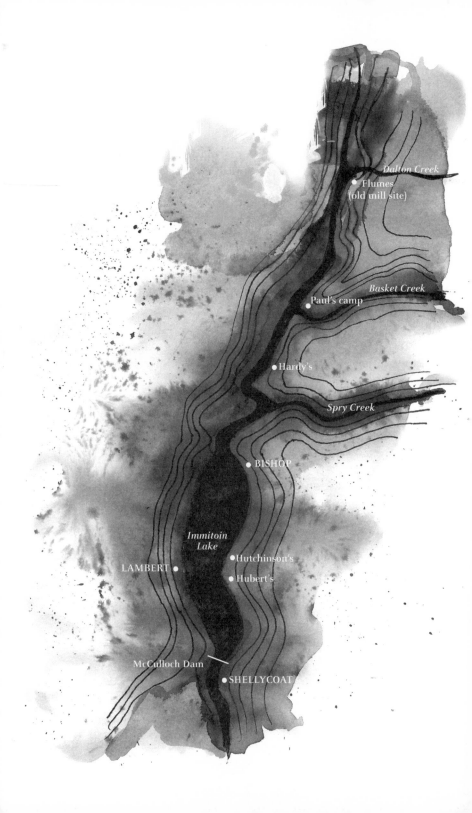

Dalton Creek

Flumes
(old mill site)

Basket Creek

Paul's camp

Hardy's

Spry Creek

BISHOP

*Immitoin
Lake*

Hutchinson's

LAMBERT

Hubert's

McCulloch Dam

SHELLYCOAT

It is the third commonness with light and air,
A curriculum, a vigor, a local abstraction . . .
Call it, one more, a river, an unnamed flowing,

Space-filled, reflecting the seasons, the folk-lore
Of each of the senses; call it, again and again,
The river that flows nowhere, like a sea.

—Wallace Stevens,
"The River of Rivers in Connecticut"

ARCHAEOLOGY

I

Paul slammed on the brakes. Duffle bags, books, and spare boots leaped from the back seat, struck doors and windows, then settled in a heap. Ahead of him, the brake lights of Tanner's trailer flashed, the wheels kicking up dust. The scene in front of him had appeared out of nowhere, from around a blind corner. Emergency vehicles crowded each shoulder of the logging road, hazard lights blinking. Cops, ambulance attendants, and Search and Rescue volunteers hefted tools, cases, and cameras, striding from task to task with tight-lipped purpose. On the far side of the gauntlet, a stocky RCMP constable waved through three logging trucks headed in the opposite direction with their loads of timber. They inched past, the drivers flashing flinty scowls at the cop. Long after they were gone, their terse, irritated chatter crackled through Paul's CB radio.

He'd just been imagining the riverbank as a good place to sleep, sunny and warm in the August heat, open to the sky and free of the oppressively dark forest on the other side of the road. He'd been following Tanner's truck and its swaying trailer for more than an hour. They'd left the town of Shellycoat in the early morning, driven north past the McCulloch Dam and along Immitoin Lake until they'd reached the upper end of the vast reservoir. There, a rusted white sign peppered with bullet holes named the collection of ruined buildings and abandoned yards Bishop, Unincorporated. They sped past the boarded-up remains of a community hall and an old general store, the occasional log house or plywood-sheltered mobile home tucked between copses of second-growth pine and power line right-of-ways. Along the lakeside, incongruous modern summer cottages—cubes of aluminum siding, trapezoidal windows—perched above the rocky shoreline, elevated by wood stilts or concrete pillars. As the road led them to the Immitoin River, the cottages became less frequent and more rustic. From there—if not for the confusion of men and vehicles that suddenly blocked their way—it would have been less than an hour to the Basket Creek recreation site, where he would spend the next forty days alone.

He felt a nagging, physical urgency, the kind that scattered most clear thoughts and deadened curiosity. But even beyond the press of his bladder, the slight dampness in his incontinence pad, and the ache above the pubic bone where the dirt road pounded the scars of his surgery, he was desperate to keep going. Hell-bent on the solitude Tanner had promised him, and deeply uneasy, as though this scene, whatever was happening here, had the power to derail him, throw everything off.

Yesterday he'd left Vancouver, where he'd lived all his life and where, for the last several months, he'd been a medical rarity in the offices of the Prostate Centre. At the first visit, the receptionists had assumed he was there to drop off his father. After that, he sensed a change in the looks the two young women gave him, the spiralling away of possible attractions, connections. He was only thirty-three.

The constable signalled again and Tanner's truck crept forward. His friend rolled down his window and Paul did the same.

"Cliff!" Tanner called to the officer. "What's it this time? Another rafting accident?"

The constable squinted at him, then walked over. He had white and grey sideburns and a walrus moustache, a body threatening to become portly. "I dunno yet. It's not pleasant." He grimaced slightly, then gave Tanner a brief smile and patted the trailer with a meaty hand. "Time to count the fish again?"

Tanner jerked his thumb back toward Paul's vehicle. "Not me this year. I got him. Old buddy of mine, Paul Rasmussen."

The cop gave Paul a curt wave, which Paul returned, mentally assessing the amount of moisture in his underpants. Tanner opened his door and unfolded himself to stand on the road, lanky and bearded, every inch a fisheries biologist in his long-sleeved plaid shirt. They glanced Paul's way, either talking about him or expecting him to join them. He rolled up his window and drummed an agitated rhythm on his thighs. His mind curled around the ache of his perineum and bladder, and he tried a few clenching Kegel exercises to distract himself.

To his left, a short driveway sloped from the road down through the trees to the river. A mossy and weather-beaten house sat along the bank, its deck overlooking a broad eddy. Beyond the gently stirring pool, the main current bucked and swirled past boulders and gravel bars, the water glinting in the sun. Along the shore, two RCMP were stringing yellow tape between two poplars that flanked the eddy, while others stood transfixed by whatever was in the water. Just as Paul considered slipping out through the passenger door and seeking the privacy of the woods, two attendants removed a gurney from the ambulance. Things would turn ugly soon. Paul turned up the CB radio and found a station that played nothing but static, cranking the volume to keep the world out. There wasn't much else in his vehicle to distract him, no music, his laptop emptied of all his old research files. Most of his things were buried in storage. This was part of the plan, to strip himself down to the essentials, see what these might be.

He remembered his last really good August, two years ago, when he'd lived at his parents' summer cabin on Salt Spring Island. He'd cobbled together lesson plans for an introductory

undergrad course in archaeology, which wasn't his specialty—
just another hoop to jump until his doctorate. He'd stretched
on the dock on St. Mary Lake with a beer in one hand and
Archaeological Theory in the other and, while his parents
lazily bickered nearby, re-learned all he'd forgotten from his
own first year at university. Sometimes he would plunge off the
dock and down, until he found a mind-numbing shock of cold
beneath the pondy surface. He would rise, towel himself dry,
and continue his list of course objectives and prescribed learning outcomes, or concoct PowerPoint presentations, slideshows
of elated field researchers gathered on riverbanks to excavate
an Adena burial mound or a Salish midden. Meanwhile he was
quite content to let his dissertation, his ethnographic study, sit
cooling on the backburner. The project seemed both ambitious
and foolproof, as most ideas do at their inception. He'd always
been good at beginnings, if nothing else. Most of his happiest
moments were beginnings.

Meanwhile, on the banks of the Immitoin, the wall of police
and rescue personnel stirred. Some of the men turned from
the water and wandered a few paces up the driveway or leaned
against the woodshed adjacent to the houses, their faces pale,
slack, and grim. He couldn't hear anything over the radio static,
but the bleakness of their expressions, so at odds with the sunshine, infected Paul with a type of hysteria, and he thought he
might suddenly grin or even giggle.

On the deck, an old man had appeared, bare-chested beneath
an unbuttoned flannel work shirt, pacing like a trapped animal,
gesturing erratically. A young, smooth-shaven policeman followed him around with a notebook in hand. Down in the water,
two SAR volunteers in neoprene wetsuits, hip-deep, dragged
something between them. The clutch of officers parted, and
now Paul could see the grey, bloated flesh. The body belonged
to someone much shorter than Paul. A child or adolescent—no,

the shoulders were too broad, the torso and belly massive. The corpse's clothing, a green T-shirt, khaki pants, and blue briefs, had been swept aside to reveal the battered, discoloured figure of an obese man. Beneath a shock of coarse white hair rusted with what might have been clay or blood, the face was pallid and bulging, amphibious. Half-man, half-salamander—a missing link.

A spasm of nausea clutched Paul's throat just as a sudden warmth and dampness hit his pad, and he unbuckled his seatbelt and threw open the door. Tanner and the cop turned toward him, eyebrows raised, and he managed a bizarre, cheerful wave before he bolted into the trees.

~

Yesterday, Paul had begun his drive from the coast, heading eastward from the Fraser Valley onto the Hope-Princeton highway and then beyond. He navigated the switchbacks and winding passes slowly and cautiously. The approach was queasily intimate, uterine. The landscape held the vehicle close to itself, and Paul was drawn forward and upward by the loops and convulsions of the rivers and mountains.

He shouldn't have been driving. "It's a little early in your convalescence for such a road trip," his doctor had said. "Sitting for too long, getting jarred around." Nearly every gas station became a pit stop. Once he pulled over along the beetle-ravaged clear cuts above Princeton, where the hillsides were stripped bare, and tossed a damp incontinence pad into a slash pile. At the edge of a vineyard outside Keremeos, he leaned against a fence and massaged his perineum while he dribbled urine into the sagebrush and wiped frustrated tears from his cheeks. Each stop was a battle between churning, sobbing brain and spastic detrusor muscle that clenched in search of the prostate gland. The body alien to its damaged self, the mind shamed by passing traffic, quick stares.

He'd been released from the hospital in late June and e-mailed the department of anthropology and his supervisor, Dr. Elias Tamba. He told them what they needed to know, or in Dr. Tamba's case what he already knew: the only thing in worse shape than Paul's health was his dissertation. Nor would he come back to teach in the fall. He spent some time with his parents, who had driven him to the hospital and then stayed for his first difficult night of intravenous drips, drain tubes, and morphine. His mother, who'd worked as a receptionist in a doctor's office for many years, arranged his apartment to make it more comfortable for him, and bought what she felt would be the best foods. She was much calmer about the whole thing than the two men. His father, a civil engineer, was close to retirement and well past the age at which the prostate ceases to be an abstract idea—Paul knew his father had been tested several times. He acted puzzled and guilty, as though he believed that through some strange karma or bad thought he'd passed on his own inevitable fate to his son.

Paul's ex-girlfriend, Christine, showed up to play nursemaid, and this had been hard. She provided sympathy, a voice, but said nothing about her own life, how her research was going, if she'd fallen in love again. They'd barely spoken in months. He suspected she might be secretly dating Dr. Tamba. She'd cut her hair and her body looked fit and toned, as though she were no longer losing sleep over her thesis or career and had started rock climbing again, her skin radiant with success or sex. All this hinted at the happiness she hid from him as he lay on the couch with his catheter and collection bag.

He'd phoned Tanner two weeks after coming home from the hospital. They'd been friends since an undergrad biology class several years earlier but had only spoken a few times since Tanner had taken work as a fisheries biologist. Paul had been caught up in research and teaching, while Tanner started a new life in the Immitoin Valley. The last time they'd talked had been after Paul's trip to Sweden, the year before his surgery. Tanner had moved in with Beth, a girl from Kitsilano he'd met when he and Paul were roommates. They'd bought a house on two acres outside Shellycoat. He had steady work, long-term contracts with Monashee Power, a hydroelectric company, and the local Streamkeepers Association. But—the weirdest change of all—Tanner had just become the chairman of Shellycoat's new film festival. Had Paul heard of it?

"Of course not," Paul had said, sighing into the phone.

"Set to run in November. I'm slammed." Dozens of films to screen before the final selections, volunteers to organize. "And meanwhile, this contract buries me in the boonies for two straight months, starting in August. August! Like, *fuck me*, you know? What's up with you?"

Paul offered up some vague details about the cancer, and his decision to abandon both his PHD and his teaching. He and Tanner were college buddies in the truest sense, only comfortable talking about sexual conquests or personal disasters that were sort of funny in retrospect—like Sweden, or Naomi, or even Christine. Anything else was off-limits.

"So you won't be well enough to teach by September?" Tanner asked.

"I could, technically, I guess. Sure. It's just . . ."

Tanner didn't probe too deep. He phoned Paul back a couple of hours later to offer him a job. "It's the perfect gig," he said. "You need some down time, I can tell. Time to reflect." Paul almost snorted: reflect. That didn't sound like his old friend. It sounded like Beth, who had always struck him as the flaky type. Still, Tanner wasn't entirely wrong.

The work was easy, Tanner told him. Live beside Basket Creek where it meets the Immitoin River and count the bull trout trapped in a set of weirs each night. Measure, weigh and tag 'em, let 'em go, write it in a notebook. Done.

Eight hours after leaving the coast, Paul reached a junction where the main highway continued east, toward Christina Lake and over the Paulson Summit to the West Kootenays, while the smaller highway cut north, following the Immitoin to Shellycoat. The sun was low on the horizon, filtered through the smoke of distant forest fires, and the light flickered orange and pink across the turbulent, shifting waters. He arrived in Shellycoat at sunset, greeted first by the towering stacks of a pulp mill that seemed too quiet and empty, even for this time of day. Only a handful of trucks sat in the parking lot, and lumber lay stacked and forgotten in the far corner of the yard. He passed a row of service stations, an industrial yard full of yellow highway maintenance trucks, an A&W, and then arrived in what he took for downtown—a handful of streets and avenues, the main street lined with mom-and-pop stores, a saloon-styled bookstore, a Mexican-themed coffee shop. Tanner had found him a room at a hotel instead of offering a spare bed or couch at his place, though Paul would have said no anyway. After that drive, the last things he wanted were questions, curious stares, and sympathy. He was haggard and wasted, especially between the legs, and was ready for an Epsom salts bath and some television.

He used to enjoy road trips, rolling exhausted into places he'd never been. Sparked by the unfamiliar, his mind would organize people and things into broad categories, even consider possible ethnographic studies, like the working lives and relationships of the female flaggers who controlled traffic at highway construction sites. Once, he would have been fascinated by the grab-bag of characters who wove their way between the hand-painted signboards that cluttered Shellycoat's sidewalks: forestry workers covered in a film of sawdust and chainsaw oil, unabashedly filthy as they sauntered into the grocery store; the dreadlocked and sandalled, filthy in their own way; tourists dragging their children behind them and gazing through the windows of closed galleries, trinket shops, and outdoor equipment stores. A dozen questions flashed through Paul's mind, an assortment of connections and possibilities presented themselves—ethnographies of resource-based communities, tourist economies—and faded. Something inside him had been snipped out, excised.

In the brown-curtained hotel room, he flicked through television stations and finally settled on the local weather network. He left the station on and ran a bath. Immersed, he stirred the water and contemplated, as he had hundreds of times in the last few weeks, his body invaded and altered.

He still resembled himself. He'd undergone no chemotherapy or radiation, so the retreat of his black curls from his forehead was natural, maybe stress-related. The unilateral prostatectomy—the removal of his prostate, including his seminal vesicles—hadn't shocked his body into complete weight loss. In fact, he'd packed on a few pounds from lying on his couch all summer. If not for his paleness, the atrophy of his arm and leg muscles so out of proportion with his expanding gut, someone might have mistaken him for a healthy man. Enough, though, of this timid circumnavigation—a bath always came down to his groin and incision site. All summer he'd carried out the doctor's measures of hygiene, done his Kegel exercises to help with bladder control, cleaned his scars and limp genitals as he might an infected toe.

The echo of sloshing water reminded him that he hadn't stayed in a hotel since Sweden more than a year ago. There was—had been—something erotic about occupying a hotel room alone. Anticipation lingered in the air, like a psychic residue left by the previous guests. No matter how drab, each room hummed—along with the bad wiring, dodgy light fixtures, and haunted air ducts—with a promise that his surroundings were a type of moral *tabula rasa*. In Skinnskatteberg, he'd heard a woman come into his room while he showered, a cleaning lady there to drop off fresh linens and towels. Her voice

("Housekeeping? Sir?") carried the unmistakable inflections of someone young and new to the job, a teenager or immigrant. As he stood under the torrent of water, he'd imagined her sitting on the corner of his bed, waiting . . .

He heard laughter, an uncontrolled hacking cough from the streets below, men and women spilling in and out of a pub, the twin slam of truck doors. There should have been a small thrill in this, like so many times before, listening to the voices of strangers drift through the clouded glass of a bathroom window. The unknown night, the unknown town. The only real possibilities in life lay in the erotic. Something he'd said once, and it frightened him now, because he still believed it.

~

In the morning, he met Tanner in front of the hotel. Because they'd spoken on the phone—and, Paul believed, because men did not readily acknowledge the passage of time—they greeted each other with a brief handshake, the same grins of two years ago. Still, it must have shocked Tanner—Paul thought he caught a startled look, quickly veiled—to see his pasty skin, his emaciated arms and shoulders.

"So," Tanner said. He grinned through a hastily groomed reddish beard. "What kind of stories you got for me?"

"Stories?" Paul licked his lips. "Oh—well, good drive here. Feel fine."

"Yeah?" Tanner kept nodding, eyebrows raised. "Whole new outlook on things, I imagine. Second chance at life and all that."

"I guess. I pee myself sometimes, if that's what you mean."

"Well, that's a start." Tanner pointed up the street. "There's the theatre." He rubbed his hands together. "Man, I'm just—hope you're around for this, it's going to be—Iceland! Did I tell you that? Two films from Iceland. Haven't even seen them yet, but that's the kind of thing I hoped for. First year, and we're already international."

"Great," said Paul. "So, groceries."

"Right. Sure thing."

Paul followed him to the store, where they bought enough supplies to last him a week or so. Then they drove out to a storage unit facility near a gas station just outside of town to pick up the trailer and the materials needed to construct the fish barrier: rebar, a roll of wire fencing, and wood for the upstream and downstream weirs. They loaded the materials, hitched the trailer, and headed out.

The highway ascended gradually toward the monolithic concrete wall of the McCulloch Dam. At the bottom of the spillway, whirlpools foamed and churned against gigantic, jagged boulders, rip-rap enclosed in heavy metal mesh. Past the dam, on the reservoir, a marina docked a few dozen boats, most of them small and rudimentary day-cruisers, although the occasional cabin-cruiser or sailboat towered above them. The marina office itself was old and poorly kept, all chipped paint and rusted metal. On the other side of the highway, unpaved roads disappeared into the hills or led to houses and fenced fields that pastured horses and cattle. Everything became more desolate by degrees, which somehow served to lift Paul's mood. He was withdrawing, and was just beginning to savour this sense of exile when they turned the corner and were met by a cop's raised hand and a crowd of sickened faces.

2

They left the flashing lights and commotion behind and continued on to Basket Creek. Another policeman met them at the top of the narrow side road that led from the main road down to the site. "Almost wrapped up here and I'll let you drive in," he said, then jogged down to a levelled clearing among the trees where a second officer was jimmying open an old truck. Paul and Tanner stood outside and leaned against the trailer, facing the sun.

"Strange place to drown," Tanner said.

"Could be someone else's truck," Paul said quietly.

"No, it's his. The owner wouldn't be far away otherwise."

A few moments passed. "What do you mean, strange?" Paul asked.

"Just strange." Tanner checked his watch. "Riverbank isn't that high, and it's stable. Water's shallow at the edge. No real hazards, unless you're some drunk teenager on an inner tube, or a child. Or stupid." Tanner started to grin, probably on the verge of cracking some joke, but stopped. Paul shuddered, still queasy.

Over an hour passed before the officer decided there was no harm in letting them set up their camp. The vehicle in question, a grey pickup, was pressed against the shrubs at the far edge of the clearing, one wheel sunk in the soft soil and moss. Paul parked and then helped direct Tanner, who backed the trailer into a shady spot beside the remains of a campfire enclosed within an old truck tire rim. They silently unloaded the bundles of wire and rebar, tarps, and wood slats and stacked them on the ground. Wary of straining himself, he took embarrassingly small armfuls. But the two officers ignored them, tramping circles through the woods, and disappearing again toward the river.

Straight ahead of the trailer, obscured by trees except for flashes of silver light, was the Immitoin. To Paul's right, twenty metres beyond a wall of alder, willow, and other bushes, ran Basket Creek, the delicate glassy notes of its running nearly overpowered by the jumbled roar of the larger river. Tall firs and cedars loomed over them, the forest sloping upward past the main road and into the foothills of an unseen mountain range. The sky above the site was a narrow blue eye that winked half-shut whenever the treetops dipped and swayed in the breeze. As he worked, Paul stole glances at the pickup.

They made several trips down the path to Basket Creek, stacking their materials on the gravel flats beside scrub willow and trembling aspen, some fifteen metres from the mouth of the stream. The banks gently sloped to a small pebble beach along a restful pool. As they returned to the trailer for the final haul, a second police car drove into camp, followed by a tow truck. "Why don't you sort our stuff at the creek," Tanner said. "I'll stay, see if they need me."

Paul wandered down the path and then into the trees. He unzipped his jeans, checked inside—he'd thrown his pad and underwear into the woods earlier but felt even more disgusting without their protection. He looked around. So this was now home: where a man had fallen, or possibly thrown himself, into the river and died.

As he finished separating the bundles of fencing wire, he heard the low rumbling of the tow truck driving away. Tanner appeared, carrying two sets of neoprene chest waders. They would walk part of the stream before building the fence. Paul, following Tanner's example, took off his shoes and pulled on the waders, the coarse, tacky material rubbing against his leg hairs. "Hope I got your measurements right," Tanner said. "It's like you got both skinnier and fatter." Tanner, Paul grudgingly admitted, had never looked fitter or more comfortable in his own skin.

There were no dead fish anywhere. Paul had anticipated, with a kind of morbid satisfaction, a scattering of carcasses on the banks, the bodies accumulating, grey, eyeless flesh piling up against the fence until he was ankle-deep in the rot. For the next forty days, whenever he stepped out of the trailer, he would face a siege of scavengers: grizzly and black bears, crows and ravens, coyotes, a type of lush destruction. On the coast years ago, he'd seen a river that roiled with sockeye salmon and had been surprised to see even innocent-looking birds, dippers, sparrows, and wrens, pluck the eyes and bits of innards from the carcasses draped over rocks and logs, fats, oils, and proteins fed to the forest by the smallest mouths, the most innocuous scat.

He'd forgotten that trout were not salmon and didn't die after they spawned. He admitted as much to Tanner. "The journey'll do some in," Tanner said. "There were salmon once, before the McCulloch Dam and the rest. Four species of them." They'd travelled from the Pacific Ocean, up the Columbia River, across three States and then north, to spawn in the Columbia's many tributaries. "Pioneers and First Nations used to joke about walking across the river on the backs of salmon. Although I've heard the same joke about different rivers, so who knows."

The creek wasn't deep, or all that fast. His waders were fitted with cleated soles for extra grip. Even so, the going was more difficult than he'd anticipated. The water buffeted his shins and knees, while the stones and gravel—round, polished, and slick—gave way beneath his feet. He pulled himself forward, trying to power through the current. Compared with him, Tanner could have been dancing, the way he lifted one foot and then hopped forward, finding solid ground and quieter water, striding with his long limbs past the riffles and treacherous pools. Paul stumbled and struggled along, head down and panting.

The way people negotiated obstacles or incorporated them into their routes: this had been a major theme of Paul's dissertation. A progression of boulders led upstream to where the bridge crossed the logging road, and he imagined that the cocky Tran Minh or the self-effacing Xi Bai, two key participants in his ethnographic study, could have gone from here to the bridge without touching the water, jumping effortlessly from stone to stone. He even imagined his old self capable of doing so. Or maybe not. Despite the hours he'd put in, the rigorous discipline, he was never a real *traceur*. Nor was that supposed to be the point of his research. Still.

For his ethnographic study, he'd placed himself in an informal group of youths and adults who practised parkour on the university grounds, around Kitsilano, and downtown. Parkour, everyone in the group had told him many times—because parkour was easier to summarize than properly explain—was about getting from Point A to Point B as quickly and efficiently as possible, regardless of what stood in the way, using only the body to conquer each barrier. Any man-made object counted as an obstacle. Parkour was both a celebration of architecture, of materials and texture, and a benign war against urban confinement. Walls, stairwells, and turnstiles were meant to corral the body into uniform, pedestrian channels, but parkour changed this by expanding the possibilities. A thin, decorative ledge could become a ladder, a means of travel. A wall of coarse brick or inlaid stone with protruding edges was easier to surmount than vinyl panelling or a stainless steel veneer.

The leader, a whip-thin political science student named Nathan Cook, picked out their routes or found structures where they could spend their sessions honing certain techniques—balances and crawls, leaps and landings, tumbles and rolls, vaults and climbs. Nathan practised parkour for the philosophical aspects as much as the athletics. The youngest mostly wanted to emulate what they'd seen in movies. But even then, obsessed as they were by escalators, rooftops, and terraces, the teenaged traceurs and traceuses (there were three women in the group) were as likely to slip into the same esoteric jargon as their older counterparts. They spoke of reclaiming space, of a new interaction with their urban surroundings. Some called it the art of displacement—a bastardized translation, Paul understood, of the French term *l'art du déplacement*. A park bench, a concrete fountain, a fence: these things stopped being themselves, or only themselves. They also became pathways, blank objects redefined by the body. A psycho-athletic re-envisioning of architectural space.

Which came across as total pretentious gibberish to most people, of course, but for Paul it was pure gold. How else to convince his department, or any source of grant funding, that he was studying something more than social misfits playing Spider-Man?

Shadows flicked past his feet, olive green, brief iridescence. "They're already here," Tanner shouted. "They're staging in the pools." His friend became more animated—crouching low to squint into the riffles and then springing ahead, his feet finding the sure ground among the loose rocks and whirlpools. The bridge and the embankments of the logging road loomed in front of them, but for all of Paul's flailing, he came no closer to it. The weight and play of the water tugged his feet down into the gravel. Worse was the rubbery constraint of his waders, beneath which his jeans had slid off his hips while the legs rode up, so that all the material gathered in goiter-like lumps around his thighs.

Paul: swaddled like a gigantic infant. Hauling himself upstream to stagger on the spawning grounds.

3

Once the sun was down, they returned to the creek, and Paul hung his lantern on a hook screwed into the frame of the measuring station. There was no moon for light, only a glow in the southwest corner of the sky, the bounce of Tanner's headlamp on the water. The stream muttered and gurgled strangely in the dark. Where the current ran slower beside the beach, they'd installed the two box weirs assembled from pre-fab frames and cedar slats, each uncovered and designed with a single opening that faced either upstream or down. From the second weir, the fence ran the width of the creek, held in place by the rebar stakes they'd laboriously pounded into the creekbed.

The measuring station was a simple frame of pine poles and two-by-fours, a square of plywood and a tightly fastened tarp for a roof. A wooden folding table took up most of the space, along with a large plastic cooler in one corner. There weren't many scientific instruments, thankfully nothing complicated or intimidating: a weigh scale, a measuring tape, a waterproof notebook, and plastic bottles marked with millilitre increments and filled with amber-coloured clove oil, a few drops of which had been added to the water inside the cooler to serve as an anesthetic. Another tool looked like a pricing gun at a retail store, loaded with transparent filaments tipped with round, blue plastic ends, each marked with a five-digit number.

"Bring the lantern so you can see what I'm doing." Tanner

stood at the edge of the creek with his headlamp. Dark things thrashed and churned inside the weirs—fish jockeying for position as they tried to continue upstream. Their meaty backs and slender dorsal fins bisected the inky surface.

"Just a handful," said Tanner. "None in the downstream. They're starting to head up now, you see. By the end, it'll be the other way around."

He focused his headlamp onto the middle of the creek, where an unnatural ripple bumped against the wire fence. "He'll be in the weir by morning." He pulled on a thin pair of latex gloves and motioned for Paul to do the same. "Otherwise your hands take the slime off their body, which is bad. This won't take us long," he added. "But you'll get the idea."

Tanner netted one from the upstream trap and held the thrashing prize in front of him as he scrambled up to the station and dropped the trout into the cooler. The fish bucked against the white walls at first but quickly calmed, moving its tail in steady flicks. The smell of clove oil clung to Paul's shirt. A minute passed, and then Tanner nudged the fish and provoked a sluggish reaction. He rolled it on its side. "See how he's all hook-jawed. That's the kipe."

There it was, the cold, nocturnal creature that would be his only company for more than a month: the lean, toothy jaw, the muscular olive-green back, white and reddish spots haloed with blue along its sides, the white-tipped pelvic fins, the belly flushed orange and red. The trout, its face reptilian and mechanical as a plumber's wrench, filled Paul with a quiet despair.

Tanner lifted and cradled the fish over to the table. His friend was deep in his element, almost jubilant with familiarity, muscle memory carrying him easily through each task.

"How it's done," grunted Tanner. In a few smooth motions he jotted the fish's weight on the lined waterproof paper, then held the measuring tape from the farthest tip of the tail fin to the knobby end of the kipe and recorded the length. He grabbed the tagging gun, lifted the dorsal fin between thumb and forefinger, then punctured the fatty area below the fin. "At an angle, not deep." The blue plastic jutted from one side. "Write the tag number down, and you're done."

With the trout back in the net, Paul followed Tanner down to the weirs again. In the shallows on either side of the fence, they'd arranged piles of rocks to create a breakwater where the fish could recover from the anesthetic away from the current. "One hand beneath its head, the other at the base of the tail. Rock him gently back and forth in the water. Get the oxygen moving through his gills."

"Do bears ever come down at night?"

"Nope. I don't know, the noise and the lantern probably scares them."

"Maybe you've just been lucky."

"Maybe. Okay, let him sit now, he's fine."

He watched Tanner process another trout and envisioned a typical night's work. At its best, the gratifying rhythm of skilled labour, like carpentry; at its worst, the monotony of the assembly line. He lifted the third fish from the cooler, and the body pulsed and quivered in his hands like a spastic muscle. The cold seeped through his thin gloves. He tried the tagging gun, hit too high up the fin, and the rectangular end of the filament stuck out the other side. Tanner snipped it off with cutters, pulled the tag free, and Paul tried again.

The next two fish already had tags in them, yellow ones, the numbers buried under a slick of green algae. "The yellows came up two years ago, you'll see lots of those. Any red tags, that's last autumn. Always amazes me, the ones that make it consecutive years. You'd think they'd take time off. It's a hell of a trip."

~

23

Inside the camper, they had stuffed Paul's gear into the overhead fibreglass cabinets and stacked canned goods, toolboxes, and batteries in the storage space under the seats. They wiped down the counters and the inside of the bar fridge, and then piled blankets and sheets on the sofa bed at the front of the camper beside the closet. The table at the back of the trailer could be collapsed into a single bed when the night's work was done. The upholstered white walls behind the gas stove and countertop, the thin beige drapes, the narrow windows—it would be like living in an egg.

They sat at the table and transferred data from the waterproof paper onto a spreadsheet on Tanner's laptop, while outside the generator rumbled and stuttered. Tanner poured a glass of scotch, and Paul sipped herbal tea, a blend that had the unfortunate slight taste of cloves. The whole process had taken them just over an hour.

"It'll get busier," Tanner said. "In a few weeks, the run will hit its peak. Just enough so you won't get bored. You'll work for three, maybe four hours straight, not including the data."

"Hope I'm faster by then."

"You'll get there," Tanner said. "I noticed your laptop—you have your own stuff to do?"

"I don't, really."

"Thought you might be picking away at your dissertation."

Paul traced his finger along the edge of his cup. "Not anymore."

"No more parkour?"

The trailer had an ugly fluorescent light that made Paul's arm look jaundiced and stick-thin. He flexed his bicep and made a wry face.

"You should go back to Sweden." Tanner laughed. "I love it—chasing Vikings and bog mummies."

Paul wanted a drink, a nice beer, so he could pretend this was like old times, yakking it up in the campus pub. Nobody said booze was out of the question, but it somehow made sense to deny himself the pleasure of alcohol's comforting lassitude. Less likely to pee himself too. "When I got back," he said, "I tried to salvage my research, tried to stay interested . . ."

Tanner nodded. "So you're done, then? In the department?"

Paul shrugged. "I told Dr. Tamba about this job. He said, 'Since you're near Castlegar or Grand Forks, why not do something on the Doukhobors?'"

"And?"

"I said, 'I'm not in Castlegar. Or Grand Forks.' Anyways, he was being facetious. He thinks I just grab ideas from thin air."

"Well, don't you?" Tanner asked and shot back the rest of his drink. "Like the parkour?"

"Maybe the parkour," he admitted. "All right, maybe every ethnography I've done. It's great fun, it really is, finding out what makes these groups tick, what sustains them. I mean, what kind of grown man would belong to a parkour club for five years? But it's true I've never found something I could really latch on to, not the way you have with bull trout. I want to keep going. Somehow." He was an academic, he'd lived so long on research grants and university money he couldn't imagine another way of getting by.

Tanner was staring at his empty glass. He suddenly laughed— a vulgar growl. "Fucking *bloated*. Like a grey balloon."

"Let's not."

"You have to wonder."

"I don't."

"Who it was, I mean." Tanner poured another drink. "They ushered us out pretty quick after the corpse hit the stretcher. Once you were, you know, back from the woods."

Paul flushed, a sudden surge of anger at the drowned man, the way the body had intruded on his life and made everything about the camp feel ominous and unsettling.

"Guaranteed I'll know him," Tanner said. "Hopefully not well."

"I'm not going to think about it either way."

"So, what's the deal, then?" He gestured irritably at Paul's body, maybe because he wouldn't be suckered into talking about the dead man. "Didn't bring any booze or steaks with you, you're drinking tea. You look like crap. Are you okay or not?"

"They got all of it, for now. If that's what you mean."

"How about . . ." Tanner pointed again, this time toward Paul's crotch. "I hear, sometimes with the surgery . . ."

"Yeah." Paul fidgeted with his teacup. "I'm out of commission."

"Nothing at all?"

"Not a twitch."

"Wow."

Both men looked out the window. The wilderness all around them, the generator their muttering lifeline to civilization.

"Not for long, though, right?" Tanner turned back to him. "You're young, geez. Haven't even had kids yet."

"I can still have kids."

"Sure. Artificial insemination, test tubes. Fuck all that—the mechanics are what's important, right?"

"The doctors say—well, doctors say a lot of things." He raised his teacup in a mock toast.

"So is that—you know—is that all right with you, then?"

Paul struggled for a moment to speak and ended up laughing, helplessly. "I don't have a lot of choice here. It's better than the alternative, I'll give it that."

Tanner yawned. "Time for bed. And up early to count. Will the table-bed be comfortable enough?"

"Sure. I should warn you, I'll probably have to get up a few times."

"Won't even notice. I'm more snug out here than at home, but let's not tell Beth I said that." He winked, then paused. "We're trying to get pregnant. Figured it's time."

"How about I go out and kill the generator," Paul said.

"Sure, yeah. Get ready for the silence."

4

Before he stumbled across parkour, Paul had been in limbo, having finished, with partial success, a study on cycling clubs. The overwhelming trend among Paul's peers at the university was ethnographies of the "sporting body," a reaction against the abundance of netnographies, studies of online communities that saturated journals and publications. Or maybe a natural outcome of living in a city obsessed with recreation and its own greenness, or even the upcoming Olympics. Students conducted fieldwork among cultural groups formed by marathon addicts, competitors in extreme endurance races, or transgendered wrestlers. There was always pressure to find original, eclectic material, a community that occupied a very particular or unusual niche. Sometimes it felt like you were spinning so-called cultural groups out of nothing, just to keep pace with your fellow academics. But he enjoyed the challenge of identifying some obscure, tenuous cultural phenomenon and then mining it for publishable work that actually said something about society. There were risks, of course, like chasing an idea down a dead end—his master's thesis had come close—or simply becoming stumped for ideas.

He'd been dating Christine for a few months, and she was teaching him sport climbing. Her dissertation was a study of families who climbed at a gym called The Edge. Usually she worked with the binaries of broken or strained marriages: mother and daughter, father and son, and so on. Each parent had his or her own reason for climbing with a child, different values. Teaching him to rise to the challenge, a divorced father might say about his eight-year-old. Teamwork, the parallels to ambition and hard work. Companionship, a single mother would admit. To teach courage and independence.

Paul had his own reasons for climbing, one of which was the spectacle of Christine, the feline way she formed her body to the wall, fabric stretched against her, jaw taut with predatory grace as she reached for the next brightly coloured hold. A real beauty in her motions, not the ugly lunge that marked Paul's progress. He was all raw strength and desperate clutching. He admired her Zen-like poise, but the real turn-on was her competitive, almost hostile drive to outperform Paul in the climbing gym. Which she easily did.

He learned to trust the rope, his harness and the bolts and hefty carabiners that made up the anchor system at the apex of the climb, and he suppressed his fear of heights. But the equipment (minimal as it was) and the fear (unfounded as it was) distracted and took from his pleasure. He only wanted to think about the problem in front of him, the necessary series of moves, the crux he had to surmount. Mostly, he wanted to think about Christine.

They were alike in many ways, both of them ensconced in academia for most of their adult lives after brief, unsatisfying forays into the "real world." After high school she'd been a wait-ress, then a bartender, while Paul had started in construction for one of his father's buddies before switching to retail during summers while earning his undergraduate degree. Neither of them had brothers or sisters, and both had spent their early, angst-ridden university years imagining the world as an infi-nite number of cultural groups, none of which they belonged to. They both preferred to think they'd outgrown that stage of their lives. She liked, he knew, his cleverness, the way he could connect obscure ideas and make something from nothing. He was ambitious but not serious. She was both.

When Christine joined her research participants in their climbs, Paul would retreat to the so-called Cave at the back of the gym, a room of overhanging walls, big, grippy handholds placed on a low, sloping roof, and a floor covered in thick crash mats. Different colours of tape marked the routes that traversed the room. To move from one hold to another might require an upward lunge from a near-supine position, or a long reach from one razor-thin toehold to another with only one divot crimp for his burning fingers to grasp in between.

In the Cave, he met the person who would become his first research participant, Xi Bai. Thin and quiet, the teenager had gone back and forth along the rear wall of the Cave several times without resting—Paul had to step off the wall to let him pass. He had an unorthodox style, showy and acrobatic, and went from hold to hold at a precarious speed, his wild swings threatening to rip him from the wall. Xi explained to him, in whispered, faltering English, that he'd decided to train here for parkour only because of the rain. What was parkour, Paul wanted to know, but the boy couldn't say. He invited Paul to the next practice session. If it hadn't taken place on campus, a few minutes' walk from Paul's office, he likely wouldn't have gone.

As a subject, Xi Bai didn't make for an easy interview. Or Paul was trying too hard to make immediate intellectual connections, forcing theories before the fact. "Do you think, maybe, that parkour is a means of defining a foreign landscape on your own terms?" Paul asked. "A way of claiming a space for yourself?" The boy looked blank, a little frightened.

"Fun," Xi finally stuttered. "Have fun."

Xi was not the only member of the group who found it difficult to articulate why he practised parkour. Paul's scratch notes, recorded in a small notepad, were filled with little more than comical macho posturing and weird cheerleader platitudes. From Tran Minh, international student: "To go higher, better, really kick the wall's ass. That's what I'm talking about." Or Nathan Cook, BA candidate in political science: "Break out of those set rules of movement, the prepackaged, so-called reality of our surroundings. Reinvent."

The group also had a desire for fame. They filmed themselves obsessively, edited and synched the footage to hip hop and heavy metal, and then uploaded it onto their own YouTube channel. Nathan, ever the purist, tried to lend an instructional bent to the videos by adding voiceovers, but most clips were all bombast and rhythmic jump-cuts, testosterone with a soundtrack. Filming his fieldwork proved to be a headache, and Paul quickly abandoned it—participants were too eager to be in front of a camera, it became a fetish object instead of an unobtrusive means of documentation. That might have posed some interesting meta-ethnographic possibilities worth exploring—except, really, he just wanted to play.

He spent the summer learning how to do proper rolls and tumbles on the grass, something he hadn't done since he was a child. Parkour wasn't meant to be competitive, but Paul found a friendly rival in Tran Minh. They competed at kong-vaulting picnic tables and ledges or muscling over walls, and taunted each other when a manoeuvre was bungled. But Tran also proved to be a willing teacher, perhaps revelling in the novelty of instructing someone much older than himself. By October, the physical enjoyment of becoming a competent traceur, of his own unexpected transformation into a faster, stronger, more limber man, far outweighed the pleasure of conducting interviews, writing up field notes, or instructing archaeology students. A fact that didn't escape the notice of either Christine or Dr. Tamba.

One evening after a long session with Tran and Xi, Paul went to the lounge where he often met and drank with a handful of instructors and grad students. He liked his department. They were mostly younger and, like him, still valued the academic life over family, children. Tamba was putting in a rare and unfortunate appearance and sat at the head of the table with Christine and the others gathered around him. In his late forties, smooth-shaven and blessed with Mediterranean skin that rendered him both exotic and ageless, Tamba was more charismatic than handsome. He never spoke loudly or with any real vigour, never intruded or forced himself on a conversation, but always caused a stir. The female students in the department, even Christine, cheerfully confessed to having a crush on him. He'd made his reputation at conferences lecturing on the participant-observer oxymoron and the ethics of conducting consumer, or mobile, ethnographies. In public he spoke with a self-deprecating tone noticeably absent when he met with Paul inside the confines of his office.

Paul slipped into a chair at the far end of the table. He sported a fresh purpling bruise on his forehead and a scraped chin. Dr. Tamba stared deliberately at Paul's wounds. He raised his glass—a clear alcohol, garnished with a sprig of mint and a lychee—and gave him a thin smirk. "I see you're going native," Tamba said and made it sound like a bit of martini-dry humour. The crowd chuckled. It was, in fact, an old saying among ethnographers, an accusation that Paul had lost his objectivity and gone beyond the acceptable limits of participant observation. Everyone heard and registered the undertone of contempt.

When Paul had first suggested the project, the two men had had a lively discussion about the philosophical background of parkour, from Georges Hebert's "Natural Method" to the *dérive* and Guy Debord's "hurried drifting." Tamba worried that parkour, in and of itself, was a difficult subject to take seriously. Still, with diligence, connections and parallels between parkour and larger social issues could be made. Diligence being the key word: ever since Paul's master's thesis—where there had been anonymous accusations of unprofessional, unethical behaviour on Paul's part—the professor doubted his work ethic even more than the subject itself.

Paul shrugged it off. The bantering between them, he figured, only raised his status among his peers. A few looked up to him, mostly because he wasn't afraid of Tamba.

He returned Tamba's smile and tapped his finger against his scraped chin. "These are my field notes, pal."

Later, Christine sat at the edge of the bed while he stood naked before her. She ran her finger over a yellowing bruise across his ribs and frowned. "Do you think maybe he's got a point?"

"Who?" He grinned and motioned for her to lie back. He took her feet and pressed them against the relatively firm planes of his abdomen, and then up over the bruise onto his chest, her arches fitting to his pectorals as he ran his hands along her calves. He shifted his weight from one leg to the other, a swagger to his movements as he pushed her heels back until her knees pressed against the bed, her legs wide. She brought her hand between her legs, and he did the same. Lately, this manner of foreplay had become habitual. They increasingly put each other at a distance and watched, as though sex would eventually require viewing each other through cameras and computers from separate apartments. When he was ready, he signalled her with an indolent spin of his finger and she turned over onto her knees and, just as languidly, arched her backside toward him. He held back, still the triumphant observer, savouring his own flesh, scraped and stinging and about to be satisfied, and had a brief vision of his body as a sublime machine, a beautifully humming engine.

~

The next semester, things came to a head. Spring meant Tamba's big conference, an international symposium on postmodern ethnography. Recognizing the chance to get on Tamba's good side, Paul had offered to present a paper called "Urban Geography and the Sporting Body." Of course, presenting a paper implied he was making good progress on his dissertation, that theories were emerging and the possibility of broader application or meaning existed. Nothing could be further from the truth. He and his participants accumulated bruises and aches and babbled philosophically—and rather pointlessly—about a physical activity that was only hypothetically useful: it might help them rescue someone or, perhaps more likely, to run away from someone. His research, barely begun, already carried the slight whiff of the stagnant, the frivolous.

He knew good research took time—Christine was in the third year of her own dissertation—and that much ethnography could appear thin on the surface level. The title of Christine's paper, "A Childhood on the Rocks," sounded like a one-person play, not a PHD paper. He'd once read a study concerning a handful of widowed grandmothers in Chicago who sewed quilts on Wednesdays. Once you dug into the meat of the project—but it was exactly that, the meat, which eluded him. He loved the sport, but the idea of spending the next three years coaxing something profound from it was painful. Tamba's warnings were coming true.

Teaching, which had felt like an anchor and distraction before, now became a refuge from the frustration of parkour, the dread of writing a paper that would largely be fluff. He immersed himself in lesson plans, marking or updating the class website and forum. He posted links to upcoming archaeological digs hosted by different universities from several countries that gave students the opportunity to join field schools in excavations around the world. The majority took place in either the States, Spain, or Italy. There was a dig happening later that spring in Sweden, the second year of an ongoing project.

The stark fields and wetlands featured in the website photos for the Vastmanland dig looked both alien and familiar, perfectly suited to his rather bleak mood. In the forefront of one photo, several muddy young men and women dressed in colourful raingear grinned wildly at the camera, arms around one another. They were likely as lost and bewildered as he felt—why Vastmanland, when there were the Roman baths in sunny and grand Pollena Trocchia, for God's sake?—but they seemed happy with the prospect of searching for Viking artifacts in the muck.

Of course, the notion of putting his dissertation on hold to pick up an archaeologist's shovel was laughable and dreadful. Tamba would eat him alive. It was too late to enrol in the field school—it was intended mostly for undergraduates wanting to learn basic archaeological methodologies—but the school encouraged observation or volunteer participation from doctoral students. He sent some e-mails and put himself on the volunteer list, just for the hell of it. If he could at least toy with the possibility of an exit strategy, it might take the pressure off writing his conference paper.

"What would you say," he said to Christine one night, "if I ditched the conference to travel to Sweden?"

"I'd say it was hilarious," she said. He lolled in the middle of the bed, post-sex, while she checked e-mail on her phone. She'd showed up at his place late, after drafting the paper she'd be presenting at the conference, a summary of her work over the last year.

"I've been thinking I'll be busy over the next while," she said without looking up. "Probably won't have much time to spend together."

"We don't already. Stay with me while you work," he said lightly. "That way we'll see each other nights, at least." He admired, maybe loved, how she was less interested in theory than the emotional core of her research—the myriad inner thoughts of parents who anchored themselves by rope and harness to their children and watched them climb, grasp, and slip.

"Thanks. Thank you." She put her phone away and placed her hand on his chest. "But I need my desk, my books. I like our arrangement."

"It does keep things exciting," he agreed, both relieved and disappointed. They were silent for a while.

"Actually, I wouldn't find it funny," she said. "It'd be a colossal fuck-up."

He laughed softly, trying to reassure her. "I'll be all recharged, get a whole new perspective on my work. Much better than me serving up some bullshit about Guy Debord and dérive."

Later, too late, he would realize he'd made the classic male mistake of thinking that if she didn't want anything serious with him, then she didn't want anything serious at all, with anyone. There was a line in a movie he'd liked—something about how you end up hating the person for the same reasons you fell in love with them.

In May he withdrew his conference paper at the last moment, bought a plane ticket, and flew to Stockholm.

5

In the morning, Tanner checked the ratio of clove oil to water in the cooler, Paul's tagging technique, and all the other details that would make the job run more smoothly. They processed the handful of trout in the traps, then entered the data and made their eggs and oatmeal to eat on the edge of a small but sheer bank at the confluence of Basket Creek and the Immitoin. The river was three times as wide as the creek and ran different shades of blue and silver midstream, steel grey and pale green along the forested banks on the other side. Paul watched a slate-coloured dipper bob from stone to stone and then plunge underwater.

"So, you feel comfortable with everything?" Tanner asked.

The thrill of finally being abandoned and left alone jolted through him. "Sure," he said. Anyone, really, could do this job as long as they didn't mind being alone or working outside at night. If a person actually *understood* fish, or even liked them, that would be better, but anyway, here he was.

Tanner crouched, swished his plate in the creek, and then dipped his mug into the river. He rose and drank deeply, eyes closed. "Okay." He grinned and tugged at an imaginary cap on his head. "Time to put on the film critic hat. Try not to screw anything up." They walked back to camp, where Tanner packed up and drove away.

For a while, Paul wandered in circles around the camp, unsure what to do with himself. Before he could properly register his being alone, vehicles rumbled up the road. Their approach was slow, and the violent shake of equipment and the laboured mutter of truck engines in low gear echoed through the valley. He could see the road through the trees, a hundred metres or so uphill from where he stood beside the camper. Two large crew cabs hauled long white trailers, followed by some smaller trucks, their cargo boxes loaded with chainsaws, shovels, jerry cans, and other gear. Clouds of dust drifted through the trees, and by the time the air settled, the last rattles and engine noise had faded.

First task: clean the fence. He grabbed his waders from where they hung drying beneath the camper's awning and went to the measuring station. Except for the weirs near the shore, the fence ran across fast-moving, choppy water and sizable rocks where the female trout wouldn't lay their eggs, so there would be no redds to disturb as he followed the length of the fence.

He picked at the twigs and bark bits piled against the mesh, grabbed handfuls of alder and aspen leaves and tossed them downstream. Then he scrubbed the mesh with a wire brush until the matted leaves had flaked away. There were branches stripped of bark and nibbled to sharp points by what he guessed were beavers. Tanner had warned him that after several days of bad weather there'd be so much debris piled up that either the fence would be blown out or the creek would flood. A chainsaw was stored in one of the camper's bins in case a tree swept against the fence. He'd never used a chainsaw and thought that standing knee-deep in storm-tossed currents wouldn't be the best place to learn.

Midstream, a small fish, a rainbow or cutthroat, had wedged its sloped head in the fencing wire and snapped its spine, the body rubbery and clammy. A sad waste, but learning to gut and cook a fish was beyond him today—another foreign, unfamiliar task. He threw the trout downstream, and it floated on the surface for a moment, pale underside flashing in the sun, then disappeared.

Ten o'clock. Waders off, and his work done until nightfall. Now what the hell was he supposed to do? He returned to where they'd eaten breakfast at the confluence and crouched on the shore to absently scoop warm pebbles and sift them through his fingers.

On the other side of the Immitoin, a broad, flat forest stretched along the shore before it ran into the hills and mountains beyond, a range of conical and boxy peaks with snow-covered ridges and cols, suspended in hazy air. The woods across the river were dense and marshy, a place where a hundred elk could disappear.

His thoughts were erratic, flighty. Whatever he wanted from his mind, it was impossible to access. He became drawn in—downward, it felt like—by the sound of the river, the rhythms and counter-rhythms, the layers of melodic and discordant voices created by unexplainable surges and shifts among different currents. The noise pulled his mind along, stripped it of language, and left him with a tattered patchwork of disturbing and fleeting images. White, claustrophobic images: hospital rooms and hospital sheets, a toilet bowl with a trace of blood spiralling in the water, snow falling in late May outside a bar in Skinnskatteberg.

The report of stones hitting stones made him jump, and he spun to face upstream. A woman stood on a dirt bank undercut by the Immitoin, her hands shoved in the back pockets of her cargo shorts, a ball cap shielding her face. She was nudging small rocks with the toe of her boot, pushing them off the bank and into the water. Or no—she stepped back to reveal a boy, about four or five years old, trying to throw stones that slipped from his small hands. Paul waved once, a little reluctantly, and walked over to them, tripping here and there over exposed willow roots.

"Usually a different guy up here," she said. "A skinny man."

"Sorry," he said. "I'm the substitute, I guess."

There was something solid about her. Not that she was stocky, exactly, but she wouldn't be easily knocked off her feet. Tanned, freckled—an outdoorsy woman. About his age, faint crow's feet at the edges of her eyes, laughter lines around her mouth, a strand or two of grey in the dark hair that stuck out from under her cap.

The boy wanted to show him a stick, and squinted up at him, sandy-coloured hair draped over his forehead and eyebrows, a slight scowl.

"This is Shane," the woman said. "I'm Gina. Hubert."

"Were you cooking hot dogs?" the boy asked. He held up the stick, a thin willow branch whittled to a point at one end, and whipped it back and forth like a fencing foil. "It's nice and bendy."

"Paul," he said. "So, are you . . . what brings you . . . ?"

"On our way up to camp," she said. "I'm a camp cook for Pinewoods Forestry."

"Tree planters," said Shane. His r's came out as w's.

"Spacing this time," Gina corrected him. "Chainsaw work." The child had sauntered off and was wildly swinging the willow branch at a tree stump.

"I don't even know what spacing—okay," Paul said. "So you're part of that convoy from earlier. Thought they were loggers."

"No, the mill's shutting down again. Trucks are still hauling, but most loggers are on their boats floating around the reservoir and drinking beer." Her eyebrows narrowed a moment, annoyed at something, then she shook her head and laughed. "I should be ahead of everyone, but it's a pretty bumpy road for a kid. Shane needed a break."

"I had to go poop," Shane said. *Pewp.*

"How far up is the camp?" he asked, looking upriver. Worried they would be around the corner, within shouting distance.

"Another fifteen K." She turned and led them back toward the site. "Where are you from?"

"The coast." He waved his hand in a vague direction.

"We saw police cars," Shane interrupted. He was tapping his finger against the camper's propane tank.

"We did, didn't we?" Gina said. She looked at Paul. "Know what happened at that cabin down the road?"

"No." He suddenly felt drained.

"Drive down and check it out. You look like someone desperate to keep himself amused." She laughed. "Sorry, that came out wrong. I meant bush work's kind of tough if you're not used to it. I'd invite you up to camp to share dinners with the crew, but the foreman wouldn't like it. Lunch, though. No one's around for lunch."

Maybe he'd slept even worse than he thought—he was growing resentful of their presence, the energy he had to expend. What was it, exactly, that kept normal conversation going? What was the impetus, the drive that allowed strangers to lob words back and forth? But her offer was remarkably generous when they'd only just met. "Hey. I should show you two the fish fence. It's kinda neat," he said to the boy.

"It's a fence," Shane said.

"We should go. Got a kitchen to put together," she said. She opened the truck and helped Shane into his seat. "We're at the end of Branch 65. Swing by for a coffee some afternoon. Keep yourself from getting bushed."

"Bushed?"

"Thinking yourself to death," she said, then started the engine. Paul gave her a weak, uncertain smile and wave, baffled by her friendliness.

After, he put together a simple lunch and thought again about the sheer effort of conversation. Was this his future with women from now on, a series of emasculated exchanges? Or was he just being paranoid? After all, whatever impression he'd made on her, she'd gone and made a neighbour out of him anyway.

~

When he closed his eyes after his first night alone at the measuring station, the scene played out on the back of his eyelids as though he were coming down from some sketchy drug. The slime on the bodies of each fish, their haloed spots, their ivory mess of teeth. Out of the weir, into the cooler, onto the scale, back into the dark. He could both hear and feel the dull piercing of the Floy gun's metal tip through fatty flesh, and the unfamiliar weight against his forehead where his headlamp had rested. Everything smelled of clove oil, and the lantern's ambient hiss, long extinguished, carried on in his ears.

He'd spent a half-hour before bed entering measurements and tag numbers into the laptop while he drank his herbal tea. Then he'd gone outside to shut off the generator, and the sound of the river and creek had immediately filled in the lost noise. If the generator sounded like civilization, like humans, then the water was the babble of fish heading for the fence. The alien, unblinking trout.

So much could go wrong. He could kill a fish with too much anesthetic, or maim it with the tagging gun. If he released it into the main current too soon, the trout would drift helplessly and smash into boulders and log jams. Fish were hard to relate to as living things, so cold and robotic and unceasingly one-minded, so given over to their constant movement. And yet, it was the fact of their aliveness, the specks of dark blood that sometimes appeared when he punctured them with the Floy gun, their mouths and gills desperately working at the air, that kept Paul awake.

He rolled over and the camper swayed, the plastic and vinyl components creaking. He hadn't taken any time to sort through the cupboards, take a few of his less vital belongings out of their bags, or do anything that would make himself feel at home. He'd eaten his dinner outside, tin plate on his lap. The evening air had been warm and sweet with the scent of tree pitch, and sparrows, thrushes, and juncos came down from the trees and pecked and scratched at the edge of the clearing. If only everything he saw or did wasn't shot through with the anxiety of handling fish, he might have been content, almost blissful, a man on a camping trip.

He'd imagined his days here would be exactly like a vacation, free of worrying about his future or his past. He'd forgotten, though, that a person goes into vacations backward, feet first, the head still back at home or at the office, still stuck in traffic. His troubles followed him to the outhouse or along the path to the river, finding fertile soil in the solitude he'd been so eagerly anticipating.

~

The Vastmanland excavation took place on a hobby farm several kilometres outside the city of Skinnskatteberg. The field school concentrated its search on the far corner of the property, where rolling fields softened into a *schwingmoor*, a quaking bog. The excavation faced an enormous obstacle: the owners of the farm had forbidden any dredging or draining of the bog. A crude system of boardwalks had been built, a grid established, and the students took turns using a long, thin metal pole to probe the deceptively thin mats of vegetation, searching by feel the black murk beneath.

The most common finds in that part of Sweden were burial sites, artifacts and weaponry from the Iron Age, and petroglyphs from the Bronze Age. The property was filled with signs of past civilizations, once you knew to look for them. Foundation stones lay randomly around the fields, the crumbling, hand-chiselled granite squares hidden by tangled grasses and sedges still brown from winter. Each time Paul pushed aside the weeds to examine a stone's markings, midges swarmed his face. The air was filled with the songs of insects, thrushes, and cuckoos.

One of the organizers casually mentioned bog mummies, dismissing the possibility of finding one here. Too far north, not the right tribal history. Paul detected a wistful tone and suspected that bog mummies were precisely what the professor was hoping for. From his lesson plans and slides, he remembered Dan Boothwell, who wrote about Lindow Man, and P.V. Glob, who had investigated Tollund Man and Grauballe Man, the two men forever connected to some of the most famous artifacts in anthropology. He felt for the professor, for the sheer romantic folly of his secret ambition, the audacity of betting on near-impossible odds.

The landscape, though, invited belief. In spots along the narrow boardwalk, the blanket of reeds and heathers on either side of them rippled, a quagmire sloshing beneath. He could have punched through the illusion of solid ground. The dead could be down there, centuries old and perfectly preserved in their tannic state, resting among the weaponry and tools the field school hoped to find. The mummies might have been thieves, farmers, or priests, sacrificed to pagan gods—ritually fed and then strangled, throats slit. Was the ritual meant to sustain the bog itself, the corpse a homunculus that kept the wheels of the land turning, the plants growing, the birds and animals returning? And if you pulled out the body, took it away, did that mean everything would wilt and die?

He'd travelled very little in his life, apart from some family trips to Mexico and the States, and he enjoyed the energy of the field school—the near-manic camaraderie, the swiftness with which friendships were made. Nearly everyone admitted that, like him, they'd left behind some sort of responsibility at home. The girls were excitable and flirtatious, and there was talk about spending Friday night at the campus pub in Skinnskatteberg.

Paul, along with some other male students, shunned the boardwalks as much as possible and moved through the grid by hopping from one hummock of earth to another. The dangerous gaps between solid ground enlivened him. Once, the soil gave way beneath his feet when he landed, and he pitched himself forward, the reeds and grasses cushioning his roll. The solidity of each mound was an illusion: his impact shook a stunted birch six metres away. When the whole field school descended on the bog each morning, the land shook like the hide of a dreaming animal.

On the Thursday afternoon, Paul struck something four metres down, near the end of the probe's reach. It was a large object, at least a metre and a half long, solid but slightly spongy. The field school spent the rest of that day securing the object with ropes and slings, and then setting up a winch and platform that would allow them to pull it onto the boardwalk. It proved to be a tremendously difficult and exhausting operation. At twilight, the object finally surfaced with a great sucking sound, wrenched through the immense weight of mud and tannin-coloured water. The students shovelled away mud and grasses to ease the strain on the winch. The rope was black with peat rot, silt, and muck. The thing came to rest with a sodden thump.

"Wood, I think." Two of the professors cautiously scraped the object clean with trowels and wire brushes. "A log of some kind." A few of the students groaned with a giddy sort of disappointment.

One professor said, "Both ends are even, smooth. This wood may have been cut for posts and beams. Carved, perhaps, with an adze. So it might be an artifact. Of a sort." The other professor, the hopeful one Paul had spoken to earlier, shrugged and wiped his hands on his jeans, his weathered face glum beneath his thick eyebrows.

Some of the students were billeted in farms near the excavation site, but Paul stayed at a hotel in Skinnskatteberg, in a room that had a small sauna off the bathroom. That night, he scrubbed himself with a coarse loofah in the shower, then sat in the sauna, exhausted from the hours of shovel work. He held his right arm out and turned it back and forth in hypnotic half-circles, noted the veins that protruded, the shadowed definition of biceps and triceps. His legs, pressed against the cedar bench, revealed the curved, impressive knolls of his quadriceps, his thighs yielding only the slightest undercarriage of fat. The orange, fire-like glow forgave every blemish and mole, the wiry copses and ridgelines of body hair. His member was thick and partially engorged from the pleasurable heat, his scrotum relaxed and heavy between his legs. In that moment, Paul thought he understood something about an athlete—how his body, unlike his mind, didn't differentiate between victory and defeat. His body felt the deep satisfaction of physical labour, it wanted to celebrate and find release. It was amazing, all things considered, how good he felt right now. Physically, at least.

He was finished with the dig. The moment that waterlogged piece of wood hit the boardwalk, he'd lost all interest. All that remained was the pointless folly of coming here, the comedy of self-deception. The trip had cost him dearly, and not just the money he'd thrown away. There would be repercussions at home, even beyond the ones he could easily guess.

Something surged through him, a deep, wild impatience—he needed to seek a crowd, noise, women. There'd be lots of students from the local college as well as the field school and instructors at the pub. Tomorrow it would be time to go home and take his punishment. But right now, he would give himself a night out, while he was still an ocean away from the consequences.

6

The grey body being pulled from the water, a man on each flabby arm, the head and chest sagging toward the water. The men's faces both straining from the weight and recoiling from the touch of dead flesh. If only he hadn't seen that. The memory cast an insistent shadow, made it impossible for him to forget the wildness of where he was, the vast, unforgiving space. It had left the traces of its horror on the water like a film, like oil or fish slime.

By noon of each day he'd run out of things to do, even if he took his time cleaning the fence or entering the morning's data. There was nothing to do but wait for night. Sometimes, in the idle time while he sat by the river or in the shade outside the trailer, minutes went by with his mind gone wonderfully blank. But then the image of the corpse would flicker into sharp focus and cut through his reverie. When it faded, he'd find himself trailing after a gloomy thought, and the river would become something menacing.

He was angry, too, about pissing himself again, this time in the simple act of bending to scoop a fish out of the weir. His underwear hung on a line by the trailer, rinsed in the creek. He thought he'd gotten the humiliation out of his system—the humiliation of surgery, of the catheter. He'd been invaded by people who knew more about his body than he did. When they sent him home, he'd known even less about his body. Not technically, because since the diagnosis he'd learned more about his inner workings than he'd ever wished to know. No, the surgery had made him ignorant on a gut level—disconnected him, as if part of him had been left behind, a part that now belonged to clearer, higher minds.

After his diagnosis in the late winter, the possible repercussions of his approaching surgery laid out before him, he sent Christine an e-mail: *I won't miss it. Sex, that is. I feel like I've been drifting away from sex these past months—I don't know whether it's a case of testosterone collapse or just too much on my mind.* The doctors had told him it was not a symptom of his cancer, nor had there ever been a connection between loss of desire and the disease. *It's purely mental, or hormonal, or whatever. But (how to put this) my desire to feel desire isn't there anymore. It's a relief, in many ways. Maybe for you as well, though I guess it's a bit late for that.*

So many of life's decisions were based around sex. Consciously or otherwise. Hilarious, really, how pliable a man's life was, how easily it was tipped and upended, blown off course by lust. Before Christine there was Naomi, a participant in his study of the cyclists. Bubbly, idealistic—and young, bordering on too young, that was his first mistake. She was the one who'd complained to his department about unethical behaviour. They'd been sleeping together for weeks already, but then he'd made some suggestions, a little high or drunk or both, maybe pressured her to do certain things. Or she'd found out about other women—there'd been a strange sexual dynamic within the cycling club that any sensible person, a good researcher, would have avoided or documented from afar.

There had also been Sweden. Christine had not been around when he arrived home from the excavation, a small mercy—she missed the spectacle of Tamba openly mocking him at the pub, the final blow to Paul's rapidly diminishing reputation in the department. She was away writing her paper at a cabin she'd rented (she did not say exactly where) and had plans afterwards to climb in Squamish with friends. He couldn't tell her over the phone about his night in Skinnskatteberg, in the alley behind a bar. He would later, in person, after she'd returned from her trip with her hair cut short and a torn ligament in her wrist. With or without his confession, their end was inevitable. Chasing whims, chasing women: she found them equally distasteful, equally damning. They sat on his bed one last time and tried to look back on things with a fondness they didn't feel. Their relationship had become so coldly physical. "We had good sex," she said, as if that were all, and he said that was true. After the breakup, Paul had gone to his parents' place on Salt Spring and prepared to teach another semester. Tamba and Christine became a single person in his mind, a figure of disapproval who made him feel crass and low.

Fall semester came and dragged on. He reached a plateau in his parkour training and couldn't push himself any higher. He had hit his peak, and it was underwhelming. This shouldn't have affected his research, but it did. Around the same time, urinating became a painful, difficult, and frequent adventure. Or, really, hadn't it been a little difficult for a long time, a year or more, and he'd just been ignoring the faltering, stop-start stream? Then there was blood and he wondered if he'd caught something in Sweden. Avoidances, tests, finally the Centre. Patients he met there identified themselves with their Gleason Score, the results of their biopsy—his was a Score 7, mildly aggressive. This earned him a solemn high-five from Tim Holcomb, Score 8, whom he met in the waiting room. "You'll do well," Tim said.

After the night count, unable to sleep, he looked for distractions. The things Tanner had left behind in the trailer were the dregs an old roommate leaves behind: half-empty packs of matches and melted-down candle nubs, playing cards stained with cola, a wine cork. There was a book of local history, published twenty years ago by a press he'd never heard of, the last several chapters water-damaged and unreadable. He warmed water on the stove and then washed himself with a cloth, tracing the scars that furrowed his perineum. He was the sum of his body's failings, and he was well within the age at which failure mattered.

~

He slept heavily and woke before his alarm only because a door had slammed. He peeked through the curtain to see an old blue pickup, parked as far from his own truck and camper as the site would allow. He slid out of bed and dressed quickly. When no one came to knock on his door, he opened all the curtains in the camper and looked out each window. No doubt the visitor was a fisherman, here to cast for cutthroat—Tanner had said to expect some anglers—and desired human company no more than Paul.

As he put on his waders outside, he heard a sharp crack. He pulled the suspenders over his shoulders and started down the path to the fence. Another shot echoed—a gun, he was sure now—ahead of him. He brushed his way past the wolf willow and alder and stumbled onto the gravel bar beside the measuring station. A broad-shouldered man in a ratty purple fleece stood over the upstream weir, the creek pouring into his rubber boots. Water had wicked up his jeans past his knees. A mess of grey and white hair stuck out of a stained ball cap that sat too high on his head. He looked vaguely familiar, but Paul was distracted by the small rifle the man was pointing into the weir, the butt tight against the inside of his shoulder.

"Stay fuckin' still, will ya." The man's growl was coarse and phlegmy. He swung the gun barrel in wild circles, then fired a shot into the water.

"Whoa!" Paul yelled, not meaning to. He had already turned to dash back to the camper, but the cleat of his left foot slid on a rock, and he stumbled two steps toward the creek instead. The old man spun and pointed the rifle at Paul's head. The man's eyes widened, and his mouth contorted and worked soundlessly, trying to get words out.

"Garbage fish," he stammered finally. "That's what they are!" The man turned toward the trap, about to take another shot, but then began to lurch downstream to the Immitoin. "Fuckin' garbage fish!" He shouted it again as he scrambled up the bank, water spilling from his boots, and disappeared into the trees.

Paul's knees buckled, and he collapsed heavily onto the gravel. Almost as quickly, he rolled back on his feet, unsure what to do. He went down to the fence and saw two bull trout, male and female, floating on the surface of the upstream weir, their bodies pressed by the current against the back of the trap. The male had its eye shot out, the upper part of its skull split open. The other bled from a hole in front of the dorsal fin; she was still alive, flicking her tail fin as she tried to right herself. He heard a truck engine start. The waders made running nearly impossible, but he managed a straight-legged reel back to the site and arrived in time to see the truck tear onto the main road in a sepia cloud of dust, skid a hard right, and head south.

He paced frantically, in and out of the trailer, and then finally returned to the fence to carry on the morning count. The other fish couldn't be left in the weirs all day. The dead male he scooped out and kept on the measuring table. He'd freeze the trout in a Ziploc as some sort of—what, evidence? There were three more trout, but he couldn't process them properly: the tagging gun trembled dangerously in his hand, he couldn't get the angle right. He returned them to the creek. Maybe he'd get them on their way back down.

The last fish, the injured female, hugged the bottom of the stream. When he netted her, she came alive, wiggling in short frantic bursts. She was the biggest female he'd seen so far, a little over the length of his forearm, her fins and sides weathered and scarred. The bullet wound looked bad, an ugly divot in her back.

She was tagged already, red from last year. The plastic nub was buried under thick algae, like something from an ancient wreck. He scraped the green algae away, and for a moment he could almost picture the gloom and murk of the lake bottom where she'd come from.

A host of purple spots danced in front of his eyes, and he sank to his knees, trying to keep the netted fish from hitting ground. He took a few deep breaths, and his vision cleared, his stomach settled. What to do with the fish—she'd be too weak, the anesthetic would do her in. He took a guess at her length and weight and remembered the tag number before he released her. No doubt her body would end up pinned against the fence some-time later today. Too bad you can't bandage a fish, he thought.

～

Tanner on the satellite phone: "Explain again what happened." Static or a breath of exasperation. He'd told Paul to use the phone only for the direst of emergencies. He'd been uncharacteristically sour when he said it. Paul realized then what the most important part of his job was: to let Tanner focus on the festival. So the phone had sat in a cupboard, and Paul had resented the mere presence of it—an unwanted lifeline. He enjoyed the way his cellphone would signal to him, the icon flashing and spinning in futile circles, searching, searching, and coming up empty. On any other occasion, he might have disliked hearing Tanner's voice as much as Tanner probably disliked hearing his.

He repeated his story. "Garbage fish. What the hell does that mean?"

"Some old-timers say that. The bulls aren't as much fun to catch, you see, and the big ones eat cutthroat. Was a time some fishermen used to kill them and throw 'em out. That was mostly back in the late seventies, before people realized bulls were the endangered ones, not the cutties or rainbows."

"That's a very strange vendetta."

"Probably drunk." There was noise in the background, a television, laughter. "I'll give the conservation officer a shout, or maybe the cops. That'll put the fear of God into him."

"Whichever. I just don't want to get shot."

"Sounds like you scared him off. I'm sure he's gone for good."

"Give me a break. If he wants to kill trout, what better place to do it?"

"Like shooting fish in a barrel." Tanner laughed suddenly. "Nice."

"Glad you're enjoying this."

He spent the rest of the day pacing around the rec site or sneaking through the brush to Basket Creek, expecting the man to be there with his gun. It was worse after sunset. While he sat inside the camper waiting to go down to the fence, something moved outside the window. He recoiled, then swore—it was the underwear he'd hung on the line.

At the measuring station, none of the equipment had been disturbed, and there was nothing wrong with the fence. Eight fish were in the weirs, the flick of tail and dorsal fins catching the light of his headlamp. He worked with one eye toward the forest, his ears straining to hear over the water and the lantern hissing on its hook. He struggled to find his rhythm: he bungled a couple of tags and measurements, and re-entered the data into his notebook with quick, furious scribbles.

When the traps were empty, he dumped the used-up water from the cooler, closed the lid, and sat down. He'd only rested for a minute or two before he heard a splashing. A cutthroat hovered near the surface of the downstream trap, and he released it into the main current. He peered in again and saw two other fish, bulls that swam near the bottom. They flashed colour—both tagged, thank God. The first was a male with a blue tag, the number perfectly familiar. "I saw you an hour ago, you sonofabitch." He marked the number in the notebook and then released him.

He lifted the last fish and saw the red tag and then the bullet wound. She'd come back. "Gave up, did you?" he said. "Or got confused, poor girl." He let her go, as he had the male, but didn't expect to see her again.

The RCMP showed up late the next morning after Paul had finished his morning count. Paul recognized the driver as the officer who'd stood with Tanner on the road. The other, younger than Paul, had a cocky swagger, good-looking but rugged, a hockey player who'd somehow avoided breaking his nose or losing any teeth. The older cop greedily sniffed the fresh air as he approached, his face lifted to the warm breeze.

"Pretty sweet set-up you've got. I haven't been this far up the mainline since a fishing derby two summers back, I think." He introduced himself as Cliff Lazeroff and the younger man as Davis.

"Coffee?" Paul asked.

"Please." Lazeroff looked a little apologetic. "Should talk about yesterday, but it'll wait. Let's pull up some chairs here."

They grabbed two log ends near the fire pit and dragged them close to the camper. Paul kept the door open and listened to the men talk idly while he brewed coffee and herbal tea for himself. Lazeroff was saying something about dry fly casting. The younger cop owned a powerboat and spent most of his time on the lake. "New motor on it. Hauls ass out to my favourite spots and back in an afternoon. Have to watch out for deadheads, though, especially the north end," he told Paul. "Sometimes an old snag that's been standing underwater comes loose and pops straight up and out. Like a rocket."

"It's a spooky thing to see," said Lazeroff.

"There's a whole forest underneath the reservoir," Davis said. "It's gotten better over time, but it's best to stay out of certain areas."

They went quiet, as men do when they're given an image of

danger, envisioning deadly scenarios, savouring, in a way, the possibility of disaster.

"So about yesterday," Lazeroff said, once Paul sat down. "Going by the description you gave Tanner, I'm pretty sure we know who it is." Davis shook his head and smiled into his coffee.

"Oh?"

The constable gestured downriver. "His name's Hardy Wallace."

"Hardy Wallace," Paul repeated.

"You know the day you came up with Tanner?"

"You were directing traffic."

"That man who drowned. An older fella, Caleb Ready, not that the name's going to mean much to you." Lazeroff coughed. "Hardy spotted the body from his kitchen window."

Davis interjected. "He was pretty shaken up."

"I remember him now. He was standing on the deck."

"He's got a history. Gone off the deep end before," Lazeroff said. "Lives alone. Always has, from what I understand. A Lambert local, as they say."

"Lambert? Is that the place with all the shacks and summer homes?"

"No, that's Bishop. Lambert was a village across the lake from Bishop, before the dam. Lambert folks were given property in Bishop as compensation for getting flooded out. From what I understand."

Paul nodded impatiently. "So what do you mean he's got a history?"

"This isn't the first body that's ended up below his house," said Davis.

"First time, a young woman, a rafting accident upstream," said Lazeroff. "He took that okay. A real tragedy, was all he said. Then that child on the May two-four weekend."

"That's right, three years back," said Davis. "Horrible. Fishing trip near the falls, kid stumbled off the bank."

"Threw him for a major loop. Some folks had to look after him until he got his head back together. And now, Mr. Ready."

"That's—that's a lot of bodies," said Paul.

"It's the current," said Davis. "If the corpse doesn't get caught on a sweeper upstream, or stuck in spin cycle beneath some falls, it'll end up in that eddy."

"Bad luck, the house being where it is," Lazeroff said.

"This Ready guy we haven't figured out," said Davis. "He certainly wasn't a kayaker, or fishing."

Lazeroff gave Davis a quick glare, then shrugged. "Damned shame. Bottom line is, maybe Hardy's still a bit rattled. It's partly up to you, of course, but we'd like to not make much trouble."

Paul shook his head, confused. "Trouble for whom?"

"I'm just saying, there's not much to gain. Did he, in fact, threaten you with his firearm or point it at you?"

"More or less," said Paul. This was all because he wasn't a local. If he was someone like Tanner, things would be handled differently. "I don't know."

"Hard to say he did anything on purpose?"

"Except shooting the fish."

"Any dead?"

"One. He wounded a female too, but it looks like she might make it." Which made him laugh a little crazily. The cops looked at each other. He went inside and brought out the killed trout he'd kept in the freezer. They hummed and hawed, and finally said they'd take it back with them. "We'll probably end up eating it," Lazeroff said.

Paul sighed, irritated. He didn't want complications either—or more visitors. But he didn't want to be shrugged off.

"Look, I'm willing to let it go," he said. "But I need to know I'm safe. I need to work in peace."

"You will." Lazeroff looked relieved. "We'll go talk to him right now. Maybe turn things over to the conservation officer. He'll likely get a fine." Or nothing, Paul thought.

"Might be worse than going to jail or a hospital," said Davis. "Can't imagine he's got a lot of money."

The cops nodded at him, looking for agreement, so Paul obliged them, still unhappy. Did they expect him to feel sorry for the old loon?

"Hey," said Lazeroff suddenly. "You mind taking us down to the fence? I'm curious for a look."

At the creek, Davis appraised the equipment in the measuring station as if he were shopping at a rummage sale, holding up the Floy tag gun and vials of clove oil, his eyebrows narrowing and then rising, his lips pursed. "Huh," he muttered indifferently when he finished. Lazeroff, meanwhile, stood at the edge of the fence, the water touching his boots. When he spoke, which he did with a low, almost wistful voice, he pointed out every aspect of the stream—the straight riffle, the curve upstream that created a pool along the far bank.

"You call this a job?" he said. "This is a vacation."

Paul grimaced. "You aren't here at night."

"You getting bushed yet?" said Davis. He grinned at Lazeroff.

The constable laughed. "Oh, it's too early. Give the man another few weeks until the cold and the rain hit, with nothing but a pack of cards to keep him company."

Lazeroff gave him more assurances before leaving. "Pop into the station when you come into town," he said. "I'll let you know how it turns out."

For a long time after they'd gone, Paul paced the camp. The cops made the old man sound harmless, an object of pity. Not much sympathy for an outsider—didn't he know madness was par for the course out here? Apparently he'd soon be half-mad himself.

7

He decided to head to Shellycoat the next morning. Food and clean clothes were running low. And it might be best, he thought, to get the trip over with, not have it lurking in the back of his mind all week. When they'd talked about being bushed and coming into town, the younger cop had given him a wink. Oh, yes: women. That's what Davis had implied. Go see some coffee shop girls, cashiers, women jogging in their shorts and yoga pants along the lakefront. That built-up tension, the blue-balled bush man. But what he felt was slightly anxious. He certainly wasn't starved for people's company. They were dropping by camp on a regular basis, for Christ's sake.

While he drove, he kept the CB volume turned up and set to channel 5. A trucker's voice came through the radio's static. "Empty, twenty-eight on the Immitoin." Paul looked for one of the orange kilometre markers so he could call his location. That was how to do it, according to Tanner. Empty when driving up the road, or north, and loaded when heading south toward town.

He passed Hardy's cabin without realizing where he was, and as he looked back in his rear-view mirror, a logging truck swung around the corner, the semi's grill staring him down. "Fuck," he shouted and tapped on his brakes, too hard, and fishtailed through a water bar, the nose of his vehicle slamming down hard, then skyward. He jerked to the right, his tires plowing through the soft shoulder as the truck slid past him. The driver gave him a long, angry blast on the horn. Paul cranked the wheel again and skidded back onto the road. *Jesus H. Christ*, he breathed.

"Hey, Fred." An irritated voice crackled over the CB. "Some cocksucker in a Pathfinder doesn't have a radio, heading your way."

"Okey-doke." The accent sounded Russian. "Empty, twenty-eight."

His face burning, Paul waited until he saw the next marker. "Loaded pickup, twenty-nine," he mumbled into the receiver. He pulled close to the shoulder and slowed down. A few moments later, another logging truck rattled around the corner, a cloud of dust billowing up beside it. The driver lifted two fingers off the wheel in greeting, a smirk on the broad, red-cheeked face.

"Fuck you too," said Paul under his breath as he sped up again. A few hundred metres later, where a power line right-of-way crossed the road, he pulled over. Thimbleberry, bracken fern, and dogsbane, all caked with dust, hung in rows above the ditch. He walked around to the passenger side and dropped his pants. With a few swift movements, he ripped off his damp incontinence pad and flung it into the weeds.

~

He swung by the police station, his first stop. Behind his desk, under the fluorescents, the constable looked dumpy and bored. Paul asked if there had been any confrontation with the old man. "Didn't wave a gun at me, if that's what you mean," Lazeroff said. "Caught him at a lucid moment. Says he'll come by and apologize if you'd like. Told him that probably wouldn't be necessary."

"Or wanted," said Paul. "Thanks."

The constable changed the subject and asked him if he'd seen anything out of the ordinary—besides Hardy, of course. They still didn't know how Caleb Ready ended up in the river. "I haven't really explored, to be honest," Paul said. "Should I?"

"Well, yeah, for your own sake. It's beautiful country." Lazeroff chuckled. "No need to poke around on our account."

"That drowned man," Paul said. "Did he leave a note? At his house, I mean?"

"Cottage."

"Pardon?"

"Summer cottage by the marina, just up from the dam. He didn't live here year-round," Lazeroff said. "There wasn't a note."

He left and found a coffee shop with Wi-Fi, deciding to sit outside and soak up the small town buzz. He was enjoying himself far more than he'd expected, which maybe wasn't saying much. The late summer heat of Shellycoat was different than the coast, tailor-made for sitting outside. Smells didn't come and go on an ephemeral ocean breeze but hovered in the still air and accumulated in richness: deli meat, bagels and mustard, coffee and fresh bread. Mountain bikes leaned against the ornate metal-work railings, a line of men and women in cycling shorts queued up at the coffee counter, brown and grey mud drying on their calves and black apricot-shaped bums. They looked to be all ages, anywhere from twenty to fifty, all of them hard and lean with tanned and veiny arms. On the curb near Paul, two men in khaki uniforms spread maps and clipboards on the hoods of a truck marked with a Monashee Power logo, their travel mugs perched at angles on the gleaming metal.

He checked his e-mail, sent a quick reply to his parents to say he was all right, the river was beautiful, so were the fish, sorry he'd be out of touch for the next while. Most of the incoming messages he could ignore, put off, or delete. Like the one from Dr. Elias Tamba.

> Hope your convalescence is going well. I took the
> liberty of checking for a specialist in your area
> and, of course, found no one and nothing. In fact,

I would recommend avoiding any type of serious injury or disease during your stay, as apparently the local hospital, thanks to recent government cuts, has been reduced to something slightly better than an emergency outpost.

I'm obliged to ask about your plans for the future (your silence is understandable, of course, but this needs to be addressed sooner rather than later). Requisite questions: Are you registered for the next semester? Have you modified your dissertation, or considered a new direction you may want to take?

He gnawed softly on one knuckle. Tamba's stiff attempts at camaraderie grated. All he could picture was Tamba's smug smile and Christine. Did he need to reply to this right now? No. If the question was whether he'd drop out or not, Tamba probably knew the answer better than he did.

Driving back, the back seat loaded with clean laundry and groceries, he watched the monolith of the dam rise up like a mirage and shimmer under sunlight. The smell of dried grasses, hay in a field, filtered through the open window, along with the truncated notes of crows and blackbirds. An osprey perched on a telephone pole and then launched itself over the water. Cars and trucks were parked along the reservoir, and families trudged up dirt paths from the water, arms loaded with rumpled towels and empty coolers, their bathing suits wet with the last swim of the year.

At Hardy's driveway, he slowed to peek at the cabin. On the deck, a single straight-backed wooden chair faced the river, and the cabin, for all its dull-wooded wear, looked like a tourist's dream, the cozy summer cottage. Then something moved on the far corner of the deck, and there was Hardy. The old man leaned against the railing, staring down at the dark pool, at the eddy gathering whatever the current sent down.

8

In the dream, the woman was mostly Anneke, the student he'd met at the Skinnskatteberg pub, but he also recognized Christine's elfin figure. The smile, broad, sweet, and somewhat naive, was distinctly Naomi's. He wanted to kiss that smile, drawn to the memory of its silly warmth, but the shifty mouth eluded him, there and not there on the blond, plump-cheeked face of the giggling Swede.

Much of the dream was a true recollection: they'd stumbled outside to a dark spot behind the building, where the streetlight didn't reach. Snowflakes like drunks keeling over. Whenever she laughed, Anneke would press her head against his chest, and she was always laughing. "Very high on the Ecstasy," she told him. He'd taken a mix of pills she and her friends had given him and they'd made him drink too much aquavit. He leaned against the wall of the building, her forehead butted against his collarbone and her breath gathered in the folds of his coat. He kept bringing her hand down to the fly of his jeans until she unzipped and pulled him free into the cold air. Her hand kept rhythm while she laughed and muttered things into his chest. Her teeth latched on to his sweater and yanked. Time jumped around. Or a moment disappeared in a blackout. He heard the crunch of her knees pressing into fresh snow, white flakes streaking past as though he were driving fast through a winter storm on a pitch-black, unmarked highway. She was up again, her teeth back into his sweater, close to the neck, and now his middle and ring fingers worked against and inside her, cotton brushing against his knuckles. "You don't stop," she warned him, and he hadn't in real life, but in the dream he was racing off down the highway, careening wildly, and then awake.

Most of him was awake. "So do you miss morning hard-ons?" Tanner had joked the day he left, and yes, Paul did miss them, especially after a dream like that.

Two days had passed since his visit to Shellycoat, which he decided he hadn't, after all, enjoyed. There'd been too much stimulus, too much awareness of his own body: the discomfort of searching for a bathroom, the self-consciousness of being a stranger. Not a tourist, just a stranger. And then, after being surrounded by people—the half-sincere smiles of cashiers and grocery clerks, music, and the café smells—the return to camp's solitude was too abrupt, too absolute. The sunset, the red and purple light playing across the river until it faded into a dark shale grey, made him all teary.

Yesterday, he napped by the Immitoin all afternoon, lost in its ceaseless tumbling sounds. A small brown lizard had paused among dead leaves, and a dipper perched on its boulder and bobbed like the coiled spring of some benevolent toy. The hills across the river, their peaks elusive in the hazy atmosphere, stretching back over the horizon, flashed bits of yellow and orange along its crest where bushes had dried from the summer heat. Sometimes the river created the disturbing illusion of voices—a child's cry, a woman murmuring, a friend shouting from across the way—but the babble eventually won him over and lulled him.

He finished up the morning count and sat outside the trailer, drinking tea and contemplating how to ration his food, the best way to wash and dry his clothes at camp while the good weather lasted—any possible way to stretch his time away from town. Tanner had supplied a solar shower, a black rubber bladder that hung from a tree near the creek where it could absorb the sun's heat all day. It beat showering once a week at the community recreation centre. If he was careful, he could go maybe ten days between trips. So, two, maybe three, more visits to Shellycoat. That, of course, raised the question of what he would do after his final trip out, when the contract ended in mid-October, but he couldn't even attempt to answer that one yet.

Someone was driving up the mainline: a bad muffler, probably a pickup or an old model SUV. He heard a cranked stereo, heavy bass, and a rattle of loose wood and nails as the vehicle thumped over the bridge, and his heart sank. Tanner had said this place was quiet: it got more traffic than a city park. A few moments later, a rusted-out Jeep coasted down into the rec site, a stubby red kayak bungeed to the roof, the driver's window open, hip hop blaring. The driver had his arm out the window, whooping as he rolled his truck beside Paul's Pathfinder, his fist raised. He stared at the camper and at Paul, and his arm retracted. He turned off the stereo, and the door opened with a loud creak and pop, flakes of rust falling to the ground. He looked about twenty, sporting his cap backward on top of unruly blond hair, a surfer T-shirt and board shorts hanging off a toned and muscular body.

"What the fuck," he said, shuffling around in small circles. He pulled out his phone and started texting angrily.

"There's no signal," Paul said.

"Don't I know it." He tapped at the phone in disgust. Finally his glance returned to Paul. "Hey. Sorry, dude."

"That's all right." Paul still sat watching him from his lawn chair, both irritated and slightly amused. He didn't know much about kayaks, and this one looked strange: short, tapered front and back, very space-agey, like a squashed UFO. *Massive*, a decal said in sizzling letters.

"You see some guys earlier? Two trucks kinda like mine, kayaks on the roof?"

Paul shook his head.

"Fuckers." He threw his arms up in the air.

"Maybe you're early."

"No, bro, I'm fucking late. Like always. And nobody's been here waiting? Aw, man. They bailed on me. Fuckers."

"Sorry, what's the story here?" Paul asked, fairly sure he didn't care.

"We were supposed to drop half our trucks here and head up to the Flumes with the rest. We launch about ten K up the river, and we finish at the mouth of Basket Creek," he explained when Paul raised his eyebrows.

"Well, nobody's driven by this morning. Not even logging trucks." Paul sifted tea leaves through his teeth and spat. He pictured the rec site packed with beat-up trucks and shirtless teenaged dudes swilling beer. His idea of hell.

"They're probably hungover. Slept in. Shit. I was so hyped for this." His voice went up in pitch, somewhere between a teenager's whine and an adult's resigned disgust. Paul, reminded of the impatient and cocky Tran Minh, suppressed a smile.

"It's my first day off in, like, two weeks. Supposed to be our last big hurrah on the river for the year. You know?" He glanced over his shoulder to where the trails headed toward the water. "I guess I could just do some park-and-play action," he said to himself, a little subdued.

"Park and play?" Paul asked.

"You know, just session one spot close to the car."

"Here?"

"No. The Flumes. Big set of rapids."

"Doesn't sound like the type of thing you do by yourself."

The young man shrugged, his grin slightly sour and mocking. His body was always in motion, a twitch of the leg or finger tapping against his shorts. "Hang on a sec," he muttered. He jogged toward the river, disappearing down a path.

He was gone a long time. Paul stood and circled the truck. The boat's weird shape kept drawing his attention. He'd rented sea kayaks a few times in Vancouver. Those kayaks were sleek, built to slip across the surface with the least possible resistance. This craft demanded to be bashed around, it wanted dangerous places and an aggressive paddler. He was, he admitted, curious to see what this thing could do.

The young man returned, his hair and shirt soaked. He must have dunked his head to cool his temper. "Fuck it," he said. "I'm doing it. I'll walk all the way back up for my Jeep afterwards if I have to."

"I'll drive you," said Paul.

"What?"

"I'll drive you. Leave the Jeep here."

They took it slow the first few hundred metres up the road, the kayak wrapped in blankets in the back. "Sorry I was freaking out back there," said the young man. "My name's Jory."

"Paul," he said. "I'd be pissed off too." He wasn't entirely sure why he was driving the young man up to the Flumes or wherever. Maybe just to get this guy out of his camp, or maybe this was the push he needed to finally break away from the safety of his trailer and explore.

"So you a fisherman?"

"Not really. Counting fish, though."

"I wondered, but I figured that couldn't be right."

"What do you mean?"

"The guy that's normally here always has someone with him—his wife, I guess."

"Well, I'm single. Thanks for pointing that out."

"What I mean is, don't you need two people to keep up with the tagging and measuring?"

Paul looked over, surprised. "You know a lot about this project."

"My dad used to work for Monashee Power. Knows all the biologists around here."

"Retired?"

"Sorta." Jory grimaced. "He's into pottery now. Yeah, don't ask."

"So the spawning run—it's pretty big?"

"Big enough, especially when it's midnight and raining and your hands are going numb from the cold. No way a guy can do that shit alone and not lose his mind."

"Huh."

"Didn't know that?"

"Not a clue."

"Your boss is a bit of a dick, yo."

Paul was starting to think the same thing.

The road sloped upward and they climbed until on his right, across from the river, the mountains rose into view, craggy and snow-covered along their cathedral-like tops. For the first time he saw the magnitude of the range as it stretched to the north and south, the layers of peaks stacked westward, blue shapes blended into the sky. The river had disappeared behind a patchwork of clear-cuts, slash piles, and dense plantations of young spruce and larch.

"Branch 65," Paul said as they neared a fork in the road. The signpost, painted in white, hung from a broken-topped cedar.

"What about it? Keep left."

"A work crew. I met the camp cook. I think she invited me for lunch." Paul frowned, thinking he wouldn't take her up on the offer, and maybe it was too late anyway. "Kind of a bumpy drive just to get a meal and some company."

"It gets worse farther up," Jory said. "The road turns to absolute shit. You need an ATV and a jockstrap. Take a left down there."

Tree branches scraped the window, and twigs snapped under the tires as he negotiated the narrow trail's steep descent. A hairpin switchback spat them onto a clearing, a bench of land fifty metres above the river. On the far side of the bench, a forest of hemlock and fir dipped into a small, narrow ravine, where a fast-moving stream cascaded through the woods and met the river. He stepped out, stretched, and smelled rotten wood warming in the sun. Among the dried grasses, fireweed, and thistle, bits of rusted metal peeked out, the iron spokes and rim of a wagon wheel, a corroded chassis.

"What's all this?"

Jory pulled the kayak from the back of Paul's vehicle. He glanced around. "The junk? Part of an old sawmill, I think."

"Hence the name? The Flumes?"

"I guess."

Paul waded through the grass and inspected the metal scraps—an axle attached to a gear the size of a truck tire, the corroded skeletal hoops of an old waterline, the wooden slats long gone into the earth, corroded tin sheets from the remains of a sluice or drum. He tripped over the remnants of concrete foundations at his feet, the faint traces of vanished walls.

"Little help here?" said Jory behind him.

Paul stood up. "Sorry."

"I'm joking." He'd stripped down to his underwear. From a duffle bag, he pulled out a neoprene wetsuit and hood and tugged it over his muscular, mostly hairless frame and finally zipped up a sporty-looking yellow lifejacket. "I'm going to roast if I don't get in the water. You know, if you like old stuff, you're going to love living in the valley."

"Don't plan on living here," Paul said, but Jory had already slung the kayak under one arm and grasped his paddle and helmet in the other hand. As they walked through the field, the young man rattled off a list of local antiquities: trappers' cabins in the woods, cemeteries in the middle of nowhere, mineshafts, abandoned logging equipment. They reached the edge of the bench, which dropped off steeply. A well-worn goat trail led down the slope. Below them, the river roiled and surged between narrow channels of boulders, each the size of a small car, breaking the current into pockets of white froth where the water turned back on itself, all noise and chaos. Compared with this, the stretch of river running past his camp was as placid as a pond.

"The Flumes," Jory said proudly.

"Are you for real?"

Jory was already halfway down, negotiating the trail with ease. Skidding on his heels, Paul followed him down to a rocky beach beside a narrow strip of relatively calm water sheltered from the rapids.

"There's no way you paddle this," Paul said.

"Fucking rights we do. Some big holes, stoppers, and some pour-overs. You go through that chute"—Jory pointed out a spot between boulders—"and play in those waves for a while, then shoot downstream."

"You've done this a lot?"

"Oh, fuck yeah," said the young man. He hesitated. "Well, Cordell usually takes us through the tricky spots. He's our guide."

Paul shuddered and shook his head emphatically. "You know, I'm the only guy up here and I really, really don't want to see a body floating past my camp. They already fished one out of the river last week."

Jory snorted. He was stretching his arms above his head, limbering his wrists by turning them in circles. "Heard about that. Probably some douchebag looking to rip off someone's patch o' weed."

"He was an old man."

Jory edged the front of the kayak into the water and lowered himself into the seat. "See you back at camp." He laughed again as he dug one end of the paddle into the gravel. "You don't have to watch if you don't want to."

"That's why I brought you," Paul said. Jory pushed off, pointing the kayak's nose upstream. He tucked in with a few hard paddles until he hit the main current. Just as quickly, he spun to face downstream and slipped between the largest of the boulders.

For a split second he vanished, then shot over the ridge and into the waves. The kayak wrenched around, and then the front end plunged straight down in a pirouette. Jory arched his body until his head touched the back of the kayak, and the boat popped out and then surfed across the length of the wave. Every time the river threatened to topple the small craft, Jory would thrust his paddle down, lean in toward the ridge and vortex of the stopper, and launch back into the waves. He could have been a bit of spray, a droplet of dyed water, the way he crested and spun and cartwheeled, airborne. Paul shifted from foot to foot, and his hands and shoulders flexed and flinched at each of Jory's twists and spirals. He felt sick with how useless he would be if anything went wrong.

He paced the shore, angling for a better view, but there was no imagining the rapids from Jory's perspective. Certain features of the river obviously required specific techniques—the way a bouldering problem or parkour route was solved by a particular sequence of moves. In those sports, your body worked directly with static things, a type of conversation between your limbs and a climbing hold or structure. Kayaking looked far more complex and dynamic. The river was always moving and changing, dangerously influenced by things hidden below the surface. Within the deafening pandemonium, a frenetic dialogue was taking place between water, rock, and gravity, which produced currents and forces that spoke to the kayak with their pummelling and pulling, their suctions and expulsions. And these wordless signals reverberated through the fibreglass shell and into the paddler, who reacted. Or if he had some mastery—and Jory did—he could accomplish more than basic survival, just getting through the rapids. He could choose his course, take pleasure in his technique. He recreated, he played. Always on the edge of disaster.

Suddenly and inexplicably frustrated, Paul turned and climbed up the trail, panting and sweating at the top. Hands on his hips, he sucked in a huge breath and then wandered into the clearing to slow his heart.

He parted the tall weeds, prodded and nudged bolts and rivets embedded in the ground, cleared away brush from wire coils and decayed wood. A set of cogs and gears, caked with clay and attached by an axle to an empty metal drum, bore serial numbers on their corroded sides. The white ceramic emblems and metal-work of an old stove peeked out at him from under a clump of yews at the edge of the forest. An Adanac, the wooden handle on the main oven door rotted away. He tried to pull open the smaller compartments, but some had rusted shut, while the rest were filled with collections of leaves, twigs, and moss, the nests of packrats or squirrels. The date on the upper ledge above the iron top read 1930. They were strangely compelling and peaceful, these old and inert things, like artifacts carefully placed in an open-air museum.

With a shock of guilt, he remembered the young man on the water and ran back to the edge. The Flumes churned and roiled, empty—but there, downstream, a flash of red, then the yellow blade of the paddle, the kayak and paddler cutting through the smaller rapids, around the bend and out of sight. The river must get easier from there, Jory would be safe enough. But what did he know? The Immitoin was a mystery to him.

~

The Jeep still sat in the middle of the site when he returned, but the kayak, dripping wet, had been bungeed back on top. Jory was here somewhere. Trusting his gut, he ducked inside his camper and grabbed a beer Tanner had left in the fridge. He walked through the woods and found the young man sitting on the bank, his elbows resting on his knees, and his fingers kneading his temples.

"I had to sit and get the shakes out," Jory said with a laugh. His hands trembled slightly, and he looked a little stunned.

"Hit a rough patch? Rougher than the Flumes?"

"Let's just say the river's full of surprises."

Paul nodded. "Split a beer?"

Jory took one long drink, head back, then rose to his feet and handed the half-empty bottle back to Paul. "Hey," he said. "I have something for you. To say thanks."

"No need."

"Seriously. I know what I did was stupid. Like, really fucking stupid. You didn't have to give me a ride up."

"Guess I didn't feel it was my job to say so—I mean, I'm like a guest here."

Jory laughed. "Counting a few hundred trout'll make you feel right at home."

When they returned to camp, Jory pulled a metre-long piece of broad PVC pipe from the back of his Jeep. He grinned. "It's like a scope. For spotting fish. Dad made it. See? He glued a circle of Plexiglas on one end here, and the handles he salvaged off old cupboards."

Paul rolled the pipe in his hands. The handles were brass, almost dainty. One end of the pipe had been carved to rest against a person's forehead and chin. At the other end, a crust of yellow epoxy fringed the Plexiglas like icing. "I don't get it."

"He cheats. We go fly-fishing and he makes me wade to the edge of pools and eddies to scout for cutthroat. Pretty hilarious. A real fisherman would shit if he heard that."

"If I meet one, I won't tell him."

"Guess that was it for the year." Jory had opened his truck door and leaned on it, his eyes toward the river. He sighed. "Fucking summer clearance sales."

"What do you do, exactly?"

"Me and a couple of buddies have a little shop. Skis, bikes, boards, all that."

"Should have guessed." He saw the young man a little differently. If he could run a shop, there must be more to him than a simple adrenalin junkie.

"Catch you in town soon?"

"Of course. I have to get this back to you, don't I?" Paul held up the scope.

"No rush. Enjoy." Jory tilted his head and sniffed the air. "It's going to be a cold fall."

"Really?" The air was dead, and sweat trickled down Paul's back.

"Yup. Hope you got some decent porn on your laptop, because you'll be cooped up in that trailer before long." He hopped into the driver's seat. "Later."

That evening Paul was wondering about the old mill site at the Flumes and remembered the musty book Tanner had left behind. He dug it out of the cupboard: *Dixon's Gold: The Pioneer Years of the Immitoin Valley*. He thumbed through the chapters, but the book's mildewy smell drove him outdoors. Light shone dimly through the trees, the sun's last rays banking off the tops of the mountains to the south. He thought it a strange juxtaposition, to read of the Immitoin's first white explorers while he sat on the same banks a century and a half later, similarly lost and disoriented in his own, modern way.

Dixon arrives in Shellycoat.

The town of Shellycoat was named for a sturgeon.

1857: Bruce Dixon, a flame-haired and rangy man who'd once travelled from the mouth of the Columbia as far north as Kootanae House and Boat Encampment, finds himself in a hellish portage up the Immitoin. He and his expedition seek easy passages west, to the coast. It's late spring, and while the journey down the Columbia was tumultuous and deadly (a fatal capsizing at the appropriately named Death Rapids), the gruelling nature of their journey threatens to wear their spirits down entirely. The river is less majestic than the Columbia or even McGillivray's (later called the Kootenay), but equally savage: a younger, yet more primitive cousin of those greater rivers. Along the shores of McGillivray's, there existed pools, meanders, and braided channels that gave the explorers respite from the undertows and whirlpools. Here, the Immitoin gibbers in lunatic fashion across its entire width, and if it pauses for a breath, it is a space too short in which to launch boats.

He and his men have come upon a place where the land forms a long bench at the base of steep hills. Between forests of slender lodgepole pine and lush bracken fern are copses of trembling aspen and meadows saturated by ephemeral streams and two substantial creeks. On the face of each surrounding hill, at least one waterfall can be seen cascading through the blue trees. Kekulis and the charcoal remains of fire pits mark the camps of native fishermen, but the Sinixt and the other tribes will not arrive until autumn, when the salmon are running.

Twilight approaches. The older men rub Balm of Gilead into their palms and wrists and tell stories around the fire while the youngest ones groan from the day's labours. On the pretext of washing his tin plate and mug, Dixon has gone down to the river to watch the bats and hovering caddis flies, and to think. He knows that before the end of tomorrow, they will reach the place where the river widens into the first lake, and they will be blessed with a full day of easy paddling before the short portage to the second lake. Where they are now is a habitable place. He wonders if they would be derelict in their duties to not explore some of the small creeks here for minerals. There have been tentative explorations by others before him; but while otter, beaver, and fox pelts were harvested from the valley, no claims have been struck.

As he squats at the water's edge and dips his plate into the steely rapids, he feels a cold upwelling in his stomach and knows something is about to rise from the water, and then, less than twenty feet from where his heels dig into the sand, something does. The rattle of shells and coins accompanies the figure that launches itself above the spray and surging currents. A Shellycoat, Dixon thinks in horror. The bogeyman of the rivers in Scottish lore. The creature, the size of a young man, beckons once with a splayed hand as it arcs, naked and grey in the pale orange light of sunset. It holds itself in the air long enough to wrench Dixon's fate away from other explorations or, more precisely, to fix his fate to this particular place.

Then it vanishes, and he finds himself sprawled on the ground, terrified and struck by a newfound sense of purpose. Some men might have taken the creature as a bad omen, but he knows, even as his jellied arms and legs refuse to lift him, that he and his men cannot simply pass through here. Nothing like this would have occurred in a place that didn't hold great promise. They say a Shellycoat is a joker as much as a demon, and likes a good song as much as a drowning.

A year later he will wonder if the wind had displaced the rattling sounds from their true source, or if the gesturing limb was only the combination of skutes and jaw and fleshy whiskers—by then, he will have seen men haul one of the great fish onto their boats. It won't matter. He will already be building what will become a trading post and, in another twenty years, a prosperous mining town. For the time being, it will remain a desolate outpost waiting for the first prospectors to arrive.

9

The job's repetitiveness began to overwhelm him, the thousand identical twists of arms and shoulders and hips from weir to cooler, cooler to measuring table, table to river. Kipes and mossy scales, pale bellies, the fluttering gills beneath the bony operculum. The slight give of fish flesh against his latex gloves, fish smells, clove oil. The night, full of eerie sound and cold silence. When he tried to fall asleep, the same motions played out over and over against the back of his eyelids.

Deep down he'd expected the work to transform him physically back to what he had been, or something even more lean and rugged. He'd grown stronger—not enough—from constantly netting fish and scrubbing the fence, and could wade through the creek for longer periods of time before growing tired. But his beard made him look older and dishevelled, not rugged and manly, and his returning strength was overshadowed by soreness. His elbows, wrists, and fingers began to ache and seize from the cold water.

And yet he spent his afternoons in pursuit of the trout. At first, he hadn't understood what the scope actually did, as simple as it sounded. One morning after breakfast, he went down to Basket Creek to maintain the traps and fence. As he scooped a handful of twigs and leaves off the wire mesh, he suddenly realized he could use the scope to check for holes and damage underwater. Returning from his quick march to the trailer, he plunged the fish scope into the middle of the channel. The sudden clarity surprised and delighted him, and for a split second he remembered (or imagined) snorkelling in a lake as a boy. What water did to light, and what light did to rock, looked almost artificial, like a digitally enhanced photo. Near the vivid orange and white of larger stones lay pebbles flecked with red and black glitter, or streaked with cheerful jades and pinks, the subtle varieties of colour and grain magnified. Flakes of bark slipped through the gaps in the wire, the current tumbled pebbles downstream. A tiny stonefly nymph clung to the underside of a rock near the toes of his waders.

Stooped over the scope's eyepiece, he worked his way along the length of the fence and then upstream, sinking into the type of reverie a silent film can induce. Things drifted past the narrow circumference of his view. He even heard the creek differently, as though his ears had become more invested in the polyphonic roar of the stream, more receptive to sounds occurring beneath the surface.

He reached the bridge that crossed Basket Creek and kept going. At the edge of a pool, he spotted a flash of movement. He crouched and angled the scope until he saw a broader portion of the creek. Cutthroat hovered close to the surface, their small, football-shaped bodies dwarfed by the bull trout staging below them. The bellies of the male bulls blazed, iridescent and molten. In the shallower water, a female trout with one of his new, bright blue tags scraped the gravel with industrious flicks of her tail. As she dug her redd, the finer sands rose and glittered. Diffused, refracted light in the floating sediment created a distorted world—each pebble, each blue-tinged halo on the trout's flank, preternaturally glorious.

~

No one had come by the camp since Jory, and he finally felt alone—felt it too keenly, choked up by certain sights: the silver flash and distant rumble of a jet passing overhead, a satellite breaking loose from the static cluster of stars to continue its monotonous loop. Clouds blew in toward the end of the week, and the night air grew colder. Huckleberries ripened by the paths down to the water, and the leaves of the ash and willow began to turn. Sometimes a mist rose in the early mornings and filled the river valley, the landscape showing the grey face of its isolation.

He began following the Immitoin upstream with the fish scope, a little smug that he was getting into the secret stretches of river reserved for people like Jory. *Dixon's Gold* said that nearly every tributary of the Immitoin had been prospected. He searched for old things—pans and tins, a knife, the sole of a boot. History gave context to the wildness, mapped and defined it somewhat. He was someone who needed scale, limits. The early stories of settlement were all tipped lanterns and lightning strikes, avalanches and mudslides.

> In the hills are the charred or buried remains of villages that had believed, for brief, shining years, that they would become prosperous cities, hubs of culture and wealth. They imported pianos and established health spas on the mineral spring that some prospector had stumbled upon. They became expendable when the railroads changed the face of the frontier. Towns died before their names could be put on a proper map. They were reclaimed by the forest and forgotten.

One day he wandered up a small stream, its banks lush with false hellebore, arnica, and foamflower. The water tasted floral, alpine. He saw nothing of interest, other than a few rainbow trout and sculpins, and returned to the Immitoin. A shadowy cluster of large fish dashed into a trough that ran along the opposite bank. Water buffeted his knees and hips as he squatted in the gravel to peer through the scope. The riverbed, beautifully illuminated for most of its width, dropped away into indigo darkness as it met the trough.

As he manoeuvred to get a broader look, he stepped deeper into the current and, forgetting himself, crouched too low. Water poured into his waders, the loose substrate slid away beneath him, and the torrent yanked him underneath, slamming his face into the riverbed. A high-pitched note sang in his ears as he began to slide downstream. He planted his arms and thrust his eyes and nose above the surface—he needed to cough water out, but the river battered his lips, seeking entry. His body seized with the shock of frigid water, his hands numb, the swamped waders a heavy sack he would drown in.

He managed to wrench himself sideways and turn over so that he looked downstream, the current buffeting his shoulders as he coughed and sucked in air. Then the bottom dropped out again and he tumbled forward and beneath. The water was silver and disordered, flecks of light within bubbles that gathered and attacked. His feet hit the shallows, and he managed to take another quick gulp of air. The river hauled him over rocks and tumbled him this way and that, as if he were wood. He flailed his arms trying to stay upright, and he choked and sobbed between breaths.

He twisted toward the shore and clawed at the ground. His fingers were stiff and nearly useless, but his momentum slowed enough to let him wrap his arms around a boulder at the edge of the bank. It shifted, slid a few inches, then held. He kicked and squirmed until he pulled free of the waterlogged waders and hauled himself onto ground. Retching up water, weeping, he reached back for the waders and tugged them to shore. He wiped the water and mucus from between his nose and upper lip and saw that his numb and trembling fingers were scraped and cut. He wiped blood from small gashes on his cheeks and dabbed the raw mess of his forehead. His ribs and shoulders throbbed with every movement. He rose unsteadily, legs threatening to cramp and buckle, and staggered through the willow whips and cottonwood saplings. On his way back to camp, he found the scope precariously lodged in a cluster of driftwood and debris along the bank.

In the trailer, he piled blankets and sleeping bags on top of himself and passed out for the rest of the afternoon. He woke up in the dimming light, exhausted and battered, and troubled by a feeling that he'd been watched while he slept, exposed to a strange witness.

Last winter, he'd felt this same fear and loneliness. His body's quiet betrayal had been not unlike the babbling menace of the Immitoin. Here, animals passed by at night, snapping twigs and snuffling outside the trailer while he rolled onto his stomach trying to ignore his bladder. At home, it had been the walks down the dark hallway to the bathroom six or seven times after midnight. Dribbling into the bowl, frightened by jolts of pain. Then waiting for the doctor's word. No comfort, no refuge: not in other people, not in one's own body.

He was hot under the blankets, feverish. He held one arm tight across his sore ribs, hand in his armpit. With his other hand, he reflexively pawed and cupped his groin. No pleasure in it. His cock and balls lay warm, soft, and limp in his fingers, and after another light, testing squeeze, he brought his hand up under his other armpit and settled deeper in his blankets.

The next morning he woke to a light rain hitting the camper roof. The air smelled sweet when he opened the door. A raven called, a single note, *tock*, like a pebble being dropped into water. The sounds were muffled, as though the air had turned to loam. He stepped outside and saw that the hills had disappeared under clouds and the trees shone with rain. His waders, which he'd turned inside out to dry, were still saturated and cold. They'd been torture during last night's count. He pulled them on and shuddered. The huckleberry bushes and rhododendrons drooped across the path, their leaves soaking the shoulders and arms of his fleece pullover. The rain and overcast sky conspired with the creek to hide the fish beneath the grey mirror of the surface. His world had become increasingly and unpleasantly aquatic.

Last night the traps had taken four hours to empty. Stiff muscles and a chill made him inefficient and slow: whenever he thought he'd processed his last trout, five more would swim into the upstream trap. The spawning run hadn't quite hit its peak, and would only get worse over the next week or so. He needed to rest and then dig in for the long haul.

Nine days had passed since he had last gone to town, seven since he'd driven Jory to the Flumes. Food was running low, and a trip to Shellycoat loomed on the horizon. Dr. Tamba's e-mail still nagged at him, surfacing now and then with an uncomfortable sharpness: procrastination induced its own particular nausea. If he went to town, he would feel obliged to reply, which required a plan for the future, and he had none. He thought about life back on the coast. The fieldwork and writing he would have to continue in order to maintain his income, all the lost momentum he would have to regain. A desperate, strung-out sort of restlessness gripped him over breakfast. Bad weather would end the wandering that distracted him from his thoughts. He wasn't ready to be trapped inside the trailer yet.

~

The tree-planting camp appeared in a shallow valley clear-cut on both hillsides. Clouds in the treetops and mist along the ground framed the scene, dreamlike. Among the burnt stumps, the dry streambeds, thistles and fireweed, bloomed a colourful collection of tents, trucks, rusted GMC vans, and Volkswagens. Two long industrial trailers, the ones he'd seen drive by Basket Creek, formed the hub of the camp along with a pair of large, dirty canvas tents. Off to one side of the camp, near a small copse of ash and rhododendron, stood three porta-potties spaced a few metres apart. The camp looked like a post-apocalyptic shantytown. He stopped for a long time at the crest of a hill where the skid road descended to the camp, and might have turned around then if someone hadn't stepped out from inside one of the trailers and given him a wave. He tapped the gas lightly and rolled down to her.

"So you finally come visit, right on the last day," Gina said. Flour clumped and clung to her hands and wrists and sauce stains covered her apron. Beneath, she wore shorts and a grey, long-sleeved shirt. She let the rain soak her hair, the early grey strands damp and shining.

He stared at her as he stepped outside. "Last day?"

"Every contract ends with lousy weather. I don't know why." She brushed off her hands. "Lunch?"

He followed her into one of the trailers, knocking the mud from his hiking boots on the edge of the steps. A rich smell of broth, onions, and baking bread greeted him. Rows of cupboards and long countertops stocked with fruit, vegetables, and tins lined the counters on both sides of the trailer, except for a space near the back where a small table and two chairs rested against the wall. A pair of fridges and a large grill, a four-burner propane stove and oven, and a double sink completed the kitchen. A shotgun was mounted on a rack above the back door.

"A bear comes by every now and then," she said, following his glance. "He scares easy, so far. Coffee?"

The smoky, nutty smell of it, set against the damp cold outside, was impossible to refuse. He edged his way into a chair. "Where's your boy—Shane?"

"Just started kindergarten," she said. "He's back in town. With his dad." Her tone was a bit too neutral, but he said nothing. She poured coffee from a French press into a chipped yellow mug and set it in front of him. It was perfectly brewed, strong and earthy, not bitter. He closed his eyes a moment.

"So, are you going bush yet?" she asked.

Must be, he figured. The mere texture of good coffee in his mouth had him swooning, emotional. He knew he looked terrible, his forehead and cheeks scabbed and bruised, yellows and purples in the folds of skin beneath his eyes, a dark scruff of a beard harbouring bits of food and twigs. He probably smelled— his nostrils were perpetually clogged with clove oil and fish slime, so how could he tell anymore? "Do I look the part?" he asked.

"A little rough, yeah." She grinned. "Should I ask about your face? Some guys don't like being asked. Pissed off they got hurt in the first place." She scooped a ladle of soup into a bowl. He stirred the vegetables in their yellowish broth and lifted some to his lips, tasting cracked black pepper and turmeric.

"Thank you," he said. Soup dribbled off his lip into his beard. He took another sip of coffee, the beginnings of a giddy euphoria rising from his chest.

"You're the first person I've talked to in days that isn't a trout," he said. "Except for this young guy—Jory. Gave me a fish scope, and I almost drowned. That's why the cuts and all that." He pointed to his forehead as he spooned more soup. "I'm sorry I'm babbling like this."

She nodded, a smile playing at the corners of her mouth.

"I was feeling a little pinned down with all this rain," he continued. "Thought I should get out now, before the roads get worse."

"I don't mind the rain much," she said. "Prefer it, in a way. At this time of year, sunshine feels like a cheap lie. Summer's come and gone, and I worked every damned minute of it."

"Yes," said Paul. He leaned forward, half aware that he was

stirring his coffee in manic circles. "But when the weather turns, you know winter's on its way, and you have to know what you're going to do next. And, me, I don't have a clue."

She'd gone back to the oven, pulling out trays of buns and dinner rolls. He set his coffee aside, trying to slow himself down. He rested his hand on his tender brow and breathed in the warm, buttery smell of fresh bread. A moment later, a bun appeared on a plate before him. Gina sat across from him, and they angled their chairs to face the window, to the rain and mist in the trees outside. The bread yielded softly to his fingers as he dipped it in his soup.

"Won't you go back to the coast?" she asked.

"Probably not." He laughed a little wildly, surprised at his own answer. "I guess I don't really like anything waiting for me there."

She turned from the window and smiled sadly. "That used to be the best part of bush work—the winters off. I used to go to Mexico with my friends, live on the beach. Dreamt about buying a little house down there. But now that Shane's in school, I'll be sticking around. I don't ski or snowboard, so there's fuck all to do. My ex and I . . . disagree over child support and visitation. And other things. I'd work through the winter if I could."

"I hate the thought of going into Shellycoat, checking my e-mail, watching people do their real-life things," he said. "But I'm running out of food. I like being at camp, getting to know what's around me. I like the history of the place, the little I've read. Sinking into that."

He told her he could barely keep pace with the spawning run, and that at his rate he'd soon be working all through the night, or close to it. "When I try to speed up, I forget to record my numbers or I stab a fish with a tag."

Her brow suddenly furrowed. "No one's helping you during the peak?"

"What do you mean?"

"I've seen the camp operate other years. I'd swear there were always two people there."

"That's what Jory said. It was probably Beth." He shrugged. "Tanner's just lucky enough to have a partner, I guess."

"Or too cheap to hire you one," she said, more to herself than him.

She stood up and grabbed an empty cardboard box from the counter and began filling it with food from the shelves—a box of crackers, a dozen apples and a few bananas, tins of olives, tuna and black beans, a small jar of salsa, and a bag of coffee. Then she took another box and piled in stuff from one of the fridges: cucumbers, spinach, beets and carrots, plastic-wrapped ham and turkey slices, a dozen eggs. Two Tupperware containers filled with leftovers: penne with bacon, peas and Manchego cheese, and a chicken curry.

"Think that'll hold you over for a while?" she asked.

He leaned back in his chair. "But—how much would I owe you?"

She snorted. "Nothing, obviously. They're just leftovers. Company's already paid for it."

"Well." He reached out with his hand, about to shake hers— then quickly brought his hand back, clasped his fingers and stared at the table, a lump in his throat. God, he was so not ready for people.

"It's nothing." She took off her apron. "Gotta run to the outhouse. Back in a few. Help yourself to coffee."

He waited until she'd left before greedily pouring himself another cup, his hands shaking from the caffeine. At the end of one counter, newspapers were stacked in a small pile. He sorted through the papers until he found the most recent one, dated from five days ago. *The Shellycoat Observer*, mostly filled with advertisements, classifieds, and a calendar of community events.

A few small articles in between half-page ads. Scores of a round-robin softball tournament, another round of layoffs at the mill. But nothing about the man who'd drowned. He skimmed some articles, and then stopped when he recognized the name and face of Hardy Wallace, his photo a small square above a large block of text. Not a police report, nor an obituary. No, the old man had written and paid for a full-page ad.

To all Monashee Power Criminals:
Wouldn't you know it—another year gone by, another year wondering when the folks of Lambert, not least the owners of Lots 4205 and 4209 to 4313, will be fairly compensated—those of us that are still alive. Yes, it's our anniversary again, forty years since Lambert vanished from the map. Can't you tell by the wasteland of stumps that appear every fall on the northern shores of what you call the Lake? The fruit that must be imported from the Okanagan because our best farmland is under-water? The mill shutting down, "seasonally," as it has ever since you drowned the forests and opened the valley to the foreign logging companies that buried all the little guys?

You may treat me like some stranger, even after all these years, but you know me full well—you watched the valley, every house, go up in flames. Our past was nothing but ashes before we even arrived at our new home, exiled, shunned for being "north of Shellycoat."

So happy anniversary to us "Lambert locals." Maybe I'll spend the day remembering, now that our creeks and rivers are full of nothing but garbage fish and a handful of cutthroat, how the whole

Immitoin once ran red with salmon. The pool below my exile's house used to be filled with them, back in my father's day. Now it gets sucker fish and the occasional dead fisherman—suckers of another kind, people who think they know the river.

And the place where you folks sit with your boats and fill your coolers with mercury-poisoned fish—right in that very spot, some hundred feet below your keel, we once grew apples and pears, plums and cherries. Even watermelons, if you can believe. Try growing them now, with the best soil gone.

Still waiting for justice. How long now? Forty years, more.

10

Several events marked his last two weeks on the Immitoin, the first being the rising of Basket Creek. On his way down from Gina's camp, new streams had leaped the ditches and culverts and cut channels across the road. His wipers rubbed frantic arcs across his windshield but could not stop the valley from disappearing behind the spray of mud and rainwater. Back at camp, twigs and sticks had piled up against the mesh of the fence. He waded out to the middle of the creek, the turbid water battering his knees with an unfamiliar force. The makeshift pools where the fish recovered from the anesthetic had been absorbed into the current. The rest of the afternoon he kept watch beneath the tarp of the measuring station and waded back out when the fence took on too much debris. Before he went back to the trailer for a brief dinner, he gathered stones and rebuilt the pools. If a half-stunned trout was swept into this current, it would be battered to death against the rocks.

The rain kept on for days. Despite the rising waters, the spawning run reached its peak, and the numbers of trout mounted. Perhaps it was a projection of his own exhaustion, but the fish appeared more haggard and worn. Dorsal and pectoral fins were torn, and scratches and small gouges appeared on their noses and flanks. Their gasps, as they lay on the scale, were more pronounced and desperate. The numbers in the downstream trap increased, as bull trout began to make their way back home to the lake. The females had worn their tail fins ragged digging their redds, and their bodies, emptied of eggs, lay wasted and hollow in his hands.

There were other things he'd have liked to pursue, such as the meaning of Hardy's letter and why the newspaper would print something so bizarre, even potentially libellous. He wondered about certain things the old man had mentioned: the lot numbers, the houses going up in flames. The orchards—he'd never noticed any on his drives between Shellycoat and Basket Creek. And the mysterious Lambert locals, the "us" and "we" of Hardy's letter, which suggested there were other folks like Hardy in the valley, people who shared his history and maybe even his particular brand of rage. Now that was an fascinating possibility. People were Paul's thing, even when they really weren't.

But all this would have to wait. The creek, the rain in his eyes, rain hissing against the hot globe of the lantern, the dark eyes of the gaping trout, all these things were part of the same entity, appendages of a body composed of infinite water and the limits of his endurance.

On the fourth day of rain, Gina drove into the site pulling a camper behind her. The way she worked the truck back and forth at different angles until it was perfectly level, he knew she was staying. For a moment, he felt guarded and irritable, possessive of his isolation. He avoided meeting her gaze at first, trying to quell his annoyance. She wore a wide-brimmed oilskin hat that she'd pulled down low on her forehead to try to conceal a bruise on one side of her face near the eye and a swollen, discoloured cheek. She looked fierce and stubborn.

"I know you don't want anyone here. But I thought maybe you could use a hand," she said, and Paul knew better than to ask why she wanted to help someone she'd only met twice.

"I was up until two last night," he said. "Fingers got so numb, I couldn't record data. Had to repeat the numbers aloud while I warmed my hands against the lantern."

She shuffled her feet, looking down and away.

"Honest," he said. "I'm ready to fall down."

"I even brought my own waders," she said. A price tag hung from the strap.

One handled the fish, the other recorded the numbers, switching when the handler's fingers went numb. After a tentative first hour, they settled into a steady pace. The rhythm that had so often eluded Paul came easier with two people. The first night, he netted a massive trout that would only fit into the cooler at an angle, from corner to corner. He and Gina both hovered over the giant male and waited while the fish slammed its thick body against the sides of the cooler and splashed them with anesthetic. Its back was a map of scars and leathery skin, its kipe knotted like a piece of wood and bristling with thorny teeth. Gina wrestled the bull trout onto the table, unafraid when it suddenly bucked and flailed in her hands.

Each night after the count, they would sit at the table in his camper, and he would serve herbal tea and enter data while she watched. The small space smelled of fish, wet fleece and wool, and her damp hair. Rain pounded on the roof, the rattling veneer muffling the sound of the generator. Condensation blanketed and dripped down the windows.

"You've always cooked?" he asked once. They'd been laughing about his archaeological dig in Sweden, the sad lunches of potato cakes and cinnamon buns he'd packed each day.

She shook her head. Without her hat on, her bruised face shone and reflected its different dark colours under the fluorescent light, one eye half-closed like a wink, the freckles on her cheek hidden or distorted by purple skin, pooled blood. "I used to do the work, the planting, brushing, spacing. I'm pretty good with a chainsaw."

She had to explain what all those things were, how brushers went in after the planters and cleared the competing vegetation from around each planted tree, and how spacers would, years later, thin out those plantations with saws. It paid per hectare, she said, so you were always pushing yourself harder to make more money. But you had time to daydream and think too, because the work was simple and repetitive.

"What made you stop?"

"Shane, partly. My body. Tree-planting beat up my knees and wrists, brushing did my shoulders in. Got tired of gas fumes and the noise, always dealing with a broken saw. Men love to dick around with their chainsaws. They have their rituals—eat the same breakfast, smoke their cigarettes, and sharpen their saws after dinner. I knew one guy, he'd crack his beer the exact second the truck started. He had the timing down."

"I have beer, if you'd rather," he said.

"You don't drink?" she asked.

He thought about it. "I could, I guess. There were antibiotics, painkillers before. I've had . . . health issues. It's easier if I don't." His trailer was a bit of a disaster—he took a quick glance around, praying he'd stashed his incontinence pads.

She didn't dig any further, nor did he ask about her bruises, or Shane's father. She respected what wasn't said, and likely hoped for the same from him.

Each night's work took them past midnight. When her eyes began to close, Gina would retreat to her own camper. Paul always followed her outside to shut off the generator. He'd cut the engine and urinate under a tree as the rain fell on him. A dim light would turn on behind the curtains of her camper. Sometimes he'd watch until the light went out, unsure why he did, too tired to pin down what exactly he felt beyond an uneasy comfort in the presence of the lit windows.

"If you hadn't given me all that food, I would have needed to make a trip to Shellycoat," he said on her third night there.

"Think you'll make it through now?"

"Food-wise." He hesitated. "Can't put things off forever, of course. People in my department are waiting for answers."

"You have answers?" She arched an eyebrow, her wry smile marred by a swollen lip.

He blushed. "No. I've been thinking about the lake, though."

"The reservoir, you mean. Why?"

"Hardy." He told her about the old man trying to kill the fish, and the rant he'd seen in the paper. "I don't get it. What was he saying in his letter? I understood everyone got compensation, cheap property in Bishop."

She hissed with dark humour. "Who told you that?"

"The cops."

She shook her head. The clock read one-thirty. "I'll show you something. When the work slows down."

He laughed, a scratched sound from his dry throat. "You actually want to stay that long?"

She was already pulling on her boots. "Told you I'd work out here all winter if I could. Besides, if I only stuck around for the tough part, I might get the mistaken impression this job's terrible. Good night, Paul."

~

The next morning Tanner showed up. He climbed stiffly out of his truck, his face blank and stony-eyed. Paul stood in front of the campfire warming his hands, Gina was napping in her camper.

"When I said keep the calls to a minimum, I didn't mean fall off the face of the earth," Tanner snapped. "I was starting to wonder if you'd died." He gave Gina's truck a long stare and then turned back to Paul. "You've done your morning count?"

"And all the data. I was just about to clean the fence."

Tanner reached into the truck and yanked out his waders. "Let's go down and check it out."

Paul was jittery and hollowed out—too much of Gina's coffee, not enough sleep. His stomach was knotted, ready to catch hell from Tanner. What am I, he thought, sixteen at McDonald's again?

"Who's that?" Tanner growled quietly.

"She's from a bush crew up the road. Their job ended, so she offered to help out."

Tanner stopped and turned. "You've got her handling bull trout? This is government work, man. Only authorized personnel can lay their hands on these fish."

He laughed at Tanner's formality. The two men faced off in front of the measuring station. "Was Beth authorized?"

Tanner hesitated. "By me, yeah."

"Well, then, you can authorize Gina," Paul said, suddenly flushed and shaking. "Because there's too many trout for me to do this by myself. I was practically pulling all-nighters until she came on board. Running myself fucking ragged."

Tanner's gaze broke away first. "I couldn't bid high enough to pay for two workers. Had to lowball the other contractors."

"She's not asking for money. And I'll pay her myself if she does."

The two men pulled on their waders. They walked down to the fence and Tanner scooped up the twigs and leaves that had piled up against the upstream side of the weirs. "That's your call," said Tanner. "Paying out of your pocket, that is. Lotta crap on the fence."

"I think there's a beaver upstream."

"I can give you a gun for that."

"Fuck you."

Tanner stopped tossing sticks over the fence and roared with laughter. "You *are* getting bushed. You don't sound anything like yourself." His knees buckled in the current, and he braced his foot against a rebar post. "Creek's really risen, hasn't she?"

Paul didn't say anything. They finished cleaning the fence and waded back.

Gina stood outside her truck, waiting for them. Tanner introduced himself in a friendly enough voice. Her own smile was guarded and equally professional—she was someone who knew contractors and bosses. "I just came to check on things," Tanner said.

She nodded. "I'm off for a walk anyhow. Fresh coffee's in my camper. Feel free to grab some." Paul and Gina exchanged a quick glance, and he rolled his eyes before ducking into the trailer.

Tanner spread the notes in front of him and flipped through pages. "Looks good," he said. "Did you two beat the hell out of each other or something?"

"I fell in the river. Can't speak for her."

Tanner closed the books. "Look, I get a little tense at this stage. They come by, you know, on the last day. Biologists from Monashee and the government. To check our work."

Paul sat up straight. "Here? How many?"

Tanner counted on his fingers, mouthing silent names to himself. "Eight. More, if some of the Streamkeepers Association tag along, and they usually do. We all walk Basket Creek and count redds—that's the easy part. Hard part's listening to them talk about the quality of our work, asking if the numbers are right."

"Like those brutal oral exams," Paul said. Being grilled by a panel of professors and associate deans for his thesis defence. Trying to field their questions with the minimum amount of stuttering, umm-ing, and er-ing. Would they ask Paul about the hours he kept, or make him demonstrate his tagging technique?

"Except they bring booze. Actually, it's more like I'm hanging out with my older brother's friends, and I'm always one mistake away from becoming the loser of the group." Tanner grimaced. "Anyway, that's my problem, not yours. You get to stand there and pretend to laugh at their lousy jokes."

"I can do that." He leaned back and looked out the window, both relieved and troubled. The end of his time here became more real, while life after his job still had no shape or form. It was a mist made of things he didn't want to do, or be. Money was not an urgent issue. His daily costs had been covered by his per diems, he'd spent hardly any money on food thanks to Gina, so his paycheque would be waiting for him at the end, untouched. On that amount, he could survive two or three months in Vancouver without working, four months anywhere else. So he would not starve, but then, that had never been the problem.

"Think you'll stick around for the film fest?" Tanner asked, as though he'd read his mind.

"Isn't that a ways off?"

"Not when you're organizing it. Feels like tomorrow," he said. "I screened a documentary about parkour, by the way. Kind of ethnographic—they do some interviews—but mostly there's a crappy hip hop soundtrack and kids showing off. Probably won't make the cut."

Paul sighed ruefully. "Maybe I should have made a film after all."

"So you're not with that woman?"

"Do I need to answer that?"

Tanner grinned. "No. But what an opportunity. Be a shame to miss out."

"There are reasons, you know, why I might miss out."

"Right—yeah." He smiled sheepishly. "Well, never say never."

Paul waved his hand dismissively, but he admitted Gina's presence was unsettling. Their two trailers faced each other with no trees and shrubs in between, exposed. The distance between them changed at night, a trick of the darkness. Were they situated too close or too far apart from each other? If there was tension, he lacked the physical capacity to gauge it.

11

After the morning count, Paul and Gina warmed their hands over the campfire, their jacket sleeves damp and reeking of fish. The sky had cleared, and frost brightened the hills. "We should get out of camp for the day," he said.

"Not town."

"No. You said you'd show me the lake."

"Reservoir. Why so interested?"

"Maybe because you keep correcting me," he said lightly. "Obviously something about the reservoir's a big deal."

"I never said it was." She returned his amused stare with a blank expression. Slowly, she gave him a half-smile that raised the faded bruise on her cheek toward her eye.

He dared a wink. "If you don't want to come," he said.

"No. I'll take you. There's a couple of places you should see."

She drove his vehicle and didn't speak much. The levity between them had vanished. He pointed out Hardy's cabin, and they passed through Bishop without speaking. Nearly halfway to Shellycoat, they pulled over at a picnic area. A pile of bleached, abandoned logs separated the road from the beach, a series of low ridges of river rocks between small islands of fine-grained sand. "Goosen's Beach," Gina said, but Paul was looking at the lake or, rather, at the moonscape where the lake should have been. Beyond the benches and ridges of sand and rock lay a vast plain of cracked, dun-coloured mud. At first, the sight didn't strike him as unusual; it reminded him of low tide on the coast, the pebbly beaches that became magnificent stretches of sand perforated by the subterranean breathing of clams, marked by the tracks of gulls and crabs, the beach crackling with unseen life. But here, the only signs of life were sprigs of horsetail and pale, wispy algae that covered the exposed rocks and boulders, a few crows tip-toeing among them. No tidal pools, no creatures biding their time underneath boulders, waiting for the ocean to rise—only stillness, the light sound of rain, and a faint, metallic smell. The water was a good half-kilometre away, sunken at the bottom of the valley. On the opposite shore, black-stained bedrock marked the high water line like a bathtub ring.

"You know summer's over," Gina said, "when it's drawdown."

"It's like this every fall?"

"When I was a kid, you never knew what the reservoir would look like from one day to the next," she said. "Now Monashee Power keeps the levels steady over the summer for the boaters and tourists. What you're seeing is close to what the lake really was. Level-wise, I mean. The land looked a lot different, obviously."

He walked down the edge of the beach and she followed. He stepped onto the mud flats and the ground compressed like stale cake, the damp crust breaking into shards. At the north horizon, a forest of pale dead trees stood like leached bones or blasted pillars. He remembered what the young cop, Davis, had said about the places you avoided, how snags uprooted and burst out of the water.

She pointed to the south, where the diminished lake nar-rowed like the neck of an hourglass. Paul shook his head, not seeing. She leaned into him so he could sight along her stretched arm, wisps of her hair brushing against his neck. Her sweater smelled of tree pitch and coffee.

"It's only a bump. You'd have to know what to look for," she said. "It's only visible when the reservoir's dropped. Close to the waterline."

"I wish I had binoculars . . . it looks skeletal."

"My parents' tractor. They left it behind, and no one bothered to remove it."

Now he could make out the frame of the machine shrouded in black dirt and river slime. He wanted to turn his head and see the expression on her face, but she stood against him, her arm thrust forward, and their faces were too close together.

"Now look farther up, toward us. Those piles of stone are what's left of the wharf where the steamships used to dock." She spoke in a sing-song voice, like someone telling an old tale. "Near that was the Hutchinson farm. The forest was theirs too, it led to the old road."

She paused, but he didn't know if he should say something, or more truthfully, he didn't know what to say. "It's hard to picture," he said apologetically. "How it must have been."

She stepped away. "On the other side, across from my parents' farm, that's Lambert. The shoreline you see, the mud banks and flats—all that used to be meadows and forests. And orchards."

"How many lived there?" he asked.

"Three, four hundred. But there were dozens of families like mine on this side of the lake too. More than a thousand people were displaced."

He imagined everything preserved beneath the water—a wrecked paddlewheeler, the drowned frame of a country house. It was a romantic, compelling vision, something out of a book.

"Your parents' home—is it standing, under the reservoir?"

She shook her head. "My mother and father burned it down. The day they were relocated to Bishop."

~

Bishop, Unincorporated was as ephemeral as campfire smoke caught in tree branches. "Unincorporated" implied the incorporeal, uncertain borders. The few inhabited homes hid among abandoned dwellings and lots. The modern summer cottages clung to their islands of manicured lawns and shrubbery facing the lake, away from the ramshackle homes. Their owners had all fled back to the States or Alberta, the houses winterized and closed up. Gina took him down a side road crowded by alder, past a lot where a trailer sat, its siding peeled back to bleed pink fibreglass. A plywood mudroom weaned itself from the aberrant structure of the trailer, taking nails and trim along with it.

Other artifacts on the decrepit properties: a dog chain stretched to its full length, rusted and staked to a thistle-carpeted lawn. Rusted El Caminos and cube vans oxidized down to their most skeletal essentials, refrigerators like ghoulish obelisks. Wild raspberry canes grew out of the empty chassis of a Ford, honeysuckle had colonized a lawn chair. An occasional sign of life—a car with current plates, freshly cut firewood, an article of junk or a toy that hadn't been claimed by moss or lichen—but mostly neglect.

She didn't say anything but took them farther down the road. She stopped in front of an abandoned log cabin, the wood old and peeling, cracked in places. The roof shingles were spongy and black, covered in sodden moss and dead leaves, the yard overrun with grasses chest-high, thistles, and mullein.

"Spooky place," said Paul.

"That's where I was born."

"Oh." He smiled weakly. "I'm sure it looked great back in the day."

She sat rigidly, staring at the house. "My father built it. Don't know that he was ever proud of it."

"So they were forced to move here?"

"Maybe *force* isn't the right word," she said irritably. "This was all that was offered, and all that most people could afford. If you had money, you had other choices." Gina put the Pathfinder into reverse, backed out of the crumbling driveway, and gunned the vehicle back to the main road. She was leaning her head toward the window with an absent, joyless expression, forehead grazing the vibrating glass.

"So, where to now?" he asked, trying to keep things light. "Was there a school you went to here? Church?"

"Let's head back to camp."

~

Gina spent the rest of the afternoon constructing a sweat lodge near the confluence of Basket Creek and the Immitoin. She formed a circle from rocks and logs, placing them several metres from the riverbank, in a gravelly spot among the willows. She'd cut a few saplings, but not enough, and they wouldn't stay upright in the stony ground. Once he figured out what she was trying to do, Paul went to grab a few spare pieces of rebar, a coil of wire, and the hammer. When he returned, she'd dug a shallow pit inside the circle. While Paul pounded rebar, Gina disappeared and came back with a blue tarp crumpled into an unwieldy ball.

"Sorry about bugging you earlier—saying *lake* instead of *reservoir*," he said. "I didn't know."

She was wiring saplings to the rebar posts to make a square frame for the tarp. "It's all right," she said without looking up. "To be honest, I kind of force myself to think that: *reservoir*, not *lake*. I mean, it was forty years ago, before I was born. It's Bishop I remember, not the farm. It's like a discipline, using the right word."

"I had a friend—well, a participant—kind of like you," Paul said slowly. "Xi. He was into parkour—like street gymnastics." She nodded understanding. "He never accepted his surroundings at face value, not a wall, or a pillar or a set of stairs. Everything had more than one purpose, one meaning—even if no one else could see it."

She shrugged disagreeably. "Sounds very rosy. Optimistic."

"I suppose—never thought of it like that."

"My way's more like picking at scabs." She mostly worked in silence after that, except to show him how they would wire the saplings to the rebar to make a square frame over the circle or deliver the hot rocks from the fire to the pit. The frame they made was sturdy but not tall. "We'll have to crawl in, but the inside will heat up faster," she said. The tarp draped easily over the frame and was large enough that it touched the ground on all sides. They weighed it down with large round stones and left two flaps, one where the hot rocks would go into the pit and another for the entrance. She gathered firewood and boughs to store under the tarp to keep it dry until night. A lot of sweat to make a sweat lodge, he thought.

At midnight, when they'd finished the count, he rushed through his paperwork, feeling distracted, nervous without knowing why. Gina went to her trailer and returned, bringing with her matches, newspaper, a shovel, and a plastic basin filled with coarse, dark rocks. A bath towel hung over her shoulder. She had gathered the stones, she explained, while at the camp on Branch 65. They were igneous, mostly basalt or blends of diorite and granodiorite. "Good sauna rocks," she said. River stones, she explained, could store moisture inside them for hundreds of years and might explode in the fire.

"So you planned to do a sweat here, what, weeks ago?" he asked.

She laughed. "I collect a few rocks from every camp I work and keep them in my trailer."

"Why?"

She shrugged. "Souvenirs." She borrowed his headlamp and disappeared.

Once he'd finished the data, he began to putter—stacking a few unwashed dishes, organizing folders—but finally stopped, took a breath, and grabbed his towel. He took the lantern with him, cut the generator, and walked through the woods. A small fire burned outside the sweat lodge. Gina, already undressed and wrapped in her towel, prodded the embers with her shovel. They quietly watched the rocks heat up. She shovelled up a stone, and he parted the tarp for her so she could drop the glowing rock into the pit, one arm against her body to support her towel as she held the shovel. She brought three more rocks over. "It's ready," she said. "Go on in." He slipped out of the firelight and quickly stripped down, swore at the cold wind off the river, and wrapped the towel around his hips. He ducked under the entrance flap and left the lantern behind. It was still warming up inside, not at its peak. Gina followed, put her head-lamp in a corner where her clothes were stacked, and covered it with a shirt so that it cast a dim orange light. "You haven't poured the water yet," she said and lifted the basin over the hot stones. With an explosive crackle and sputter, steam billowed around them.

The sweat lodge was small and cave-like, humid and smoky. The logs they sat on were damp, caked in dirt, sand, and charcoal that smudged and stained their towels. Neither of them had big enough towels to safely leave alone; his wanted to fall away from his hips, while hers rode up around her thighs. He and Gina sat across from each other low to the ground, their legs awkwardly extended, their left knees meeting in the centre of the lodge and brushing against each other. The stones glowed, and sweat began to bead across his shoulders and back.

"Not bad," she said. "I've made worse. A beer would really top this off."

"I should have brought one for you."

She shook her head. "I don't like me that much when I drink."

She poured more water, one arm across her to keep the towel in place, and dipped her other hand in the basin. Steam washed its moist heat over them. The fire crackled outside, sounding near or distant as the breeze shifted. The perpetual noise of the river tumbled around and over the stillness inside.

"I smell like clove oil," she said. "It's awful."

"It's probably just in your nose," he said. "I lost my sense of smell a few weeks back." The spot where their legs touched became tacky with sweat, and he wondered if he should pull away. She threw small boughs of cedar on the hot stones and they smoked and hissed, filled the space with a resinous, bitter fragrance.

He said, "Can I ask about your bruises?"

"If I can ask about your—what did you call them—health issues," she shot back, her mischievous grin somehow hard and unyielding.

"Where to start," he said.

"Exactly." She sat up and awkwardly stepped over his legs. "We need more rocks."

"I can go."

"It's all right." She went out, and he heard the sound of the fire being disturbed, the snap of coals. A metallic sound of metal on stone, and a moment later, the shovel appeared and slid three more rocks into the pit. He took the basin and poured the water. The steam nearly scalded his face and lungs, tasting of soot and minerals and acrid cedar. She returned and struggled under the low tarp, her towel covered in charcoal, mud, and dirt, slipping off her breasts and bunching around her hips.

"Oh, fuck it," she muttered. She stepped over him, naked, spread the towel on the wood, and took her place across from him, her legs slightly bent and beaded with sweat, her hands on her knees. She tilted her head back and breathed deeply. The heat and steam married the unclean smells of their bodies: the intimate funk of armpits and groins, the watery clove-tainted musk of the sweat on their backs and chests and limbs. Gina smiled at him, eyes unreadable in the shadows.

He fidgeted with his towel, shifting on his rough wooden seat, intensely flustered, nearly angry. What did she want, exactly? Their friendship was too new, definitely not ready for her nakedness to feel companionable in a hippy sort of way, which was maybe all she intended. Or was this where everything had been heading, beginning from the first sapling she'd cut this afternoon? He'd forgotten how to read signs, had tuned out the signals: he'd learned to shut down that instinctive part of himself. A conversation should have been taking place between two bodies, but his body neither spoke nor listened. Before, everything would have unfolded naturally—which didn't mean sex necessarily, he wasn't certain what was happening here—but he would have been able to acknowledge arousal, choose to act on it or not. He was confronted by expectations, and his body shrank from them.

"You asked me—listen, I should tell you," he said and without any preamble described his cancer and surgery. Possible nerve damage, vesicles, incontinence, impotence, the sound of each word, the clinical language, meant to discourage, push away. He ended with Christine, his bungled academic career, as though they also made things impossible. "I don't have much to offer. Even assuming you wanted, in the first place—maybe I'm being a loser here . . ."

She said, "A lot of people pick this kind of work, you know, because they want to run away, live like monks."

"I sort of *have* to live like a monk," he said. "In some ways."

"You came here to mope," she said. "Am I interrupting your moping?" She'd sat up straight, pushing her chest toward him, the aureoles of her breasts coppery in the muted lamplight.

"Well, a little." He looked her up and down deliberately. "But don't worry about it." Her laugh was soft, guarded.

"You know, I could have just moped at home," he said. "I mean, I was. So I came here, to do something useful."

"You came to mope. It feels more manly to go somewhere

else and do it. Otherwise you just sit in front of the television and feel pathetic." Now she pulled back, knees against her chest, arms wrapped around her legs. "I met my ex-husband in a tree-planting camp. Billy Wentz. A true Lambert local."

"You're kidding," Paul said, brightening a little. "He must know Hardy."

She shrugged. "Maybe. Billy was one of the last children born in Lambert before the flood. His grandfather was one of the first loggers in the valley, an important man. That shouldn't matter, just like it shouldn't matter I'm really from Bishop, not my parents' farm. But it does. So many times, I've watched him sit in front of the campfire, piss-drunk, just staring at the flames and bitching about the mill, or the missed payments on his truck, or what he shoulda been, coulda been."

"You're both bitter. A bitter couple."

"Anyways," she said. "What I was getting to. I met Billy in the bush, and now I come here to get away from him."

They were mostly silent for the rest of the sweat, the heat drawing the air from their lungs in long sighs. Whenever he opened his eyes, hers would be closed. He studied her body again, the darkness around it. A protest rose up from his chest, a desperate sense that they were both wrong about something, only he didn't know what.

12

Gina drove back to town after the morning count. "My mother and Billy probably passed Shane back and forth all week. I'll be in shit for that."

She left him her phone number for when he went to Shellycoat. "Or pass through, if that's the case," she said. He offered to pay her for her help, which made things even more uncomfortable. He wanted to tell her that he'd stayed up most of the night turning things over in his mind, that he'd tossed and twisted, nearly in tears, humiliated and lonely. But why the hell would she want to hear any of that?

When she was gone, he took the laundry he'd stashed in a cardboard box and washed it in the river, which was ice cold and beautifully limpid. The clouds had lifted to reveal new snow on the mountaintops. The hills ran yellow and crimson with changing huckleberry, false azalea, and mountain ash. He took the fish scope and explored Basket Creek. There were more redds, each one a patch of gravel more long than wide, plowed and turned by the female's tail, and lighter in colour than the algae-covered rocks around it. Males hovered in side channels, weary and resting. If he remained perfectly still, they brushed the scope's Plexiglas with their spotted and haloed sides. He imagined the first movie projectors, or the first person to look through Edison's kinetoscope: his intimate and startling encounter with light and motion, his primitive response.

Across the river, something moved on the hillside among the fall colours, a black bear foraging for berries. He and Gina had stripped all the bushes along the trails to the creek for their own breakfasts, and he was glad now they'd done so and left no food for animals. Later, a bull elk on the other side of the Immitoin lowered its antlered head to drink, and the rutting beasts bugled uncannily all through the night.

~

On a morning when he counted only twenty-four fish heading downstream, the female Hardy had shot appeared in the upstream trap. The missing chunk of flesh where the bullet entered still gaped, not quite healed. This time he put her in the anesthetic so that he could look at her on the measuring table. Most of her fins were tattered, her flanks scratched by branches or claws. But she had some weight to her: she had not spawned yet. She was the only female heading upriver that day. "You'd better hope someone saved you a male or two." He recorded her number and returned her to the creek, and watched until she recovered and swam away. He never saw her come back down, though maybe she simply remained in Basket Creek until he and the fence were gone. It was possible she had to go farther than the others to find the place she needed.

~

The next day, sparse, slow flakes of snow fell. He drove to the Flumes one last time. Ideas and plans flickered insubstantially in his mind, and he hoped a return to the mill site would make them more real. As he went to turn down the narrow skid road to the bench, he saw a vehicle parked below on the landing. It took him a moment to recognize Hardy's truck. He thought about turning around, or driving on, but instead he pulled off to one side and cut the engine. He closed his door quietly and crept into the brush, keeping the truck in sight. Something moved near the crumbled foundations of the old mill, and he crouched behind a fir. Hardy waded through the dead grass, cloaked in a torn rubber parka, a fishing rod and a green plastic tackle box in his hands. He walked slowly past the axles and gears and sheets of metal, a slight limp in his left leg, and when he disappeared down the steep trail to the riverbank, Paul followed and watched him from the edge of the landing.

Hardy sat on a short log at the edge of the water, near where Paul had stood when Jory launched his kayak. A corroded metal band girdled the wood, and black-stained divots marked where nails had been. A piece of the flumes, maybe. The old man wasn't using a dry or wet fly, and the hook was bare. He didn't stand up to cast his line, didn't have much technique at all. The plastic bobber dropped into the water at Hardy's feet, and it took nearly a full minute before the current caught the line and pulled it taut.

The rapids had diminished somewhat, the boulders of the Flumes standing stark and dry above the water. The bobber drifted playfully through the whirlpools, then vanished downstream. Hardy reeled in the line, so slowly it didn't appear to be happening and let it back out, as if the fishing line were a finger that traced the contours of a material he owned, a familiar-textured thing like a favourite coffee mug or a beach pebble kept in a pocket.

~

He grew restless around camp, filled with a need to move, to do something. This had been a good refuge, and in many ways he didn't want to leave. But there was no real way forward here. According to *Dixon's Gold*, the word *immitoin*—from either the Shuswap, Kuntaxa, or Sinixt language, it didn't say—meant "sheltered place." Before Dixon and the white settlers, the valley was mostly abandoned by late autumn. The different tribes and nations that had gathered for the salmon runs, or for the deer and elk, would have returned south to the more temperate Columbia River valleys or the Okanagan. This was a place to hunt and fish, to gather and collect, but not to dwell.

He read and re-read the newspaper clipping he'd kept from Gina's cook trailer. Even though it was a false image, the idea of a house or an entire town resting below the water had lodged in his mind. The people who'd been relocated—were they like Gina, harbouring bitterness? Or like Hardy, bewildered and half mad from loss? He certainly wouldn't be the first ethnographer to study people who'd been displaced, not by a long shot—but maybe that was a good thing. Or maybe this was just classic Paul, grabbing another idea out of thin air.

Deeper signs of autumn came: geese overhead, silhouettes in the narrow corridor of sky. Crossbills, jays, and finches appeared in the trees and shrubs by his camper, and he startled spruce grouse from hiding spots when he walked to the river. Frost hung on the fence and weirs in the mornings, and he could see his breath as he scrubbed the fence free of an astonishing palette of leaves: elderberry, alder, ash, cottonwood, red osier dogwood, birch, and willow. The Immitoin became sapped of light, the snow creeping farther down the mountains. At certain moments, he felt as if he'd already fallen in love and moved past heartbreak into an old, time-worn sadness.

He *was* sad, which, as Gina pointed out, was what he'd been going for the whole time. Yes, he'd come to the Immitoin to feel sorry for himself—maybe he should have savoured it more, really committed himself to being miserable and get it out of his system. But it was getting a bit late for that.

Each night, with the last fish tagged and released, he found his resolve. He drafted letters and a proposal, recalling the language and tone of academia. It was easier to consider his future at night, surrounded by a darkness he'd never grown accustomed to.

The morning before Tanner would arrive with the biologists, he counted only three fish. This was his last true day here. Tomorrow, he would have an hour or two of peace, and then the site would fill with trucks and a bunch of men standing around in a loose circle, sipping from travel mugs and laughing at inside jokes. He would be the stranger among them but also an object of curiosity. They would ask a dozen questions, examine the fence, and be disappointed there were no trout in the weirs. Tanner would say, "You should have saved us one." Everyone would split into groups to walk the different reaches of Basket Creek and the Immitoin. Afterwards, he and Tanner would dismantle the traps, pull the rebar, and roll up the fence, and that would be that.

So he had lots to do on his final day. Take the fish scope up Basket Creek one last time, careful not to step on any redds. Find a stone from the creek, another from the Immitoin. Sit and drink something hot in front of the fire, roast his dinner in the coals, smell the woodsmoke, watch the ash drift. Feel the trout struggle in the net, all muscle, all willpower and motion.

ETHNOGRAPHY

Subject: Proposal for Ethnographic Research
From: Paul Rasmussen
To: Dr. Elias Tamba

Eleven hundred people were forced from their homes in 1970 by the construction of the McCulloch Dam on the Immitoin River. This is less than the estimated two thousand or so people displaced along the nearby Arrow Lakes and a far cry from the millions of people who will have been displaced by China's Three Gorges Dam upon its completion. Still, the Immitoin Valley provides a unique opportunity to conduct an ethnographic study of those who have been displaced by hydroelectric dam activity.

The displaced were farmers, ranchers, loggers, and veterans from both World Wars living along the valley bottom where the river widened into two lakes. Four hundred and fifty of them lived in the largest community, known as Lambert, which had resisted incorporation and had, for much of its existence, depended on steamships for transportation and access to the outside world. Unlike most nearby communities, including Shellycoat, Lambert began not as a mining claim but as a cherry orchard, planted by Dutch and German settlers. At its peak, Lambert's fruit production rivalled that of the Kootenays and the Okanagan.

The valley has undergone remarkable physical change. For most of those who lived in places like Lambert, the very landscape of home has ceased to exist. How did these rural farmers—many of them descendants of the valley's first European settlers—respond and adapt to this deep, irreconcilable loss? On the other hand, how have the children and grandchildren of these displaced citizens (as well as the displaced citizens who still live) benefited from the more modern communities created by the dam? These are some of the questions I hope to answer in my study.

One of the significant effects of the relocation has been the widespread dispersal of these people after the flooding. The government relocated many citizens to Bishop, which is now a ghost town. Thus, no concentrated population of displaced citizens can be studied through observation or immersion. There's no physical, tangible community, nor a virtual one (there's no forum or chat room for displaced Lambert locals, for example, and I doubt many would show up if one were created).

My methodology will primarily be face-to-face interviews with those participants still living in the Immitoin Valley. Gina Hubert, a Shellycoat resident whose family was relocated prior to her birth, will act as a gatekeeper and key informant, providing names and access to potential participants. This includes her mother, Elsie Hubert, old neighbours, and friends of the family. Also, her ex-husband, Billy Wentz, and his father, Cyril.

Those are the bones of the proposal, anyway. Will send you something more thorough and formal once I settle in. I should mention that I expect hostile reactions to the study from some participants, particularly Billy and Cyril. Not for the reason you're probably imagining—they're just generally hostile toward everyone. One potential key informant, Hardy Wallace, has shown signs of mental instability and may be impossible to interview (at

least without being shot at—or was that the level of
seriousness you've been hoping for?).

Convalescing,

Paul

Agnes Hutchinson (b. 1929, 80 yrs old)

Partial transcript, taped at her home in Shellycoat, October 27, 2009.

Agnes was a neighbour of Gina Hubert's parents prior to the flooding of the Immitoin Valley. She lived and married in the house where
she was born, on an acreage next to the ferry landing across from
Lambert. Her family raised and sold cattle, lamb, wheat, potatoes, and
corn until they were relocated to Bishop in 1968.

She lives in a small house only a block away from Shellycoat's
main street, a few minutes' walk from my own place. In her kitchen
and living room are things from before the flood: medicine bottles,
candleholders, matchboxes, doilies. A framed sepia photograph on
the mantle shows her in her twenties—a tall, lean woman standing
on a split-rail fence. When she notices my interest in the picture, she
brings out her old photo albums.

Before my visit, I'd come up with a number of questions, based
on the literature and comparative studies I'd been reading for the last
week, which I hoped to ask all my participants. Following this interview, I'm considering a few changes.

Paul: **How did the flood alter your perspective of the landscape?**

Agnes: Pardon?

P: **I mean, in the absence of familiar landmarks and structures,
how did you go about redefining your sense of place?**

A: I'm sorry, I'm not sure I . . .

P: **Right. Of course. Let me just rephrase . . . What do you miss
the most about your old life? Besides your home, of course.**

A: I suppose the steamship—a sternwheeler, which was the best boat for getting through the shallows between the two lakes. The *Westminster*. I miss seeing it come in. A cable ferry replaced all the steamships in the fifties, right up to the flood. Our kitchen looked out on the water toward the wharf. <She opens a photo album, points out a picture of the *Westminster*—a sort of gigantic, ornate houseboat with an immense wooden paddlewheel at the rear. On the upper deck, gentlemen loll against the decorative railings, while on the lower deck, crew members are opening the cargo doors.>

Those are apple boxes being unloaded off the ship. 1925. The photo's a bit worn, my father didn't take great care of his pictures. The apples are from Lambert, of course. We used to trade meat for fruit and jam and quilts the Mennonite women made. No one ever paid for eggs back then. Knew a Swiss fellow and his wife from Lambert, produced their own cheese and sausages. Quite lovely. We had a root cellar for our own vegetables and homemade elderberry wine.

That's Harry leaning against the truck. Gina Hubert's father. This is around 1963. Man standing with him is Cyril Wentz. Cyril or Sid, I can't remember. A faller and bullbucker. His wife cut hair. She could smoke half a pack in the time it took to give your bangs a trim. Now, this photo's from . . .

P: **1925.**

A: Yes, right . . . those are my parents on the left. The Fruit Growers' Association would hold a dance every fall at the town hall in Lambert. Donald Wallace was president of the association in the valley and he organized the shipping and distribution.

P: **Bit of a coincidence, eh? The hall dance in 1925, you were born in '26.**

A: Pardon?

P: **Never mind.**

A: This is me in '75. My photos are out of order here. That's
        Bishop's schoolhouse behind me. It was also the library and
        the firehall. I taught there for almost eight years, but there was
        hardly enough children to justify the work. It was mostly older
        folks who were relocated to Bishop. I think the government
        hoped it would grow into a proper mill town. John, my hus-
        band, had to get a job in Shellycoat, drove there and back every
        day for ten years until we moved.

        It was Bill Newcomb from Monashee Power that dealt
        with us. We'd known him for years. We did okay with the sale.
        Enough to put away savings. Drew a good number in the lottery
        too: we picked out a lot set back from the logging road, a quiet
        place with some timber and southern exposure . . .

P: **Sorry, what do you mean by lottery?**

A: Bishop used to be a steamship landing with a few houses and
        farms. Monashee purchased all the surrounding Crown land
        for, what was it called, "restitution purposes" and divided it
        into lots. Everyone who was going to Bishop entered a lottery—
        well, we had to enter if we were to live there.

P: **What did people think of that system?**

A: Well, some complained it was rigged, but how could you prove
        something like that? Anyway, we were lucky, because Bill quit
        about as soon as he started, and most other folks had to deal
        with this other fellow. I heard he liked to put the scare into people.
        You didn't make out so well with him, I think is what happened.

Paul moved into an apartment, a one-bedroom suite on the
main floor of a house uphill from Shellycoat's main street. He

converted half the bedroom into an office and bought a desk, a filing cabinet, and a chair from a garage sale. Tanner had given him a spare television, a gigantic, boxy thing that dominated one corner of the living room, which had a partial view of the river flowing past town. Gina had promised to bring over some plants. He liked the height of the bathroom sink—this was a sink in which a man could properly wash his penis, now that the days of solar camp showers and plastic water basins were behind him.

The kitchen and front entrance of his suite faced a quiet avenue lined with maples and chestnuts. On the southwest side, a back door opened onto a long covered porch facing downtown. The porch, cluttered with snowboards, kayaking gear, a table and chairs, also served as the entrance to the upstairs suite where Jory lived with his girlfriend, Sonya.

The first day after his job ended, he'd popped into Jory's shop to return the fish scope. The shop was chaotic, mountain bikes shoved into a dense row along the back and snowboards, jackets, and ski goggles crowding the display window, while teenagers pawed through shelves of discounted T-shirts and used skateboards. The young man clasped his hand enthusiastically after an aborted attempt at a complicated handshake, and Paul was grateful and relieved that their one brief meeting had counted for something.

On the drive from Basket Creek back to Shellycoat, he'd been desperate for a solid plan, his mind still generating and discarding ideas that felt like the remaining wisps of the morning's clouded dream. The trailer, hitched once again to Tanner's truck, bounced along ahead of him, and the sight was sad and frightening. Once in town, he'd booked a room and spent the night and the next morning rearranging his life, making calls and e-mails and fine-tuning his proposal to Dr. Tamba and the anthropology department.

The housing gods were on his side, at least. It turned out the tenant downstairs from Jory and Sonya had taken a job on the rigs outside Fort McMurray. He didn't want to pay November's rent and was leaving early—Paul could move in before Halloween. "And you won't have to worry about us partying and shit," Jory said. "We keep a quiet house, the old lady and I."

"I wasn't worried." Although he wondered how a guy who ran a shop that looked and sounded like a traffic accident defined quiet.

"Take it you're not here to be a ski bum," Jory said.

"No." Paul scratched at his beard, feeling very old and out of place. "There a decent stylist in town?"

"I say grow it out. Lot of dudes sport the woolly look here."

Paul shook his head. "How about the museum—where's that at?"

Jory laughed. "We have a museum?"

~

His fieldwork began in an old brick Scandinavian church owned by Monashee Power and leased to the Shellycoat Historical Society. On the outer walls of the building, interpretative panels showed black-and-white photos of orchards and mills, narratives of the past. Elmer Kindiak, the head archivist, was a bald little man in his late fifties who tended to bustle from filing cabinet to storage room as if to avoid making long conversation. He clearly found it strange that someone who wasn't from Monashee or the Society was in the building of his own free will. Paul asked for a list of the names of people who'd been displaced by the dam.

"A lot of them have died," Elmer said. "Or moved away." He showed him a ledger book, the jacket made of thick, scuffed leather. "This'll get you started, the Acquisition and Resettlement Commission. A record of the transfer of property deeds from private owners to Monashee."

Paul flipped randomly through the ledger. "It'll give me names and compensation prices?"

The archivist gave him a conspiratorial wink. "Between you and me, I wouldn't trust the prices listed. The numbers don't tell you much. But the names are important, you can track down the living."

In a sudden flurry, Elmer grabbed papers and books from different rooms until he'd practically buried Paul with maps, articles, and folders. A series of black-and-white photos of Lambert taken in 1910 showed a docked steamship loaded with boxes of fruit, rows of cherry trees in bloom, a man standing underneath, his face grainy and indiscernible except for a white walrus moustache. Wagons full of nursery stock, rootwads wrapped in burlap, a dog sleeping by the wheel. A farmhouse surrounded by flowering trees, the lake in the background.

"They used these photos in promotional pamphlets," said Elmer. "To bring settlers over from Britain and the prairies." He brought out aerial photographs of Lambert in 1956, reproduced onto large sheets of paper. Contour lines, property boundaries, and lot numbers, marked in white, overlaid the physical features, the differing shades of blue ink.

Lambert was fan-shaped, a flat delta at the base of hills and forests, bisected by a creek hedged with dark conifers, fringed by cottonwoods along the shore. With a magnifying glass, Paul could pick out the wharf and ferry landing, the adjacent ware-houses and fruit-packing sheds, and, farther inland, houses and perfect rows of fruit trees. Most lots were perfectly rectangular, and included expansive orchards and pastures. He found the lots from Hardy's letter easily enough: 4209 to 4213 were the largest and ran the width of the delta, from forest to orchard to pas-ture to beach. Elmer leaned over his shoulder and pointed to a contour line. "1,450 metres is the high water mark." The contour curved and cut through Lambert—most lots would be completely submerged. Paul hovered uncertainly above the monochromatic blue world.

"Well," he said. "Now I know how much I don't know."

"Always a good start," Elmer said.

~

He met Gina for a late dinner at a Thai restaurant, a dozen tables squeezed into a narrow and cozy space. Gina, for some reason, was babbling. "This used to be a Chinese smorg. Ten years ago, we had three in town. Then a Mexican place." She fidgeted and stirred her rice noodles.

Anxious, like on a date? A lingering awkwardness from the sauna? Unlikely—the awkwardness that night had been all his. Or was it the people? The young, attractive women in yoga gear didn't pay them much attention. Same with the loner boys with their stringy hair tied back, staring at their food and at the walls, stoned and astonished. But there were the lanky, middle-aged men in oil-stained fleeces, fresh off work and spooning up red curry, a tall glass of beer at their elbows. They stole quick glances at Gina and muttered to each other.

For the benefit of their audience, he swung the conversation around to something professional-sounding, thanked her for the names and ideas she'd given him, and described some of the literature Dr. Tamba had recommended: a study of the Allegheny Tribes displaced by the Kinzua Dam, articles on the nearby Arrow Lakes, and *The River Dragon Has Come!* by Dai Qing. Tamba, deeply skeptical, was demanding a bigger sample list of participants, proof that Paul was committed to the project and already engaged in the research. He needed volunteers, and quick.

"I'm glad your mother has agreed to this," he said.

"She hasn't. I only suggested her name. She doesn't like to talk about those days. Could be a tough sell."

Paul's fork wavered in front of his mouth. "How about your father?"

"They divorced in the eighties. Might be in Fort St. John. That's where my brother works—we don't talk much. I'm sorry about Mom, but don't worry, she'll come around." She talked between mouthfuls of pad Thai. She tossed out a few names and he jotted her suggestions down on a notepad.

One of the men kept trying to catch his eye. Paul leaned closer to her and whispered, "I feel under the microscope."

"You get used to it."

"Do you?" He pictured a bar brawl, chairs and fists flying. When they rose to leave, one of the men said, "Gina." He cocked an eyebrow and thrust his chin, just slightly, toward Paul. She said nothing.

They stood outside the restaurant, in view of the fogged windows. "I should go rescue the babysitter," she said. "She's got school tomorrow."

"That wasn't your ex in there, was it?" Paul said.

She chuckled without much enthusiasm. "No. No, that would have been a different scene altogether. Believe me."

"Something to look forward to," he muttered.

"Those were his sledding buddies. Snowmobiles," she added when he gave her a confused look. "I'm glad you decided to stay."

"Are you?" he asked. She looked tired, her face blank, eyes heavy-lidded. He couldn't help but wonder again if he'd disappointed her back at camp. Or maybe she was worried he had expectations and would be constantly phoning and following her around. She didn't let him walk her back to her car, and in full view of the restaurant windows, they went their separate ways.

Peter Woodbury, forester (b.1900–d.1983)
I spent part of the afternoon at the Shellycoat Historical Society watching a video tape of an interview conducted in 1980. The tape was in rough shape, the VCR ancient. I transcribed bits of the interview, just the things that jumped out at me. I worried that if I rewound the tape

too much, the machine would eat it and Elmer would banish me from the archives.

Peter: I came to the Immitoin Valley for the orchards. For me, it was either falling trees or picking fruit . . . I knew some veterans who'd been given land grants under the Soldier Settlement Act. A beautiful place . . .

I worked for Donald Wallace—well, I worked under his head arborist, Marcus Soules, but it was Wallace's orchards. Soules was a magician at pruning and grafting, getting the trees through a rough winter. Good man, good teacher too. I still use all his techniques on my trees in the backyard.

Fruit industry went downhill by the end of the Second World War. So I stuck to logging and the like . . . Lambert had its own crew after the war, and they were an ornery bunch. Frederic Wentz ran the operation, then he and Wallace partnered up.

They started off horse logging in the lower elevations for Monashee Power, which was just a small lighting and power utility company at the time. They also built flumes so whatever they didn't mill on site they could run as raw logs down the Immitoin. It was a damned impressive set-up.

Interviewer: **Did you work for them at all?**

P: Never did, no. There was unrest between them and the community. Once whispers about the dam started, people got worried about their future. Neighbours in Lambert started fighting each other, and I didn't want to get mixed up in any of that.

Halloween night, while typing out his notes on Woodbury, he was interrupted by a knock on the back door. He found himself wandering downtown with a couple of zombies, a bloodied and unidentifiable superhero, a nun with a rather revealing habit, and a bare-chested devil—Jory with his hairless, buff torso covered in red paint. The nun was Sonya, Jory's girlfriend.

Paul had only seen her once since he'd moved in. When he'd finished unloading his vehicle and piled his few belongings outside on the porch, she'd come downstairs with Jory to help. Her natural dull blond hair was streaked with black and a faded electric blue, cut just short enough to reveal the series of piercings in both ears. She'd worn a tight-fitting but unremarkable grey T-shirt underneath an unzipped black hoodie, both tops covered in the logos of a snowboard company. She and Jory almost could have been brother and sister. Unlike him, though, her smile was forced, a brief creasing of alabaster cheeks.

"Don't mind all the crap," she'd mumbled in a low voice and shoved aside a garbage bag full of empty beer cans.

"The last guy was never here," Jory apologized, "so we kind of took over."

"I don't have much," Paul said. Sonya gave his duffle bags a wary look, perhaps disturbed by his lack of possessions.

"Aren't you, like, a university professor?" she asked.

"My dad's shipping the rest of my stuff," he said and watched as the last hint of respect or interest vanished from her eyes.

They wandered into a nightclub, confronted by a grab-bag of aliens, undead, superheroes, and devils crowding the dance floor. Here and there he saw grey ponytails and weathered faces, aging hippies oblivious to anything but the music, which was tribal, all afro-Cuban percussion and robotically incessant synths. The people his own age were invariably couples, and carried the look of careless affluence, throwing their summers' earnings into pitchers of beer and oversized martinis. Big, hip fish in a little pond. Sonya had dressed conservatively next to the sea of lingerie, bondage gear, and angel wings that drifted past their table. He sipped his gin and tonic, his first drink in months—he wasn't wearing a pad—and wondered when he could slip out of here without offending his new friend.

Jory leaned over to Paul's ear. "Analyzing the situation?"

"In a way," he said.

"We're going to pop some E," Jory said. "You want half a hit?"

Paul laughed incredulously. "No. No. It's been a while." He'd gone through his own party phase, a pretty tame one in comparison, and was finished with it. Of course, some of the greybeards out there on the dance floor would have gone through the disco days, bluegrass and jam band revivals, the roots of the rave scene, and danced their way through all of it, picking up on the new sounds, switching to the latest drug du jour. The idea of that continuity made him nostalgic for a life he'd never had. Flares of energy charged the room, while his own spark sputtered and faltered.

"The old guys on the dance floor are impressive," he said to Jory.

Jory laughed. "Thank Christ my dad's not out there. It wouldn't surprise me at all."

"They're locals, huh?"

"Born and raised. Except if they're draft dodgers. But that's as good as being born here. Like my dad's friends. They run the tree-planting companies, the health food stores. Shellycoat wouldn't be what it is without the dodgers." The music was pounding now, and Jory's breath condensed against Paul's ear as he leaned in to talk. Sonya looked bored and twitchy.

"Shellycoat wouldn't be anything without the orchardists and miners," Paul said.

"That's way too far back for me." Jory slipped a few pills out of a small tin of mints and pressed one between Sonya's lips. They nursed their drinks in silence, eyes on the crowd. Minutes passed, and then Sonya whispered something to Jory and they stood up and wandered away. She danced with her eyes closed, with modest, subtle motions—she had a sensuality some of the more daring girls lacked. Or maybe their eroticism was too overwhelming, white noise to his long-deprived senses, and Sonya's operated at a level he could handle. She danced for herself, while Jory bounced up and down, conscious of others, inviting them in. High-fives over people's heads, a pause for a quick, sweaty hug with a bro.

The music dropped to something low and throbbing. He heard a faint click and realized he was tapping his finger on the table, keeping time. He wondered what effect the drug would have had on him but brushed the idea aside. He'd stay another minute. This wasn't a total waste of time. Surely somewhere in the throng of sexy nurses and robot vampires were the grandsons and granddaughters of Lambert. Everything he did from now on was research.

~

Sheets in the wash because he'd wet himself after two gins. After his shower, he went out to the covered porch, cleared the table of its empty beer bottles and full ashtray, and set down a French press filled with coffee. Snow fell but melted instantly on the sidewalks and road. He wore a heavy flannel coat he'd found at a church thrift store for three dollars. The coat had the woody, dusty smell of mudrooms and woodsheds, of firewood and chainsaw oil. It was a relic, something outside its time.

Sonya stepped onto the porch, wearing her usual black hoodie. She was more pale than usual, her cheeks lined from a pillowcase or patterned couch cushion. "Hope we didn't wake you when we staggered home," she said, clearing her throat.

"Didn't hear a thing. Coffee?"

She gave him a slow nod. "Thanks."

Paul went inside for two more mugs, and when he came back out, she had a cigarette burning in her hand as she stared out over the valley.

"Hope you don't mind I'm on the porch," he said.

"You were here first." She squinted at him, then looked away.

They sat in silence until Jory stumbled down to the porch, bare-chested, still smeared with red paint. He shivered, wild-haired. "Fuck, yeah," he said as he poured himself a coffee. He squeezed in behind Sonya, wrapping his arms around her as he braced against the post.

"So, the night went well?"

Jory laughed, his voice burbling up through gravel. "Some guy in a gorilla suit grabbed her ass outside the bar."

"Jory lost his mind," Sonya said dryly. "So that was fun."

Paul whistled. He didn't see any sign of a beating on Jory's face or knuckles. "Anyone get hurt?"

"Aw, it's all good. We worked it out," Jory said.

"I had to tear them off each other."

"I thought everyone was in love on Ecstasy," Paul said.

"Jory can be overprotective sometimes."

"That's not true," he said. "I was being a gentleman. That fuck-ing clown." Jory chuckled, his chin on Sonya's shoulder, but Paul could see her face darken underneath her hood.

"What do you think, babe, should we make some breakfast?" Jory mumbled. His face disappeared into the folds of her hoodie. "Or go back to bed?"

She closed her eyes as he nuzzled her through the heavy cotton, and when she opened them, her face had softened, the events of last night pushed aside. Paul couldn't help watching them. He felt an upwelling of sadness almost pleasurable in its intensity. A memory of his own past, seeing the two twining into each other, amused by their own exhaustion, their bodies resilient, the deep, full well of their libido.

Paul remembered being in love like that at Jory's age—he recalled only fragments of his time with the girl, but it didn't matter. There really was nothing quite like being in love at twenty. It was unstable and volcanic. It shook the earth, then dispersed like a breeze. So elemental and simple. It was not vegetative, developing cell by cell, sending branches up and taproots down. A boy's love didn't anchor itself. It fought, as likely to linger when it lost as vanish when it conquered. Would he ever return to that again? Was that even possible?

Molly (b. 1943, 66 yrs old) **and Joseph** (b. 1940, 69 yrs old) **Kruse**
Partial transcript. Taped at their home, a few kilometres south of Bishop, Nov. 9, 2009.

Joseph was born to a Lutheran family in Lambert, growing up at a time when neighbours worried about the dam, the future of the valley uncertain. Nonetheless, after he and Molly married, they decided to stay at his family's acreage until Lambert's final day of relocation in the late summer of 1969.

Molly: Joe's father made furniture. He found all his materials along the lake and river.

Joseph: We'd canoe to the mouth of the Immitoin above Bishop and find pockets of birch, willow, and maple. Most of those groves are underwater now. He had an old lathe in the workshop . . .

Paul: **So the loss of those wetlands, that way of life—it must have had a disorienting effect on you. Confounded your sense of place.**

J: Well . . . I still miss gathering up the wood. If that's what you mean.

P: **When did you know for sure you were going to be flooded out?**

M: I remember being surprised—you know, suddenly there's this treaty. There was a town hall meeting at Lambert, where they had an engineer and someone from government explain what was going on. A lot of people were angry, very upset. Afterwards, I think this was in 1964, everyone got *The Property Owner's Guide*.

J: We lived above the flood line. Figured that meant we could stay. Of course, there'd be no more village, no cable ferry, no way of getting across except your own boat. I thought, Well, at least we'll still have our home.

P: **So basically you'd accepted the inevitable.**
J: I don't know that we accepted anything. Resigned is more like it. Young families were mostly on the dole, or they'd moved elsewhere for better work and education. Our neighbours were pensioners and war vets, mostly poor, and they just wanted peace and quiet.
M: Most old folks didn't want to leave. Fifty years in one place, you don't feel like new beginnings. You aren't going to start a farm from scratch at sixty-five.
J: Maybe the dam killed Lambert before Father Time showed up to do the job.

P: **So why did you lose your property? Did the flood line change?**
J: Nope. Monashee Power decided they needed our land for construction access, or dump or fill sites. I never got the reasoning. The land is still sitting there. They never did a damned thing with it except cut down the trees.

P: **How much did you receive in compensation?**
J: The price started at about a hundred dollars an acre, one hundred and fifty an acre for cleared land and buildings. We hummed and hawed, and the price dropped to fifty dollars an acre.
M: We said at that price, we're not going anywhere. And we'd seen the lots in Bishop. Land was stony, needed clearing. A roof for a roof, that's all we asked for. A roof for a roof.
J: Different men showed up to negotiate. The first ones were friendly enough. They'd come in for tea and ask about the

farm, our quality of life. A couple of them quit for the stress of it.

M: It was tough, what they had to do. I mean, things came at you out of the blue, government edicts and whatnot, and you had no one to confront. The negotiators were flesh and blood, so people lashed out at them.

J: Later on, this squat toad of a man kept coming by. Young too. That bothered me. I mean, he was about my age. What would he know about living here? He'd say, Mr. Kruse, I'll offer you two thousand dollars for your place. I'd tell him to forget it. Finally he said, you do know that I can and will expropriate your property. Go ahead, try, I said. So we haggled back and forth, and a few months into the negotiations, guess what?

M: Joe.

J: A forest fire breaks out on my property. In late September. Burns down two outbuildings, some fencing. A few days later, the short guy shows up again with a few of his goons. "Lightning strike?" he says. I still remember that.

M: Never knew his name. Don't recall him ever saying it.

J: Always gave his title—you know, he was "acting on behalf" of somebody. Monashee dug a deep dark hole, then turned over a slimy rock and found him underneath. I heard he burned people's houses right in front of them, before they got compensation. Before they even got their belongings out. I hope he's roasting in hell.

M: Well, he could still be alive, of course.

Had he always been this awkward at conducting interviews? Had he always blundered along, leaving behind a trail of awkward silences, stuttering replies? *Knock off the lofty theoretical questions,* Dr. Tamba advised in an e-mail. *You spent too much time with guys—nerds, if you'll forgive me—like Nathan Cook.*

His dad, who'd worked with contractors and construction workers his whole life, said much the same thing over the phone. "These are blue-collar types, practical people. You gotta be honest and straightforward or they'll tune you right out, believe me."

People didn't want to talk about life after the flood. Or, rather, they didn't want to compare the before and after of the valley. The rather ordinary things they had done out of necessity, getting on with their lives after the flood, hardly seemed the stuff of university research.

The day after he'd talked to the Kruses, he interviewed Cal and Lucy Wendish. They'd lived up the road from the Huberts, raising livestock and chickens, and growing fruit and vegetables for market. The story of people's homes, he realized, was always about things amassed, grown and built over time. Their properties had been hacked out of rough, wild land, worked and reworked from the turn of the century through both World Wars and the Depression, a long dialogue with soil, roots, and stone. And still, by time the valley was flooded, their farms had only begun to attain an air of permanence, of belonging.

Cal (b. 1935, 74 yrs old)

Cal: There was only ever a ribbon of good land here, along the valley bottom. Marshy along the river between the two lakes, but still decent for farming if you drained some land. We had one field for cold weather crops, another for early crops. Another where we kept cattle and some sheep. That was above the high water mark.

Lucy (b. 1938, 71 yrs old)

Lucy: Monashee Power expropriated it, though, because the road to Bishop was being rerouted.

C: The original dirt road hugged the lakeshore. When the reservoir is low, there's a long gravel bench—that's the old route.

Can't see any trace of our house, or the outbuildings. We had a granary, hay sheds . . .

L: <Here, Lucy brings out an old suitcase filled with small objects.> Some of these things belonged to my parents. My father was a barkeep on the *Westminster*. Birch's Black Bottle Scotch Whiskey. Label's a bit faded. Hard to believe it lasted this long without the glass getting broke. That matchbox tin dates back to the twenties. Once it was decided you were being relocated, you had to get your stuff out of your house quick. Monashee men wouldn't think twice about torching your place with everything in it. Whether you'd gotten a cheque or not. That happened to a few folks.

Paul: **People have mentioned something about a short man . . .**

C: Wasn't just him, mind you. He had help from Wallace's logging crew. They were his gang.

P: **Donald Wallace was part of this?**

C: What they'd do is come around, asking questions. See where you stood—if you'd make much of a fuss about prices. Folks who were tired of the place, or had money, sold quick—the longer you waited, the worse the money got. After a few years, the whole valley was checkerboarded out. People on either side of you had sold—but you didn't know for how much. That's when the short guy, the crew leader, would really put the screws to you.

P: **You don't remember his name?**

C: Always called himself by his title. Mr. Expropriations or whatever. He was a very arrogant fellow. He came by when I was away, trying to get Lucy to sign the papers.

L: Followed me around the garden, into the barn. He wouldn't leave. I herded him off the property with a pitchfork and our dog. <Laughs> Mr. Expropriations.

C: If you were unemployed or widowed or just scraping by for whatever reason, they treated you even worse. Piss poor. They shuffled us off to Bishop on cheap promises of good land. There wasn't any. They said there was decent farming and ranching above the flood line, but I never saw it. I'm not complaining. Just stating facts.

L: No real infrastructure—Cal helped build the storm drains and sewer system in Bishop, and there was the school and whatnot. But God help you if you had a serious accident, the hospital in Shellycoat was nearly a two-hour drive in those days. And people there treated you like a hillbilly.

C: I worked on the reservoir too. On tugs, clearing debris and deadheads. Basically cleaning up the mess they made. For years, the north end of the reservoir looked like a bomb went off—silt in the water, mudslides, dead trees. There were good folk in Bishop. But things weren't the same. People, I mean, not just the valley. You always wondered how much your neighbour received in compensation. And wondering kept you from trusting.

Paul stood in the kitchen, confronted by a whole chicken in a roasting pan, a red kuri squash he'd split in half and seasoned with olive oil and thyme. He rubbed rock salt and cracked pepper on the chicken, cut two small slits along the skin of the breasts, one more above each leg, and slid sprigs of rosemary and slivers of garlic between the fat and flesh. Gina's recipe, her favourite comfort food. She arrived holding a bottle of wine, Shane clinging to her leg and sporting a Spider-Man backpack overflowing with toys.

"I know you don't drink much." She wore light denim overalls with flower patterns on the straps, and her hair was tied back, an oddly girlish look. Her face betrayed uncertainty, and she fidgeted with the bottle.

"How about a small glass," he said cheerfully. "I'm slowly getting back to my old self. Could use a bit more exercise, though."

"I'll wrestle you," Shane said hopefully. He crouched, wild-haired, poised to tackle Paul's leg. His eyes were blue, not his mother's colour, and rather sharp and intense. He had scabs on his elbows and beneath his chin. Gina gave Paul a quick shake of the head.

"Some other time," Paul said. "Thanks, though."

"How about you play in the living room," Gina said. Paul had laid out different vegetables for a salad that he clumsily diced as Gina opened the bottle and poured two glasses.

"I don't want him to get too wound up." He was a smart boy, she told him, didn't mind playing alone for a time, but he got riled easily and was too sensitive around the other kids at school.

Gina grabbed another knife and helped Paul with the rest of the vegetables, slicing a pepper with quick and efficient cuts. "Hey," she said. "I was thinking. I know a good doctor in town, if you need one."

He paused, then resumed cutting. "Actually I will need to see doctor soon, so thank you."

"I know it's not my business . . ."

"No big deal. I'm due for a blood draw in a few months."

"Oh. I thought you meant—well, that's good."

He caught the hint and blushed. "It's probably too soon," he said. "Recovery-wise, I mean."

"Yes. Like I said, not my business." She threw her hands up in such a comically exaggerated way, he laughed despite himself.

"Can I ask what you'll do with your research?"

He shrugged, struggling to imagine a finished project. "Publish, I suppose."

"No, I mean what do you use it for? Do you go after them?"

"After who?"

"The people who made the dam. The ones who cheated folks out of their property and burned their homes down."

"It's not about going after people."

She frowned. "Then what's the point? Doesn't your work have to do something to be useful?"

He flushed. "It is—useful. Not like that. Ethnography, it paints a picture of a community. A narrative. Can't start out being biased or political."

"Ah." A pause, and then she said he should interview Billy, which, he realized, was a subtle dig, like let's see you avoid taking a side around him.

"Not sure I feel okay doing that," he said.

"Why not?"

"I noticed you didn't park outside."

"One block over." She leaned over the table and craned her neck to look for her son. "You okay in there, buddy?"

Farty-lipped truck sounds emerged from the living room. "Yes."

"Why did you park so far away?" he asked. She said nothing. "That's why I'm afraid. Unless you're keen to introduce me to him."

"Not really, no."

He stood up and opened the stove, poked at the squash with a fork. "I don't like that," he said. "The bad feeling I'm getting."

"From the squash? It looks ready." Jokes between them always fell flat.

"Whatever you have with him. It feels dangerous."

"I'm sorry," she said.

"I was more worried about you and Shane."

"I know. Let's have a drink? Please?"

"All right." From the cautious way she held it, the bottle looked pricier than what she'd normally buy. An Argentinean malbec, a dark ruby colour when held to the light. She brought her glass to her mouth and then, for a moment, looked hesitant, even strangely defiant, as though daring herself not to drink.

The rim of the glass pressed against her closed lips, pulled away, then returned, like a hummingbird at a feeder. She looked at him expectantly. He held his nose above the rim and smelled a jumble of scents he couldn't quite identify but would have called smoky. Moody? He took a small sip, unsure of what she wanted him to taste, and lowered the glass. His thumb left a perfect, greased print. Belatedly, they clinked their glasses together, and she gave him an impish grin. "To the bush," she said. "Where losers meet."

~

In the archives with Elmer, mugs of tea, a map, and a ledger between them. A faint glimmer of streetlight outside the small square windows, the white paint on the concrete walls reflecting the overhead fluorescents, a slight sheen of light on Elmer's bald head. On the map, a grid of pale blue lines showed the division of lots in Lambert. Paul was glancing back and forth between the map and the faded lines of the ledger. He had the beginnings of a headache.

Already he'd worked harder on this project than on anything in his career. Maybe that wasn't saying much. His bedroom wall was covered in maps and flowcharts as he tried to make sense of his data and look for patterns and direction. Part of him would have moved half the archives into his bedroom, just to have the maps and ledgers close at hand. Mostly, though, he was glad for any respite from his small room and cramped desk, and the tedium of transcribing the mumbling voices from his digital recorder, the hours of listening and typing, rewinding and listening again.

Elmer refilled their mugs, the small man moving delicately as he poured from the brown pot. The tea was black, strong, and had a faint hint of chocolate. Keemun Yi Hong, which Elmer ordered online from a shop in San Francisco. He was explaining how compensation for resettlement had worked. "If you signed the papers early in the process, that usually meant you had the means to buy somewhere more expensive. They gave you a compensation cheque, you usually moved to Shellycoat or the Okanagan or wherever."

But most people didn't actually sell prior to the flood, Elmer told him. "If they held out until the end, they were given a line of credit from the bank, which went toward the lot they were given in Bishop, with maybe some left over to build a house."

"So they never saw a compensation cheque."

"Not unless there was money left over from the line of credit."

"According to the ledger, all the lots Hardy mentioned in his letter belong to either the Wallace family or the Wentzes."

"Worth something, those ones," Elmer said. "Fruit trees, timber, waterfront."

"What about this little piece? Right beside the Wallace ranch." Paul tapped a spot on the map that he'd marked. "Who owned that?"

"Should be in the ledger."

"I'm going cross-eyed." Paul squeezed the bridge of his nose between his thumb and forefinger.

Elmer took the book from him and flipped some pages. "Soules, Marcus."

"I've heard that name. Worked for Wallace, an arborist?"

"The head arborist. Wallace's foreman during the fruit indus-try boom, which employed most of the valley."

Paul brushed a finger across the map. "When did the papers get signed?"

"1965. The Columbia River Treaty was ratified in '64, which gave the McCulloch Dam project the go-ahead."

"So this wasn't expropriated. Marcus Soules sold it, volun-tarily. And really early. Almost before property acquisitions had officially begun."

"Probably one of the first in the valley."

"Donald Wallace must have been furious." Paul looked at

the map again. "Strange. You have any materials that mention Wallace? I have the Woodbury interview, but . . ."

Elmer frowned. "Easy enough. He's referenced everywhere." He led Paul back to a room where a handful of books and spiral-bound reports were buried under a haphazard stack of topographical maps. Elmer fluttered his hands at the mess. "That's supposed to be . . . the shelves must have fallen . . . damn it all."

Paul helped him right the top layer of maps. Elmer put on a pair of thin gloves and sorted through the materials, flipping through a few pages and setting them aside. Finally he nodded and handed Paul a small book protected by a hard plastic jacket. "Here's a starter."

"*Dixon's Gold*," Paul said, surprised. "Forgot about this." They sat back down at the table and he skimmed through the last chapters, where the pages of Tanner's copy in the trailer had been stuck together. As the chapters detailed the mining era coming to a close, smelter by smelter, town by town, Paul finally ran across Wallace's name in a few rather brusque paragraphs.

Donald Wallace had inherited some of his land from his father, a retired military officer in London who'd purchased the acreage, sight unseen, in 1889. The elder Wallace never set foot on his property: illness kept him at home until his death in 1925. A veteran and decorated officer of the First World War, Donald was awarded fifty additional acres as part of the Soldier Settlement Act in 1919. Served as president of the valley's Fruit Growers' Association, ran Lambert's fruit-packing sheds and box factory, and wrote horticultural advice for the Immitoin Valley newspaper. It was difficult to picture Hardy the hermit as this man's son.

Elmer smiled slyly. "What does all this have to do with your research?"

"Nothing," Paul admitted. "Just background, I guess."

"I'd say you were trying to solve a mystery."

He smiled ruefully. "I suppose I am. The case of the thing beneath the water that makes everyone angry."

Elmer chuckled, a sibilant sound with his lips perched at the mug's edge. "*Reservoir noir.*"

Now Paul laughed. "Sounds like a bad mystery genre."

"Technically a sub-genre: *Drowning Day, On Beulah Height, Walking the Shadows*," Elmer recited cheerfully. "Dozens more. The formula's pretty standard: a reservoir is drained and a body, or some terrible secret, is discovered."

"Wonder what you'd find if you drained this reservoir."

"Lambert, for one thing," Elmer said. "But it's no secret what they did to that place."

~

He'd never enjoyed weightlifting. Found it monotonous and uninspiring. The equipment always carried the grime of sweat and dust, the air damp and acrid. At least this gym, on the top floor of the recreation centre, had natural light and a view toward the Immitoin that distracted from the dullness. Above the exercise bikes and treadmills, small televisions silently played sports highlights. It was mid-morning, and the weight room was empty except for a few seniors and middle-aged women on the step machines and treadmills. Later, at the end of his workout, the junior hockey team would jostle around the free weights and benches near the mirrored walls.

He began with fifteen minutes on the bike, working himself rather too easily into a sweating, hyperventilating mass. Which was depressing, not the best recipe for motivation. But then, nothing had ever motivated him for the gym except the promise of sex. Sex, not health, drove you to shape your body. He struggled through an hour of weights and stretches, bored and discouraged. The best part of the workout was the end, when he stood in front of the change room mirror with his muscles engorged, his body vaguely and temporarily resembling what it used to be.

Afterwards, he went to his favourite coffee shop, the Mexican-themed one, to look over articles and write up his field notes. The walls of the café were mock adobe, the wooden tables old and unvarnished, grey as a grandfather's sweater. He hadn't fallen for any of the girls working behind the counter, further proof that his impotence went deeper than damaged nerve bundles. In Vancouver, coffee shop girls were often the only ones worth falling for, because nothing ever came of it. You frequented the same cafés until the baristas became friendly, approachable— the pleasure lay in sustaining the fantasy.

Coffee shop girls, the men lusting after them. The same scenes were unfolding as they had for years, in every place. Nothing had changed except for himself, orbiting further from the heartsick centre of daily life. What was he doing here, more ghostly than a tourist, in danger of having no identity and nothing to do, no role to play? He clung desperately to his notebooks and transcriptions, and was comforted by those rare times when Gina or a participant met him for coffee. They grounded him, gave him ballast as he started from scratch, nothing in hand but a few tools and skills, this kernel of a new life, a new mind.

Elsie Hubert (b. 1943, 66 yrs old)
Interviewed at her home in Shellycoat, November 20, 2009. **Gina** (b. 1976, 33 yrs old) is also present.

Initially, Elsie was extremely reluctant to be interviewed, so I'm not sure how to explain her sudden change of heart. Maybe it was only a matter of Gina wearing her down, or maybe she has some particular reason she's not telling us.

Elsie lives in a small ground-floor suite of an aging apartment complex. A small den serves as an office, the walls covered in various posters: SAVE JUMBO PASS WILDERNESS, SAVE THE FLATHEAD

VALLEY, STOP THE SHANKER'S BEND PROJECT, and so on. This is the third home she's lived in since her family was relocated. Once the administrator of both a women's shelter and the town's advocacy centre, she's now partly retired. Obviously still active with local environmental groups.

On the mantle above the gas fireplace sits a framed black-and-white photo of their homestead on the lake before the dam. Near the house, a barn, chicken coops, and a woodshed. A glimpse of the fields where cattle and horses would have grazed, and a garden with several rows of raspberry canes and fruit trees. In the background you can faintly see Lambert's wharf on the opposite shore. A rope swing dangles from the branch of a willow over a pool. There's nobody in the photo: it is the homestead itself that is commemorated.

Paul: **You were born in that house.**
Elsie: Yes.

P: **And your mother or father as well?**
E: My father. My grandfather was the original pre-emptor in 1898.

P: **Your father died in the war, I understand?**
E: Afterwards. A long illness from his wounds. And my grandfather died in the war before that. Gina comes from a long line of widows. That happened to many families in the valley. Widows and their children kept the orchards and farms going. My grandmother hired help for the spring labour and the harvest in fall, usually the Doukhobors and Mennonites, who were quite industrious, and since most were pacifists . . .

P: **I've heard about the Doukhobors . . .**
E: They came up from Grand Forks and Brilliant and Thrums to work, but they never formed a community here. Gina said you weren't really interested in the past before the dam.

P: **I suppose not. Curious about the fruit industry, though. As background.**

E: The orchards were nearly finished by the time I was born. We raised livestock, grew produce and wheat, and harvested timber on our land. But fruit crops were still a big part of life. Making jam in the summer, juicing the fall. My mother worked for Donald Wallace at the fruit-packing shed in Lambert until it shut down.

Gina: I loved all her old pictures, you know, women smiling at the camera while they stack jars in crates—like Rosie the Riveter.

E: My mother and I never spoke against Wallace when he and the others started cutting lumber and poles and such for Monashee. Maybe we thought it would help our case.

P: **Your case?**

E: You know, maybe we'd get a good deal if we were in cozy with Monashee. My mother stayed friends with Donald Wallace, even after the local Fruit Growers' Association disbanded and his wife, Belinda, died.

P: **And did your family get a good deal?**

E: We bet on the wrong horse.

P: **Wallace must have had some influence with Monashee.**

E: No.

P: **They didn't show him any favouritism?**

E: <Laughs.> You've seen Hardy's place. That's no favour. Now we're getting into the whole injustice of the acquisition process. This is what you wanted to talk about, correct?

P: **Well, yes. No. Just—the changes themselves, your quality of life.**

E: The government was very optimistic. Bishop would be a booming mill town, it would draw vacationers and American cottagers interested in a wilderness setting and so on. It was all bunk. The first two years after the flood, there was so much debris no one could go in the water. And during drawdown the wind kicked up an incredible dust. Old people and children in Bishop had lung problems.

P: **The boom never happened?**
E: You should have seen it during the seventies. The government did help move some houses on trailers, but most people started with nothing. Outside investors and developers tended to get the waterfront lots—without entering the lottery. Hence the summer cottages.

  Bishop families were treated like pariahs in Shellycoat. We were squatters and hippies leaching off government handouts, backwoods hicks.

P: **Do people still think that?**
E: Well, even I think that anyone still living in Bishop these days is definitely a hick. <Laughs.>

P: **You've been involved in environmental groups for a long time.**
E: Grassroots organizations, mostly focusing on the protection of local watersheds and old-growth forests. My husband was embarrassed by all that, my petitions and signs. Part of the reason he left.
G: No, Mom.
E: Well, that and chronic unemployment. He went looking for work and never came back.

P: <By this time, it was safe to assume that she could handle one of my more abstract questions.> **So, despite the loss of** your home, an entire valley bottom, it's safe to say you're still attached to this area. I mean, your roots are still here, even though *here* is under water.

E: Absolutely. Protecting watersheds became my way of staying attached to the valley—my new roots, you could say.

P: **You were among those who tried to take Monashee Power to court.**

E: It was a sham. The courts wouldn't even discuss land value.

P: **Was Hardy Wallace involved in the lawsuit?**

E: Oh, Hardy. No, he did things his own way. A bit unstable, you know. It's a shame, he might have been a good voice. Well, in the end, nothing worked. And maybe there was no point to it. What you've put into the land, you can never be compensated for.

P: **Gina mentioned you burned down your house . . .**

G: That's about the only thing she's told me.

E: Everything was getting torched. It was just a matter of who lit the match. Monashee had a scorched earth policy. They said it was to prevent squatters from moving into the abandoned houses.

P: **What about the negotiators? I've heard different things.**

E: There were one or two good men, at first. I think one suffered a nervous breakdown and moved God knows where. I had to deal with another fellow, a thick-set sort of ape. Him and his thugs.

P: **The short man? No one seems to know his name.**

E: It's because his family wasn't local. But I made a point of remembering. Caleb Ready. He was Monashee's thumb pressing on the valley.

P: **That name—you're sure about that?**
E: Of course.

P: **You know Caleb Ready drowned recently . . .**
E: Is that right? I hadn't heard. Isn't that something. I set fire to our house just to deny him the satisfaction. I wasn't the only one. When the people of Lambert burned the whole village down, you couldn't see across the lake for the smoke.

Paul waited for Constable Cliff Lazeroff to finish talking to the old couple seated in the opposite booth. He seemed to know everybody in the A&W, even the girl behind the counter who'd botched his order. Paul fidgeted with his paper cup, breathed in the deep fryer smells and took in the yellow walls, the orange and brown trim. Bleary-eyed teenagers served sour-faced men covered in engine oil or sawdust. Outside, trucks in the queue for the takeout window carried snowmobiles, sleek machines sheathed in bright plastic and metal.

"Thing is," Lazeroff was saying, "you have to drive all the way to Grand Forks to get a decent bowl of borscht, let alone real *lapshevnik.*" Then he turned to Paul and followed his glance outside. "Boys and their toys. That kind of guy, he's worked his ass off since high school—he'll buy an ATV and sled for himself, his wife, *and* each kid. Then the mill shuts down and he's screwed." He took a bite of his breakfast sandwich. "You ever dream about those bull trout?" he asked.

"Sure," Paul said. "Not what I'd call good dreams." Blinding rain, the traps filling with infinite numbers of fish, a sort of horrifying, biblical miracle.

"Me, I have this recurring dream—well, a fantasy—that I actually have time to go fishing." He was counting the months until retirement, he explained. Trying to wrap up a few last things.

"Like Caleb Ready's death?" Paul asked.

"Him? No. Odds and ends. You know what I spent October doing? Busting grow ops. We incinerated a million bucks' worth of pot in the beehive at the mill."

Paul had read about it in the paper but hadn't paid much attention. "Gangs?"

Lazeroff nodded. "All sorts. Gangs, teenagers. Parents. Grandparents."

"Kind of ironic, all that money going up the burner when everyone at the mill is laid off."

"Probably the most action that place will see all winter," Lazeroff agreed. "Anyways, it was Ready you wanted to talk about."

"Yes. Any progress?"

"None. It's pretty much been written off as a suicide or accident."

"Any signs to say otherwise?"

"Such as?"

"Maybe he was pushed."

"Did someone tell you that?" Lazeroff leaned closer, his blue eyes peering sharply through unruly grey eyebrows. "On the phone, you told me his name keeps coming up in your interviews."

"Not his name, mostly, just who he was." Paul recounted the stories. The threats and intimidation, the houses and barns that were torched by the short man and Wallace's crew. No one Paul had talked to had actually seen him set fire to their buildings. Most of the people Ready had allegedly victimized were elderly at the time, long dead by now. But participants knew relatives and neighbours who had suffered from his fires. They made it sound like a long reign of terror, a dark smoke that hung over the valley for years. But according to Monashee's archives, Ready had been employed as a land agent for less than eighteen months.

"Listen to this—one of my interviews." Paul fumbled with

his backpack, and the constable frowned at the notebooks and folders. Paul flipped through a transcript. "Here it is. 'They did this funny thing with some landowners. You know, the man who came by with the expropriation papers would pretend to feel bad for you. He'd negotiate a private sale, buy you out with his own money for a better price than Monashee Power's. Pretend he was doing you a favour and then he'd turn around and sell the land to some developer for three times the price.'" He looked up. "What do you think?"

"Pretty thin." Lazeroff ran a napkin across his lips.

"Maybe that's how Ready bought his summer cottage. Dirty money."

"Come on," the constable scoffed. "He had a good job, you know. Lived in Abbotsford most of his life, supervised different hydroelectric projects around the province after the McCulloch Dam was completed. Brief stint in local politics, sat on city council in the eighties. Father. Grandfather. No mention of burning houses anywhere."

"He made a lot of enemies."

"I see where you're going." Lazeroff shook his head. "Ready was seventy-five when he died—that's a little late for revenge, don't you think?"

"But it's possible."

"It's a hell of a stretch," he said. "Forty years later, all these people still hate him?"

"*Hated* might be more accurate," Paul admitted. "No one knew he'd drowned just recently. For them, he stopped existing once the valley was flooded."

"Or they're lying to you." The constable sighed.

"People must have known he owned a cottage in Bishop." A thought struck him. "Donald Wallace's crew had worked for him. It's bizarre that Hardy didn't know who it was that drowned. Don't you think?"

Lazeroff shrugged, then brushed the crumbs from his lap. "Well, this is all good information. Much appreciated."

"Okay. Right." Paul raised his hands in surrender. "Just a theory."

"Didn't say it was a terrible one." Lazeroff handed back the papers. "About Hardy. You need to make peace with that man."

Paul stuffed the pages into his bag, flustered. "I am at peace. I mean—why?"

"You're telling me you're researching—what do you call it, the displacement, relocation, of Lambert—and you haven't talked to the son of Donald Wallace?"

"What, lecture him about gun safety?"

"Yeah, he's not easy to talk to." Lazeroff picked his teeth and then stood, more crumbs falling from his barrel chest. "But without him, I'd say you're just pissing around the margins."

~

The film began with a slow pan across a landscape of fireweed and black earth to settle on three broad, burnt stumps, a woman dancing on each. They bent and rose in wavering, arching stretches, in apparent mimicry of the missing trees. Someone in the audience coughed a single time in exasperation. Paul was very aware of Gina beside him. He'd forgotten how intimate it was to watch a film with another person—especially a bad film. The earlier documentary on Icelandic geological heat vents had been visually stunning, at least, and the story of a rubber raincoat filmed in stop-time animation was made bearable, at least, by its brevity and lack of dancers.

The choreographer's entry had been preceded by a film short—more of a political ad—about a proposed small dam project on Spry Creek. Most of the shots were of pristine wilderness, the eponymous creek flowing through a corridor of cedars and spruces, interspersed with quick flashes of slogans: RUN OF

RIVER = RUIN OF THE RIVER; TRANSMISSION LINES ARE NOT WILDERNESS CORRIDORS. A few boos, countered and silenced by pockets of applause. Paul remembered Tanner mentioning Spry Creek and bull trout habitat but nothing about a potential dam.

The audience around him—mostly middle-aged artsy types and a handful of wool-scented twentysomethings fiddling distractedly with their dreadlocks—frowned or smiled, nodded in appreciation or squinted in bewilderment, according to their tastes. The dancers had leaped off the stumps and were now cavorting through the clear-cut.

Paul squirmed in his chair, too hot in his bulky sweater, and feeling somehow responsible for the film's cheesy earnestness. If this was a date—but this was not a date, just a way of thanking Gina for her help. She leaned toward him and whispered in a faux-British accent, "It lacks in subtlety but compensates with its obviousness." Hopefully that meant she was enjoying herself.

She hadn't been easy to track down. She tended to disappear from his life for two or three days at a time, and then would show up out of the blue with Shane. The boy was an enigma to Paul, both affectionate and elusive, hugging his leg one moment, indifferent the next. As for Gina, she often looked rundown, with sallow cheeks and chapped, peeling lips. Before he could ask how she was, really was, she'd be whipping up a chocolate bundt cake or soup, and there'd be blenders and food processors buzzing and whirring, drowning out his questions.

Outside, he looked skyward and let the snow melt on his face. He sighed in relief, too loud. Gina was grinning, studying his face. "Not exactly the Vancouver Film Fest?"

"I wouldn't know—never went," he said.

"Kind of a missed opportunity."

"That's my life in a nutshell." Thinking about Vancouver was strange. The Immitoin Valley was a black hole—nothing got in or out, especially in winter. On grey days, the light was so flat that the mountains blended into the sky, no depth, no dimension. Time had frozen to death on some dark slope. His past life existed somewhere beyond the status updates of friends and colleagues on social networking sites: they had achieved something remarkable, gone somewhere exotic, or eaten, cooked, or bought something ethically laudable. Or their child had done something adorable and video-worthy. Where did his project, scarcely begun, fit in with all that?

"There's an after-party at the pub," he said. "Did you want to come?"

She shook her head. "I'll have to leave you here."

"Oh, come on," he said lightly. They'd fallen behind the rest of the crowd.

"The bar's a bit too well-lit for me. I liked sitting there in the dark with you." Translation: one of Billy's friends—or Billy—might see us. She glanced at the windows, and for a moment it was as if the orange light coming from inside caught and held her.

"I guess everyone knows everyone in there," he said.

"It's just a bad idea."

"Okay," he said.

"See you tomorrow, maybe." She gave his arm a quick squeeze, glancing around her. Paul watched her until she disappeared around the corner.

Inside, dozens of conversations melded into a river-like babble. A broad set of dark wooden stairs divided the pub into two levels, the upper with its bigger tables, better lighting, and plusher chairs, and the lower with dart boards and pull-tab machines. He spotted Tanner among a group of men and women—festival organizers, the board of directors and their spouses, he guessed—whose tuxes and black dresses stood out from the sweaters, denim, and ski jackets. Tanner broke away from the group and met Paul at the counter, handing a twenty to the barkeep with a grand flourish and passing Paul a beer.

"Where's your ladyfriend?" he asked, tipsy, grinning like an idiot. "Saw you sitting together in the theatre."

"Had to spell the babysitter," Paul said.

Tanner winked grotesquely. "I knew there was something weird going on at camp."

"We're just friends."

"Sure," said Tanner. Then his grin slipped. "I guess friends are about all you can be, unless—are you back in the saddle?" He raised his forearm until his clenched fist was erect, the obscenity of the gesture in bizarre contrast with his concerned expression.

Paul blinked, dumbfounded. "Congrats," he said. "On the festival. Wonderful stuff."

Tanner beamed as he looked around the crowded pub. "You said hi to Beth yet?"

"No." He spotted her among a circle of women, tall, almost his height, her blond hair gathered and held by something glittery. The women looked like they'd been at the opera, all sheer dresses and glittering necklaces. Completely out of place, though he could appreciate the effect it had on the regulars of the earthy pub. There was definitely a buzz in the air. Tanner dragged him over, but two giddy young men intercepted and swept Tanner off to their table, and Paul found himself alone with Beth. She gave him an unenthusiastic hug. "I heard you've been sick," she said—was he imagining the vague tone of distaste? Of course Tanner would have told her everything.

"Getting better." He sipped his beer self-consciously. He started to bring up the old days, but after stuttering along he could sense those things—favourite hangouts from years ago, mutual friends— weren't wanted here. She rattled off a list of what was keeping her busy, how she taught yoga and helped run the daycare for the ski resort. Took a pottery class in the evenings. Trying to get pregnant, if Tanner hadn't mentioned it. After an awkward few minutes, talk petered out, and Beth turned toward one of her friends.

Flustered, he pointed to his empty glass, a gesture Beth half-acknowledged, and he headed back to the bar. His fault, he thought sourly. During their undergrad, he'd more or less ignored her. The roommate's piece of fluff, while he was off trying to get his own. He should have invited them over this last month, tried to make amends for the past. Interesting, though, the aggressive and emphatic way Beth located herself *here*, rather than Vancouver. It took unrelenting effort to become a local, he supposed.

A group of men, middle-aged and older, hunkered around a small table in the far corner by the dart board, ill at ease with the film fest crowd that had invaded their watering hole. He recognized one of them from his last day at camp, a long-haired fisheries technician named Daryl who'd led Paul's team up Basket Creek to count redds. He'd talked in a raspy voice about the spawning habits of bull trout with a wry intimacy, a bit of fish-gossip mixed with science.

Paul weaved his way through the crowd to the table. "Rasmussen, sure." Daryl shook his hand. "Pull up a chair. We're just shooting the shit."

"Rasmussen," an obese and bespectacled man said. "No relation to Ken? The welder?"

Paul shook his head, and Daryl laughed. "In every Canadian town lives a handy fella named Rasmussen. He's the one I told you about," he said to the man, a Monashee technician named Morton. "Same cancer as you, in remission."

Morton had a mop of grey hair and an easy, toothy grin. He shook Paul's hand. "Gleason Score 7," he said and was delighted when Paul repeated the same. "It's a great life, isn't it? Every time I fart, I pee myself."

"Sounds about right," Paul managed.

Morton apparently spent part of each day in online chat rooms and forums for men recovering from prostate cancer.

They'd run through the vast gauntlet of prostatectomies— unilateral and bilateral nerve-sparing, laparoscopic radical, the da Vinci robotic—and other treatments. Transurethral resections, radiation, and hormone therapies. A lot of talk about the relative strength of one's urine stream—one either pissed like a race horse or like a kitten—or how keenly they missed the sight and sensation of their own ejaculate. Yes, Paul had skimmed similar forums, thinking this was an ethnographic study tailor-made for him—he could study his participants covertly, develop an instant rapport, because he would be one of them.

What kept him away was the language. Brutally explicit, filled with raw emotion—and courageous, he admitted, like when a forum member would joke about the best post-op underwear or announce his own imminent death. Their stories brought his own experiences swinging into queasy, too-close focus. He couldn't read a full page of discussion without feeling faint. Talking to Morton right now was making him nauseous.

Morton turned to the others. "Wife still wants sex, right? We talked about me using a strap-on. I said, you sure about that, honey? 'Cause you know I'll buy the biggest goddamn one there is. Great life," he repeated while everyone laughed. He didn't sound entirely insincere.

"How's the research?" asked Daryl. "Taking shape?"

"What's he doing?" another man asked, a hand up to his ear. "More fish stuff?"

Daryl filled him in, somewhat inaccurately. The man nodded. "Tell him about Joe Pilcher," he said with a great deal of satisfaction. "Joe fuckin' Pilcher."

Daryl rolled his eyes. "My old man," he explained to Paul. "We had a trapline and a squatter's cabin in the woods north of Lambert."

"Before the dam?" Paul asked.

"Definitely not after. It's sitting below the high water mark by about twenty metres."

"I should be talking to your dad, then."

"Not much chance of that, I'm afraid."

"Sorry."

"Could talk to me, though. It's a great story."

"If you knew what I was doing, why didn't you contact me before?"

"Waiting for you to ask," Daryl said, eyebrows raised in a hurt expression. He grinned. "No. I had to make sure of your politics. People come here, say they're doing historical research, and it turns into anti-dam rhetoric and nostalgia. Oh woe, the steamships are gone. Like we'd still be using fucking steamships if there was no dam."

"I'll mark you down for definitely not anti-dam."

"Doesn't matter." He waved a hand toward the window. "There she be, whether you like it or not. There's good and bad in everything, right? You and I wouldn't have had jobs this fall without it."

"True enough."

"From what I hear, you're impartial. So far."

"I just want people's stories."

"I'm a Monashee guy. No one's saying the dam didn't bugger a lot of things up. That's my life's work, trying to improve habitat." He waved both his hands in circles, a man describing a conjuring trick. "Fix mistakes. Bear witness. Witness bears."

Morton nudged Paul. "Here's a conundrum I've been chatting about online. My daughter's getting married this summer: do I do my PSA check before or after the wedding? You see the problem? If I wait, I might be too nervous to enjoy the wedding. But if I do it before, I might be too depressed."

There was a shifting in the wall of people, and Tanner appeared, bug-eyed and growling like a stage pirate, a pitcher of beer in his hand. Daryl fished a card out of his wallet and handed it to Paul. "Buy me a beer later this week and we'll talk."

Paul nodded, then turned to Morton. "Before. Because the news might not be bad."

"Good man—you're an optimist," Morton said, and Paul had a good laugh.

Roger (b. 1948, 61 yrs old) **and Betty** (b. 1950, 59 yrs old) **Tierney**
Recorded at their home in Shellycoat, December 1, 2009.

Roger: The road to Shellycoat back then was pure hell. Especially in spring. The tire ruts were so deep, you'd get hung up if you had anything lower than a crew cab or a crummie. That was one of the promises that came with the dam—road improvements from Bishop to Shellycoat.

Betty: It *was* easier to get around, after.

R: Sure. They wanted to get people excited about the jobs the dam would bring. Of course, that doesn't make people forget they're losing their homes. I can sympathize with that.

Paul: **So did you get steady work, then? On the dam?**

R: I worked two, three months before construction started, clearing the shores with a cat. Just before winter, a bunch of us were laid off. Told we didn't have enough experience, that we needed to sign up with the right union. All of a sudden there's Portuguese and Italians, Indonesians, all up from the coast. We said, "What about the rule to hire local?" Eventually we got our jobs back. Betty and I moved from Lambert to Bishop to Shellycoat in the span of a year and a half.

Thing about the dam, there's places you can live now you couldn't before. Spring floods downriver from Shellycoat were nasty. The dam controls the levels, everyone's properties are safer. Less mosquitoes too.

B: We enjoyed being in town. More things to do, social events and movies. Sports teams and music recitals for the kids.

R: Close to all the shops, the library, and the movie theatre.

B: You weren't so cut off from the outside world. Mind you, that's exactly why some hated being relocated.

R: They didn't want to have anything to do with the outside world.

Not everyone held bitter memories. Or they'd given up grappling with the strangeness of their land no longer existing. The children of those who "did all right" in negotiations, or those landowners who'd been starved for a more comfortable, modern life, gave a different interview than someone like Elsie Hubert. Some people were secretly relieved to give up their homes, so difficult and costly to maintain. Some had grown weary of the relative poverty and isolation, others had parents who needed to be in a rest home, not a dilapidated farm.

In Castlegar, in 1993, the Kootenay Symposium (he found a video cassette copy in the archives) had given those affected by the dams on the Columbia and Kootenay Rivers a chance to vent their anger in a public forum. There'd been nothing comparable in the Immitoin Valley. He'd got a taste of bottled-up resentment with people like the Kruses and Elsie, but he wanted more—he hoped for shouting, rage, tears. But tears proved elusive. Maybe because to show grief would be to admit defeat. Or because, really, it was none of Paul's goddamned business. Wasn't that obvious? Men didn't want to be subjects. They wanted to relate events from a distance, to be the historians of their own lives. The women wanted to talk but did not trust.

He was always aware of being the outsider. He didn't live here, he was *in the field*, the community of Shellycoat-after-the-dam. Closed within the bubble of what was called his ethnographic position, which demanded that he be both stranger and observer, that he abide—blend in if he was lucky—but not belong.

The work was satisfying, at least. He was rolling along, his mind firing on all cylinders. It was only the early stages, but he knew that what he was delving into was real and substantial— he wouldn't have to force connections from what he gathered, the patterns were already there, waiting for him to catch up if he could.

After he interviewed the Tierneys, he went to the coffee shop where Gina had promised to meet him. For two hours, he sat alone by a window with his headphones on, playing back interviews, hating the sound of his own voice more and more.

In the hallway that led to the back porch was a storage closet. It lay directly beneath Jory and Sonya's stairs, separated from the steps by a thin layer of particle board, and tall enough on one side for Paul to stand while he sorted through his stuff. Early one evening he was rummaging through one of his boxes for an old essay he'd written when he heard a soft repetitive thumping from upstairs. Someone cried out—Sonya's voice, a guttural yelp that accompanied each thump. He held his breath and moved deeper into the closet where the sounds grew clearer, amplified by the wood. They were in the living room, he guessed, on the couch close to the stairs.

He closed his eyes, focusing on the quieter, more telling layers of sound: the huff of Jory's breath, the faint smack of flesh, the protesting joints of the couch frame. Sonya groaned, an upward inflection, astonished at something, and then her cries went up a notch. He couldn't tell whether the sounds she made were genuine. Perhaps she exaggerated her pleasure to some degree, but maybe not. They were young, their own bodies could still surprise them.

He became greedy for their voices and noises, absorbed and invested in their rising joy. He knew Jory and Sonya well enough now to call them friends—he had coffee with them on the porch regularly, brought leftovers upstairs when Gina had made too much food—but not enough that decency overcame his curiosity. The creaking and groaning upstairs brought his own erotic memories to the surface, sharpened by his being deprived of physical arousal and release for so long. In his mind, he inhabited both Jory's frame and his own, younger self. He forced those playful yelps not just from Sonya, but from a procession of women from his past.

When Jory came with a ragged, socked-in-the gut moan, he left Paul cold beneath the stairs, alone in his flesh and clinging to the image of Jory collapsing on Sonya's back. They wound down with matching sighs, their wordless protests that something so wonderful should leave them.

A viscous, salty saliva filled his mouth, which he washed away with a single swallow. He slipped quietly out of the house and wandered into town. The stores were closed, the streets nearly empty except for a handful of city workers on ladders and cherry-pickers stringing Christmas lights and ornaments on the streetlights, trees, and utility poles. He kept on until he reached the park. Along the river, old-fashioned-looking streetlamps cast a dim yellow glow, and beyond their reach, the Immitoin rolled past, muted and dark. There were benches along the path, each marked with a small memorial plaque. On one lay fresh flowers and stuffed polar bears and beavers with toques. On the plaque, a woman's name, Yolanda Hayward. She'd died last winter, died young. A crossed pair of skis were engraved underneath her name. LOVED FRIENDS AND FAMILY, LOVED LIFE.

Wandering back through town, melancholy and half-asleep, he was pricked awake by coarse laughter. Three women stood on the sidewalk outside a small pub in the basement of a brick building. They gathered in a loose, wavering circle as they smoked. One of the women staggered, swore, and laughed again. He recognized

Gina's laugh. She leaned against a black crew cab with dual rear wheels, floodlights positioned on the roof above the windshield, a snowmobile perched high on a metal ramp on the back. The truck, with its dark colour and behemoth proportions, absorbed Gina as though she had fallen backward into nothingness. Paul ducked into the shadows, creeping away from the streetlight and brightly decorated shop windows. A door opened at the bottom of some stairs, and men bellowed from the threshold, calling to the women, yelling crude goodbyes to someone inside the pub. Paul hurried up the icy sidewalks toward home, sliding backward now and then, every muscle clenched and taut from the effort of staying upright.

~

The Barber Chair Pub met the requisites of a pub in the barest possible way: a few small windows (a parade of winter boots passing by—the pub sat below street level), scuffed white walls, thin wooden tables and metal chairs and stools, video lottery terminals along one wall. A single bartender served the patrons—all men. This was the daytime crowd, Daryl Pilcher told Paul. A few more women came at night, but not many. Most of the men were long past retirement, blowing their pensions on beer and lotteries. Stacks of crumpled pull-tabs and pencilled-in Keno sheets littered the tables. He wasn't sure why he and Daryl hadn't gone to the other bar. The atmosphere here was not particularly welcoming. And this was the same pub he'd watched Gina stagger out of the other night.

"Can I run this idea past you?" Paul asked. He'd set his digital recorder on the table, along with a contour map of the valley. Daryl was alternating sips of watery draught with handfuls of sunflower seeds from a brown melamine bowl. "A trapper's relationship to both the land and community would be substantially different than a farmer's, right? I've been thinking about your dad, and picturing life in the valley existing on a horizontal plane between contour lines. If that makes sense."

Daryl nodded, jaws working. Paul went on, pointing at sections of the map. "The ranchers and farmers, they occupied the low, flat plane by the lakeshore, with the fertile soil, alluvial fans, wetlands. Their whole life was there, between those broad contour lines. The loggers and miners, they belonged where the contour lines are squeezed together—the mid to high elevations, the steeper slopes, the forests. Trappers, on the other hand, they lived vertical lives—their traplines went from valley bottom to mountain top. This would have shaped their perspective of what happened. They still had something left after the flood."

To Paul's surprise, Daryl burst out laughing. A bunch of logger types glanced over. Why had he chosen this place?

"That's great," Daryl said, wiping his eyes. "That takes me back."

"To what?" Paul shifted in his chair, trying to block most of the pub from his view.

"University. You know, smoking pot with the philosophy and chem students, bullshit sessions in the pub. You remind me of some of my buddies in Monashee, good old eggheads." He stared at the ceiling, chewing thoughtfully. "Well, you might have something there. Guess I'd have to think about it." He handed Paul a sheet of paper. "Now here's something from a trapper's perspective. Brought it because I figured you wouldn't know these stats. Most don't."

Animals disappeared from Immitoin Valley, estimated count, 1971.
- 800 black bear
- 1,500 mule and whitetail deer
- 400 elk
- 150 moose
- 20,000 ducks and geese (drowned-out nesting sites, lost marshland)

Daryl said, "My first job, I'd just turned fourteen. Family had been relocated from our squatter's cabin, of course. Government hired Bishop men to drive tugs and clear up deadheads, stray lumber, plastic, and scrap metal floating around. Dad and I were on dead animal patrol. We'd use peavey hooks and whatever else to drag what we found onto a barge. Or stack them on beaches. Anything from rabbit to moose and bear. Most people think animals just wander uphill when the waters rise, but it's not that simple. Maybe they get surprised, or they're stubborn, maybe they can't comprehend what's happening, I don't know. Between the carcasses and the sludge, the valley stank the whole summer."

"Must have been tough for your dad, seeing that."

"That, and he'd already lost the cabin and most of his trapline."

"Did your family get any compensation for that?"

Daryl shrugged. "Six hundred bucks for the line, plus enough for a new shack in Bishop to call home. Well, to be fair, Monashee Power had a difficult time assessing the value of a trapline. Or any property. Even when trappers had land titles—when they weren't squatting illegally—most of those properties had barely any improvements. A cabin, a small clearing for a garden, some chickens. Squatters tended to move into old miners' shacks and abandoned homesteads. Most of them got burned out by Monashee." He paused and took a long drink. "Chucking carcasses on the barge was pretty awful. But we were lucky to have the work. When we came to Bishop, we had nothing except a couple of suitcases and a pile of furs. Yeah, furs. I shit you not."

"What was Bishop like?" Paul asked.

"Tough. No one knew us or liked us much. We were outsiders trying to live among a bunch of disgruntled Lambert folk. Not many kids my age from Bishop made it past high school, but my folks made sure I went to university, because they knew I was going to be a better trouble-maker than a logger, if you know what I mean."

A scuffling of chairs and boots from behind him, a creak of floorboards, and Paul turned around to see three old men approaching their table, followed by a man in his early forties.

"Heard you talk about burning cabins and so on," one of the old men rasped. "Weren't talking about us, were you?"

"I know better than that, Cyril," Daryl said. "Have a seat if you like."

The youngest of the men—Paul assumed it was Billy Wentz—dragged over a neighbouring table, the legs loudly scraping across the floor. He swaggered, holding his arms farther from his body than he needed to, clothing himself in imaginary muscle—though he had plenty of real muscle, easily hefting metal chairs with his veiny and scarred forearms. Beneath his oil-stained ball cap, worn, tired eyes, a hard jaw and cheekbones, a red moustache tinged with grey. He scowled at Paul, and didn't sit at the table, choosing to watch from above.

Cyril and the other old men slowly folded themselves into their chairs, all of them grizzled, lean, and bent, their lumberjack muscles atrophied but still somehow present, ghosting at the edges of their frames. They looked like those canes made from stretched and dried bull pizzle—yellowed, cracked, and leathery, brittle.

Cyril looked at him. "Heard about you interviewing people for a book or whatnot. My folks knew all those trappers, including Joe Pilcher. In the winters, my dad and I would run them supplies from Lambert, dogsledding it through the woods. One fellow, he had a cabin so deep in the hills, Monashee never found him. Maybe you remember him, Daryl."

Daryl was gesturing to the bartender to bring a pitcher of beer. Neither man looked very happy.

"That old trapper didn't have a clue what was going on," Cyril said. "Told me later he was hunting up on a ridge and saw the valley filling up with smoke, the water rising. Had a bird's eye of Lambert slowly going under." He paused and drank—flashing bad teeth beneath wet lips—then leaned closer to Paul. "I know when you talk to people they tell you Wallace's crew worked for that goon squad they called the Acquisition and Resettlement Commission. Boys in this pub know better. Wallace's crew was my crew—I was the foreman when my dad and Donald Wallace got too old. Donald Wallace hated the dam more than anyone. Hell, he lost more than anyone, except us."

"Elsie Hubert said as much," Paul said. "So you didn't work for Monashee Power at all?"

"We did—we cut and milled poles for their lumber and utilities division. We had fuck all to do with the bullying and burning."

Cyril was eager to talk about his family, sliding the digital recorder closer to himself so he could speak directly into it. He was born, he said, in Lambert, in 1936. His father, Frederic Wentz, was one of the first in Lambert to choose logging over agriculture. "It was my dad's idea to build the flumes at Dalton Creek, but he didn't have money or the backing. It wasn't until Wallace got into the business late that we had capital enough to build the flumes and mill."

"What do you mean Wallace 'got into the business late'?"

"Donald Wallace was the last big orchardist left standing in the valley. He limped along until the end of the forties, and after that, he pumped his savings into our operation. He also brought in guys from the orchards. Fruit pickers and deliverymen, the arborists that tended the trees—they needed the work, but most were green. So whenever there was an accident and someone died, it was usually one of them. Drop a tree on themselves, put a saw into their leg. Drown in the log booms. Saw men go like that."

Billy, who'd stood quietly glaring in the background, suddenly became animated. He slid into the last empty chair. "You know what a Barber Chair is, bud?" he said to Paul. "It's when the tree splits vertically as it's felled, usually because you bunged up your backcut. There's a thin strip of wood keeping the tree to the stump, and it'll twist according to where the lean is. According to its own fuckin' rules. So now you've lost control over the thing. It'll go where it pleases, usually straight back at your head."

"That's what they named this pub after?"

"Something wrong with that?" But Cyril hushed him—he wanted to keep talking about the logging days. The other old men had their stories as well—building the flumes, sending logs down the river or loading up trucks with milled lumber. Billy, obviously trying to intimidate Paul, told mostly violent stories— machinery accidents, skidders flipping over on their drivers, a bear mauling a timber cruiser.

Cyril said, "So, yeah, the golden years were mostly Monashee contracts. Once folks heard about the dam, they wanted us to pick a side, and we needed to make a living. But the funny thing was, around the same time Monashee started buying up properties, Monashee stopped giving us work. Can't win for losing. Once the land agent came along and hired away half our crew, we knew we were fucked."

"He stole half your crew?"

Cyril shrugged sourly. "He had deeper pockets. And the kind of work that didn't break your balls."

"The land agent," Paul said. "Do you mean Caleb Ready?"

Cyril squinted at him for a moment, then slowly nodded. "That's the one. Caleb Ready. Boy, haven't heard that name in a while."

Paul didn't buy that. "You didn't hear what happened to Ready?"

"Nope. Who gives a fuck about him?" Cyril stumbled off to the bathroom, and Daryl, who'd been slouching in his chair, hiding behind his beer, took the opportunity to slip away. "Think I'll play some VLTs," he muttered, then beelined for the exit.

Billy had not stopped trying to stare down Paul. "Gina ain't told me squat about you," he said, a gravelly drawl. The two old men snickered and mumbled.

"No?"

"No, and I don't think she likes you bothering her. I don't like it."

Paul, hating Daryl in that moment, didn't match Billy's stare but looked at his shoulder, which he'd heard was a good tactic when confronted by a wild animal. She must have seen something in him, some redeeming quality. Maybe the surly temper manifested itself differently in the outdoors, when the work was hard-going. And when he wasn't half-drunk in the afternoon, he was probably a handy and capable guy. Strong, obviously. He wished the word *virile* didn't come to mind, but it did.

Billy tried again. "Harassing people."

"All right," Paul said.

"Leave him be," Cyril said, returning. "I just wanted to get some facts straight, not stir up shit." He wiped a puddle of spilled beer from Paul's map, then stopped and tapped at the spot he'd cleaned with his sleeve. "That's the old family lot, with waterfront. That acreage was Billy's inheritance. It'd be worth a million by now—vacation rentals, maybe a vineyard. But no point bitching about it now, is there?"

"Did you ever try suing the government, like other residents did? To get fair compensation?"

"Lawsuits. Tie your whole life up that way. What you do, you work your ass off and get something back. You compensate yourself."

Paul was exhausted, holding his own against these gruff, reticent men. Cyril was starting to look bored. If he had any good questions, he'd better throw them out there now. "Were you there on Lambert's final day? I haven't found anyone who was."

"Most people were gone by then, that's why. I was there.

There was a squad of us, burning whatever buildings hadn't been torched already, either by Monashee or the owners."

"What about the Wallaces?"

"Hardy was in the squad too. We still had the company for the time being. The Wallaces moved into a cabin on the river we'd used as a bunkhouse for our crew. I think Hardy still lives there. After Donald died and our mill folded, I lost touch with Hardy."

"Really?" Paul frowned.

"Guess I've seen him about. We were never friends, exactly."

"Well, it seems kind of—anyways, all right."

Cyril raised an eyebrow. Paul backed off and took a deep breath. "Okay. What about your own father, Cyril? What did he make of all those changes?"

Cyril looked stunned, absolutely floored. Paul was confused—it was a logical question, it should have been expected. Cyril's jaw twitched soundlessly as he shook his head with a flat, flinty stare.

One of the old men beside him cleared his throat. "He hung himself, you dumb son of a bitch. Frederic Wentz did himself in."

Paul grabbed the digital recorder a split second before Billy swatted it across the room. He jumped to his feet. The room had gone silent. Paul looked over at the bartender, who nodded toward the door, his expression carefully neutral.

Billy was rising from his chair—Cyril briefly put his hand on his son's arm to stop him. Then he folded his arms across his chest and said, "Time to get the fuck out of here, bud."

~

A week went by without a word from Gina. Letters and pamphlets began to appear in his mail, all from the Friends of Spry Creek, a local environmental group. The stack of literature connected the proposed run-of-river project with past events—the McCulloch Dam, the displacement of Immitoin Valley citizens—although in this case no one would be relocated and the reservoir levels would be minimally affected. The group made dire predictions, though, about the appropriation of public land, the trampling of community values (whatever that meant), and the further destruction of fish habitat and wildlife corridors by construction and power line right-of-ways.

A line from a pamphlet jumped out at him: "Even after decades of court cases, belated compensation packages, and limp public apologies from government and Monashee Power officials, stories of past atrocities are still being discovered by academics and historians and are being brought to light."

Academics—were they talking about him? On a hunch, he examined the letterhead of one pamphlet and saw that Elsie Hubert was listed as the secretary for the non-profit group.

So this is why she'd suddenly been so keen to be interviewed. He'd been under an invisible microscope this whole time. People were talking about him and, worse, twisting his intentions.

He phoned Elsie but didn't have the nerve to confront her directly about the pamphlets. "Why didn't you tell me about Frederic Wentz killing himself?"

"It wasn't my business to say," she said. "I don't want to exploit anybody."

Except me, he thought. "You might have saved me some trouble with Cyril. Anyway, I went to the graveyard yesterday and saw for myself."

"It's a memorial," she said stiffly. "For Lambert's dead. Not a graveyard."

"Still. I got the sense he wasn't the only one."

"There were rumours of others," Elsie said reluctantly. "Someone would die cleaning their gun, that sort of thing. A lot of old-timers, especially veterans, they lived alone, with no close neighbours. Probably couldn't imagine themselves being shuffled off to an old folks home. But, like I said, it's only rumours."

Elmer had been the one to tell him about the memorial, but it had been a trick getting the archivist to come along—he'd hadn't been in years, and never in winter. Constable Lazeroff, surprisingly, had been eager to join them and wasn't worried about finding the place. Jory had supplied the snowmobiles, borrowing two spanking new Polaris sleds from a friend. Jory stunk of alcohol and after they'd found the memorial site, he mostly wandered around trying not to throw up.

They parked near the dam, where a set of transmission line towers climbed the hills and disappeared into the mountains. The four of them doubled up on the two sleds—Paul riding behind Lazeroff—taking the sleds up a service road that would eventually end at Fiddler's Bowl, the local paradise for sledders and backcountry fanatics. The road was hard-packed by dozens of other snowmobiles. After the first hill, though, Lazeroff led them across a rolling meadow, heading for a copse of aspen and pine. Piles of hay and salt licks soiled the pristine whiteness, the snow trampled and stained by animal tracks and droppings.

"Hay's for elk," Lazeroff shouted over his shoulder to Paul. "Rod and Gun Club does a few drops each winter. On Monashee's dime. To make up for lost habitat."

At the woods they dismounted, and Lazeroff walked them through the knee-deep snow to a boulder as high as Paul's chest. It stood between two pines like a menhir, the side facing them flat and engraved with large square letters. People had kept the inscription clean of lichen and moss. From where he stood, Paul could see straight across the lake to where Lambert used to be. He read the stone:

IN MEMORY OF THE ONE HUNDRED AND EIGHT PEOPLE BURIED IN THE LAMBERT CEMETERY, 1899–1969.

There were different ways of handling the dead of a drowned town, Elmer explained. On the Arrow Lakes, the government had covered Renata's cemetery with a big concrete pad to seal the graves before the flood. In other places, other countries, bodies were repatriated and moved. In Lambert, they had merely piled fill and boulders over the cemetery. Valley folk built the monument in 1970. Twenty years later, the government finally erected its own official memorial next to the dam.

The four of them fanned out and waded ankle-deep through the woods, walking in an outward spiral from the monument. Near a birch, Paul's toe caught against something hard, and he scraped the snow away until he found a square of granite. The lettering on the stone was faded, blackened with lichens. He found two more markers a few metres away. The names etched on the stones weren't familiar, and he added them to his notes. Underneath a clump of ash, where the snow was thin, he spotted the top of a slab with tracks leading up to it: someone had tended the stone recently. "Here we go," he called out. The others trudged over, Jory wiping at his mouth with the back of his hand.

FREDERIC WENTZ. 1901–1967. HUNG HIMSELF IN LAMBERT. THERE ARE SOME WHO WON'T BE MOVED.

Paul stood close to Lazeroff. "So?" he asked quietly. "What do you think?" The other night over the phone he'd played Lazeroff some of the recording from the Barber Chair.

Lazeroff wiped frost off his moustache. "Everyone hated Caleb. We already knew that. And now we know Billy and Cyril hate you. Not much I can do there. Except tell you to choose your women better."

"Thanks. So you're not looking into Caleb's case?"

The constable grimaced. "There is no case. Closed. Done."

"But you're here."

"Me? I'm just some old bastard goofing around on his day off." He gave Paul a quick wink, and that ended the conversation.

Over the phone, Elsie sighed. "Anyhow, that's nice of you to call. I meant to ask if you'd be interested in going to a meeting. Won't be until after the new year."

"About Spry Creek, you mean?" he said. She acted surprised he'd heard of it, a deceit that reminded him of his own mother, and he smiled despite himself. "I'll mark it on my calendar."

"If you could just observe. Wouldn't necessarily have to say anything."

Jesus, he thought. I should hope not. He paused. "How's Gina?"

"Oh," she sighed. "Same as ever. Heard about Billy."

"I was just trying to interview Daryl Pilcher." He was still beating himself up over his colossal failure. Not just his unfinished interview with Daryl, but Cyril and Billy—the last man born in Lambert, how great would that have looked in his dissertation?—and, really, an entire roomful of potential research participants. All wasted opportunities.

Elsie said, "I've known the Wentzes for a long time. Doesn't mean we see eye to eye, or deal with things the same way."

"Ms. Hubert, there's nothing between me and your daughter."

"Billy would still tell you to stay away from her."

"Oh, he did. Quite emphatically. But what do you think?"

"About?"

"Gina. And me. Not that there's anything . . ."

"I know you could use a friend. But I wonder what's best for my grandson—maybe simpler is better. Then again, I'm not sure what 'simpler' means either. I let Gina run her life," she finished brusquely. "If you can think of some people at your university that might be interested in what's happening at Spry Creek, I don't know if you have the ear of an ecologist or biologist . . ."

He waffled, made some vague promises, and hung up.

~

The next morning, after his workout, he hired Sonya to transcribe his interviews, starting with Cyril and Billy's. He knew she needed the money and something to do. He'd assumed she'd be at the ski hill every day, but discovered—Jory had never told him, which maybe said something about the young man's self-absorption—that she'd injured herself at a mountain bike race that summer, and had an operation on her right knee in September. She spent most days pacing restlessly upstairs. Still, typing out interviews was a terrible cure for boredom, and when she quickly agreed to do it he wondered if he'd misjudged her sullen nature.

The next afternoon she phoned to say she couldn't understand half of what was being said. He went upstairs and saw the digital recorder and her laptop on the coffee table in the living room. A Christmas tree stood in the corner, the strings of light glowing softly, reflecting off the strands of silver tinsel and dangling ornaments. Sonya appeared from the kitchen, holding two cups of coffee. She shrugged an apology for her flannel pyjamas. "I haven't left the house today."

He gestured at the tree. "Surprisingly old-fashioned."

She gave him a self-deprecating smirk. "I like the holidays. Jory got me the Santa skulls."

They sat at opposite ends of the couch—its familiar creak briefly embarrassed him—and listened to the moments where ambient pub noise muffled Cyril's voice. Paul closed his eyes, trying to use his memory to fill in the blanks. At his prompt, Sonya played back each muffled section. "*Widow-maker*," he said. "Another logging story." She typed and they moved on to the next problem.

"Jory at the shop today?" he asked.

"No. Backcountry trip with his friends. There's this ridge behind the ski hill, Teddy's Lemon Drop."

"They take some big risks?"

"Just being on the ridge is dangerous. Let alone the shit they'll try to pull off. People die every year up there. This one girl, Yolanda? Took a tumble off a cliff band."

"I saw the bench in the park. Her name on it."

She snorted. "A fucking bench. They named the whole ridge after Teddy."

"Who was he?"

"Hot-shit skier back in the nineties. You know, corporate sponsors, starred in films. Like Jory."

"He died on the ridge?"

"Car crash. Coming home from a party. But he's still the town legend. Live fast, die young, and all that."

They sat in silence for a while. "Let's play that one part again," he said.

Sonya stared at the ceiling, frowning, her ear toward the player as the interview rolled. "Took some balls, you know," she said.

"What?"

"The interview. Pretty tense, and the Barber Chair's a rough place too. But you kept asking questions."

A giddy grin threatened to erupt from beneath his smile. "Too nervous to shut up, is all. Thanks, though."

She tucked her legs beneath her, and the flannel tightened against her thighs and hips. When she leaned forward to stop the recorder or type on the laptop, he glimpsed the pale tops of her breasts. His body did not respond, not in the usual way, but felt rejuvenated, infused with a brighter energy. It couldn't be anything more, in his condition, than simply a keen appreciation of beauty. She had a wonderful body. He did, despite everything, remember how wonderful a body like that could be.

Sometimes at night, on his way back from the bathroom, he would pop into his storage closet for a minute or two. If he was greeted with dead silence, he would return to the bedroom. If he heard any noise, even the low rumblings of music or conversation, he would linger to see where things were headed. It was juvenile and creepy, so utterly unlike anything he'd ever done that he found it easy to disassociate himself from the weird guy under the stairs and not feel guilty when he shared coffee with Jory and Sonya the next day. One night after he'd been upstairs working on transcriptions with Sonya, he was rewarded—if one could call it that—with the steadily increasing pulse of bedsprings and, afterwards, the padding of feet toward the bathroom and the running of water. Her voice had been largely absent except where Paul imagined it. Only Jory's loud, enthusiastic gasps and exhortations made it into the mix. Paul scavenged on the auditory leftovers, the discarded sounds of their good sex.

~

Maybe desire had been present all along, existing in different forms. How else to explain his vigour thumbing through documents and texts, the delight that thrummed through him after a decent interview? Or his sudden ability to bring people together, drag three men out to a snowy field to look at tombstones? This was nothing like last winter, when his blood had stopped moving and his body became a stagnant, tepid pool where cancer quietly germinated.

He was riding a buoyant surge of momentum, and a particular urgency. His research was rooted in the past, and the past was disappearing. An event occurred, formed a community, and then time worked to erase its every member. Most of his participants were aging. How much longer would Agnes Hutchinson live to remember long-vanished steamships and orchards, barn dances?

Other things pushed him onward—disturbing dreams, lucid memories of Caleb Ready's corpse, that brief glimpse of pallid flesh. Ready emerging as the valley's sinister legend. Either his death was a bizarre, cosmic act of karma—or just irony—or someone was lying to Paul. There were voices missing from the tapestry. Like Hardy's. There was no chance Cyril or Billy would talk to him again. That fact alone made Hardy Wallace essential, unavoidable.

FIELD NOTES:

The metropolitan creeps into Shellycoat. The ubiquitous iPods, Lululemon yoga pants, designer fleece tops, designer dogs (almost surreal next to the malamutes, shepherd-wolf crosses, and mountain dogs). Australian ski bums serving tables for a quick buck between backcountry trips. Real estate prices within town artificially inflated by wealthy Albertan oil and construction barons looking for vacation properties, former Torontonians who ski all morning and run their online enterprises by afternoon. "So why are you here, exactly?" they all ask me.

It's a paradise here, at least above the tree line. Below that, it gets a bit complicated.

A chance encounter with Lucy Wendish downtown. She points out a yarn and crafts store that used to be a dry cleaner's back in the seventies and eighties. No one from Bishop would take their clothes there, even though it was the only one in the valley: a rumour the owner, a former resident of Lambert, had received an "inexplicably large chunk of money for a scrappy piece of land." But how many people from Bishop, I wonder, needed dry cleaning anyway?

Back at the McCulloch Dam viewpoint today. Most female participants remember the ugly side of the dam's construction. The hillsides and shoreline stripped of topsoil, ripped apart and compacted, bedrock blasted out, the constant sound of dynamite echoing up and down the valley. The fill piled in heaps, mercury and contaminants seeping into the river. Dangerous work, building the body of the dam. A wonder so few people died building it: six altogether, three from carbon monoxide poisoning, one from heat exhaustion, the others falling to their deaths during the installation of the penstocks.

Most men recall the construction with grudging admiration, the difficulty the crews faced fording the heavy machinery, the excavators and cranes, across the narrows. How they used barges on the upstream side to dump five hundred tonnes of fill. They compare that work with the modern hydroelectric projects in Quebec and Ontario, where engineers drill mile-long underground tunnels to divert water and the tunnelling is done so quietly it can't be heard or felt above ground. The men have made themselves knowledgeable about dams. Whatever else they feel about the past, they are unabashedly fascinated by the engineering, the sheer scale of these projects.

On the surface, my ethnography is a study of displacement and adaptation. The true project, though, is a mapping of the hidden continuity of emotions, the invisible but animate circuits that come together to affect the everyday. Time heals all wounds—wrestling with that old cliché. Generations of the displaced happily drive their motorboats over the submerged foundations of their own history. This doesn't mean anger or resentment can't still surface, the mind being less solid than earth, less solid than water.

In the winter cold I feel my surgery scars, a hollow clenching that could be all in my mind. The air around the dam is moist, an icy mist. Sheets of ice hang from the rocks above the stilling basin. Along the wall of the dam, weepholes weep icicles.

Talked to a very old man in a red Chevy at the viewpoint. This is what he chooses to do with his last years as a driver, what his truck means to him: he comes out here alone to watch the morning sun hit the top of the hills opposite the reservoir, or look at the colours of light on the water or migrating flocks of ducks. He remembers this view from a different, lower angle, when his hobby farm sat at the water's edge. When he's forced to give up his licence, he'll lose these mornings. It might just be the end of him.

On the morning of Christmas Eve, Paul prepared to embrace his first Christmas alone, without family, lover, or friends. He invested in decorations and ornaments, hung strings of lights on the back porch and along the kitchen window. Most of the town's Christmas trees had been harvested from beneath the dam's transmission line right-of-ways, sold outside the grocery store to raise money for the local junior hockey team or the Salvation Army. The young spruce he'd picked up for twenty dollars drooped under the weight of blinking lights and dime-store baubles—a Charlie Brown Christmas. He'd bought himself a single bottle of red wine, a small roasting chicken, some yams and frozen vegetables, and magazines to spend a day with on the couch.

Jory and Sonya dropped by in the early afternoon before driving to Jory's parents' house in Christina Lake, and when they left, he felt lonely. His parents, knowing Paul wouldn't make the journey home on winter roads, had flown out yesterday to an all-inclusive south of Puerto Vallarta. Snow either drew people together and enclosed them or else offered an excuse to stay apart. It was strange not to mind being alone while most people his age were all about family, or at least the idea of it. They'd procreated and made their parents into grandparents, or filled their apartments with pets or other things, and felt like their lives had come full circle.

He came across an article about run-of-river dams in one of his magazines. There was a picture of a small powerhouse beside a placid autumn river in New York State, a nineteenth-century milldam resurrected and modernized to supply hydroelectricity to the adjacent neighbourhood. The image was quaint: the preserved character of the antique brick-and-mortar powerhouse perched above the old millpond, the river continuing unabated. Of course, the reality was more complex—the article wouldn't have been written otherwise—but beyond the pros and cons of small hydro, what was fascinating about that particular dam was how it bridged and preserved both the past and present.

He had copies of photos of Lambert in the wintertime, Christmas in the valley. Black-and-white pastorals: snow stained by dung and scattered hay; roads and driveways plowed by a helpful neighbour; cattle, horse, and sheep pressed up against fences, browsing for winter grasses. Bleakness and desolation pressing at the fringes of each image. The photos were one way of tracking the physical losses directly caused by the dam—the homesteads and farmland, the milder climate and shelter of the valley bottom. But wasn't the lost intimacy of their community—the growing alienation between neighbours, between people and the landscape—the inevitable course of progress, regardless of the flood? Maybe Joseph Kruse was right, and the dam had only hastened the inevitable. To simply vilify Monashee Power would be to judge the actions of a man's limb separately from the man himself. He wondered what a contemporary Immitoin Valley would look like without the reservoir. Lambert had been a place desperately wanting to remain in the past.

He heard an engine, the sound of tires crunching snow against the curb. A few moments later, someone knocked. He walked through the kitchen and opened the front door. Gina and Shane. She gave Paul her usual grin, as though she'd only vanished for a day or two and not the better part of a month. Her chapped bottom lip was split and showed red. Everything about her looked parched and washed out, her hair dry and frizzy, a dusting of dried skin on her forehead and cheeks. He honestly couldn't tell whether she'd been beaten or was just on the tail end of a bender. Behind her, the back seat of the truck was packed to the top of the windows with boxes and bags. Shane looked as if he'd been crying, but now he squirmed from beneath her hand, happy enough to be somewhere he could set down his armful of toys.

She said, "I'd understand if you didn't . . ."

"Come in," he said.

Shane kicked off his boots mid-march through the kitchen, then tossed plastic railroad ties onto the living room carpet. The boy flashed him a quick, shy glance, and when Paul gave him a solemn thumbs-up sign, he sat and played, his chin tucked against his chest.

"Tea?" Paul asked. She nodded, and he walked past her and put the kettle on. "I left messages," he said.

"I know."

"You've been staying at Billy's."

"Sometimes he stays with us. He comes around the apartment at all hours. He gets like that."

"Must be confusing for your son."

"He doesn't really say how he feels."

"Probably doesn't know what to feel. Do you think spending Christmas with Billy would have made things simpler for him?"

"Billy's not much fun during the holidays."

Paul chuckled without humour. "I'll bet Grandpa Cyril's no barrel of laughs, either." He leaned against the counter and crossed his arms. Warmth from the stovetop crept up his back. She sank into a chair, her elbow on the table and her hand propping up her head. Shane had edged closer to the tree and tucked himself under the lowest branches, involved in a silent game, tracing invisible things on the carpet.

Paul said, "If it's because I can't . . ."

"Don't be stupid. I don't care about that."

"You don't have to care about anything. We don't owe each other anything, I know."

"I could have gone to my mother's place." She scratched at her forehead and then studied her fingernail. "I didn't want the I-told-you-so speech from her today."

"Or from me either, I guess." He smiled sourly. "Speaking of your mother." He told her about the pamphlets, how her group had used his work to further their agenda.

"I hope you don't think—I didn't have a clue. Good Lord, Mother." She laughed weakly.

The kettle hit full whistle, and he moved it off the burner, then laid out boxes of green, black, and herbal teas on the counter. "I knew, this whole time," he said. "I was worried. I still am."

"I'll try that hibiscus one."

"That's why I left those messages."

"I know. I'm sorry."

He poured water in their cups and watched the deep scarlet flowering from the tea bags in upward-reaching spirals.

"So can we stay?" She'd sat up straight, slightly turned toward the door. In the living room, Shane was still crouched under the empty Christmas tree, surrounding himself with toy trains. He'd turned Paul's magazine into a floppy sort of tunnel.

"All right," Paul said.

~

He sat on the carpet with Shane, surrounded by train tracks and scattered engines and freight cars. Gina stayed in the kitchen. He smelled chicken stock with arborio and wild rice mixed in and heard the warm sound of a wooden spoon rubbing along the inside edge of a pot.

"How can I help?" he asked the boy.

Shane slid him a section of track without making eye contact. "Put that over there." With short, not unfriendly commands he directed the layout of the tracks, and Paul contented himself with being his lackey.

If you sat on the floor beside a kid long enough, you could almost regain a child's perspective. The plastic and metal trains became lifelike against the carpet's pattern, the leg of a chair a transmission tower or grain silo, or whatever you wanted it to be. For most of his life, Paul had never understood the hobbyist's fascination with scale. Any serious model—ship, car, plane, glider, or trains—had to be made according to perfect ratio. Why couldn't it just *look* like a boat? Then three summers ago, when he'd been in Victoria for a conference, he'd taken a walk on Dallas Road in the evening, on a paved path above an embankment that overlooked the ocean. A popular spot, full of cruise ship tourists, joggers, and dog owners. On the path above a small, protected beach, a man stood with a remote control device in his hands. He looked out over the bay, oblivious to the terriers and boxers that sniffed at his ankles before dashing back to their masters. At first, the man simply looked lost. There was no whining buzz of a model engine, nothing in the air. Then Paul realized that what he had mistaken for a gull hovering silently was a white model glider. The man would send it out over the ocean, cut the engine, and let the air currents bring it toward land. Left on its own, the glider performed loops and turns, but before it could spin completely out of control the man would fire the propeller and correct its path. Then he would cut the motor again. There was something elegant about his timing.

Paul had walked farther down the line of shrubs until he could no longer see the man, only the model as it circled above him. Long minutes passed before he realized he was doing a childlike thing: he was accepting the illusion, seeing the model as life-sized, the landscape transformed—the scotch broom and roses a forest canopy, the banks heightened into majestic cliffs. He became diminished, vanishing into the scene. It had felt strangely liberating.

As Shane fit together pieces of the track, Paul bunched up part of a blanket that lay on the floor and nudged an empty shoebox near the tracks. "What are you going to use for the river?"

"The river?" Shane looked around.

"The one that connects the two lakes."

"That'll be over there." Shane dug through a duffle bag and pulled out a pair of blue underwear. He flattened them on the carpet near the tracks. Then he gathered up all his socks and lined them up across the living room floor.

"Should we make the tracks in a loop?" asked Paul.

"No," the boy decided. "Because one town's over there." He pointed at the wall. "On the other side."

By the time Gina finished the risotto, the two of them had built a pretty good replica of the Immitoin Valley, circa 1940s by Paul's reckoning. They'd piled up blankets for the mountain ranges and used the shoebox for the Shellycoat mill.

"There's your grandma's old house," said Paul. "And that's Lambert. The box of crayons will be their fruit-packing shed."

"None of it's there anymore," said Gina. She wore a blue sweater that brightened her eyes, and her cheeks were flushed from the heat and steam from the risotto.

"You look nice," he said.

"I feel better. I think I was little dehydrated before."

"For a single serving of beautiful woman, just add water."

"Sounds about right." She pointed at the television remote on the floor. "What's that?"

"Steamboat," said Shane.

"The ss *Westminster,*" said Paul. "That doesn't exist anymore either."

"Just keep my underwear out of this," she said. She returned to the kitchen but didn't look unhappy.

~

They'd washed most of the dishes, but the smells of roasted meat and onions still hung in the air. On the kitchen table stood a half-empty bottle of wine, wooden salad tongs set out to dry, and three bowls with melted candy cane ice cream at the bottom. Gina had shoved their suitcases into a corner of the living room and stashed cardboard boxes of cooking supplies and food under the kitchen table. "Just for now?" she asked. He nodded. Wrapped presents lay under the tree, most marked for Shane. The boy had fallen asleep on the living room carpet halfway through the original cartoon version of *How the Grinch Stole Christmas*, and Gina had carried him to Paul's room.

They watched television. Paul asked if it was too loud, but she shook her head. They suffered patiently through an inordinate number of commercials. This one was for a seafood restaurant. There was something obscene about the way the unseen woman in the commercial said, "Lobster." The "L" guttering up from the back of the throat, and then thrown over her tongue in the shape of the "OB," and then hissed out between her lips, "STER." It was like vomiting, like a form of reverse penetration, something retracted from her mouth in an oily, sexual way. She must have repeated the word ten times within the thirty-second ad. The word *lob* was onomatopoeic, it enacted its own meaning through the mouth. All words arose in the body, it occurred to him, passed through it like a type of test. Words were motion, and motion needed a body, and the thought of sex made his head spin.

His head was on Gina's shoulder. She touched the curls above his left ear, and the sensation dazed him. He stroked her arm with delicate attention, afraid his hand might clasp too desperately.

~

They lay stretched out on the couch, legs intertwined. They were still clothed, though her bra was balled up into a lump under her sweater and shirt. His lips were chapped and torn at. His hand rested against her belly. Her palm lay flat against the fly of his jeans. They were both breathing hard. Paul directed each breath toward the ceiling.

"It's not possible," he said. "I told you."

~

They came up with a new sleeping arrangement. Shane on a makeshift mattress in the living room, Paul and Gina in the bedroom. There would be some nights when Shane would be with his father—there was no choice in this, she said, unless she wanted things to get really unpleasant. It was important, too, that she and her son stay at their own apartment sometimes, with his own bed, his toys and familiar things. Being home, however, meant Billy could phone, cajole, and, as she put it, manipulate. When she said this, Paul heard the underlying anxiety.

Lying naked beside her was a nerve-wracking act of faith in the gods of fortune. How could it not be, when his doctor at the Prostate Centre had warned that sexual anticipation, or nearly anything else for that matter, might make him "leak a little"? To divert attention from his own body, he made a show of studying hers. Her skin's olive tone had not been a trick of the dim sauna light. "I think you have First Nations in you," he said. "Maybe from the valley?"

"No. Mom would have said something," Gina said with a wry grin. "Being part Sinixt would carry a lot of weight in her environmental groups."

Some of his participants, old fruit farmers, had mentioned a possible burial site and pithouses. Some farmers had left patches of brush and trees around the *kekulis* they found, or had been careful not to disturb the petroglyphs on the cliffs along the river. Two sets of petroglyphs had been salvaged by Monashee Power and placed in a museum on the coast, but the reservoir now hid or destroyed the last remaining evidence of stolen land. "At any rate," she said. "Think I'm just lucky."

"Lucky?"

"To have nice skin." She rolled nimbly on top of him and pinned his arms. When she forgot about Billy, she came alive.

Despite his attempts at distraction or anxious protests, she would fondle him, unresponsive as his body was, even take his limp member in her mouth, an act both overwhelmingly tender and humiliating. "I just like the feel of it," she said. He would blink away tears of shame and stifle the urge to shove her away. Once or twice he thought he felt a physical stirring, a rising surge at his core, but that was only the basic, skin-deep pleasure of being touched, no different than having his finger sucked. Phantom twitches. "Don't," she said whenever he'd apologize. "You take pretty good care of me. I'm not missing out on anything."

It was true there were things he could do for her, and he enjoyed doing them. He'd missed the pure, tactile delight, a woman's response, even after a year of convincing himself otherwise. His life had lacked the pleasure he could give to someone else, even if he didn't entirely believe that altruism, on either of their parts, belonged in the bedroom.

Some nights, though, a claustrophobic panic would overtake him, and he'd refuse to take off his boxers, could hardly stand being touched. They would grapple restlessly without any satisfying conclusion and he would lie awake afterwards, his body raw, wired, and uncertain, his thoughts a hot mud. Or, even if things went relatively well, Gina might turn away, curl into herself, and cry. She was afraid of staying at her apartment and afraid of starting over again, she owned almost nothing worth having except a few good pots and pans, and her son was sleeping on her lover's couch. He promised himself he'd buy a bed of some kind for Shane, maybe partition part of the living room.

The intimacy made them aware that they were mostly

strangers to each other, and they spent long hours whispering. Because he asked, and because he felt he'd already revealed a lot about himself that night in the sauna, they mostly talked about her. She talked about Billy, how everything had been spoiled for him from the start—the loss of his family's land, the mill always shutting down. Three nights a week he played poker with former co-workers who were as bored, restless, and dangerous as he was. The men, including old Cyril, plotted ways of making quick money—though Gina wouldn't say what that meant.

Having Shane around kept things light. During meals, they turned their chairs toward him as he told rambling, nonsensical stories about kindergarten. He explained video games to Paul. "In the olden days you had joysticks and one button, but in the newden days you need to learn all sorts of controls." But they couldn't laugh, because the boy might throw a wild tantrum at the slightest offence.

She taught Paul how to make kale and potato frittatas with goat cheese, cannellini bean soup with spinach, zucchini pesto with preserved lemon. Food was a way forward, a way of being able to talk and think about the future. She had dreams of her own café, maybe a catering business.

With Gina and Shane around, Paul didn't have much time for lurking beneath the stairs. In the evenings, they could hear Jory and Sonya drinking with friends or sometimes arguing, which happened more often since Christmas. One of the young guys working at the store had quit Boxing Day morning and Jory had to drive from his dad's to cover a twelve-hour shift. He told all the staff to go fuck themselves, and then spent the rest of the holidays filming backcountry expeditions with friends.

Two days before New Year's Eve, Paul went upstairs to give Sonya some new interviews to transcribe. She puttered around her living room in a dangerously short, cable-knit sweater dress, her legs strong, lean, and pale, her hair wet from the shower. It struck him, absurd as the idea was, that she might be teasing him or even flirting. Not in a serious way, just wanting not to be bored or frustrated, or wanting to be acknowledged. He asked about Jory and she shrugged. "He goes a bit crazy when he's stuck in town. Helps to get on top of the mountains," she said. "More sun, more open sky. But he pushes too hard. Can't say no to anything."

He remembered the day he first met Jory on the river. "I've seen him afraid before."

She looked surprised for a moment, then shook her head. "Not with his friends around, you haven't." She asked about Gina, and laughed when he became flustered. "Kind of old to blush, aren't you?" she said. She told him she was glad he'd hooked up with someone good, in a town where the pickings were lean. "You've got some swagger in your step," Sonya said. "Funny how getting laid gives you confidence."

"Oh, it still freaks me out," he said, wanting to be honest with her, but not too much, obviously. "It's your generation that has all the confidence. It took me all my twenties to figure out sex, to get comfortable with it. And now." He stopped himself.

"And now you've got all that experience. Lucky her, right?" She laughed, then gave him a look. "My generation. Jesus. You're not that old, you know."

He left, his mind buzzing. Was it because of Gina? Did Sonya see him now as a normal guy, not the mysterious loner downstairs—did that bring certain instincts to life? Or was he just imagining things, his mind becoming clouded again with sex?

Ever since Basket Creek, he'd been heading, he believed, toward a life that was less impulsive and self-serving, more rational than his old one. Gina and Sonya threatened to derail that sense of calm. Sex was becoming a renewed obsession, pushing aside his research, even the mystery of Ready's drowning. A barrage of erotic imagery, urges with no outlet. His subconsious trotted out various scenes, past performances outlining the mechanics of sex, nearly instructional in nature—just in case his impotence was rooted in forgetting. It wasn't. He remembered quite clearly, thank you, what lay out of reach.

~

Dr. Norcross was a slim man with a rugged but youthful face, despite the flecks of grey in his beard and at his temples. He had a bounce to his step and abnormally perfect posture, neck stretching upward as though he were about to levitate out of his leather shoes. Beneath his white smock he wore earthy colours, a brown wool sweater and green hemp jeans. He seemed fascinated, almost delighted, by Paul's unusual history, and went through the checkup and flipped through his file humming some upbeat tune.

"Blood draw in two months," the doctor said. "Your PSA."

Paul nodded impatiently.

"That's a significant event. Are you nervous?"

"I'd forgotten all about it."

The doctor gave him a skeptical look and Paul gave him a sheepish grin. "How about the incontinence?"

"It still catches me by surprise."

"Don't be disappointed by the rare event, but I think in your case, being so young, you'll have fewer incidents as time goes on." He pencilled something on Paul's file. "You said you had questions about exercise."

"I spent a month lifting things, back in October."

"No harm done, it seems." Dr. Norcross chuckled. "I knew a man in his sixties who played tennis a month after his prostatectomy. How about sexual function?"

Paul shifted on his seat, wary. The doctor nodded. "Sometimes it takes a year, maybe more, barring complications."

"I understand." He was, in a sense, relieved. Absolved. The

comfort of a professional opinion, the way it permits you to settle into your state of being, the truth of things.

"Still, I'm a bit surprised. Maybe you're setting too high a standard."

"How do you mean?"

"Have you heard the term *stuffable erections*?"

"Have I . . . no."

The doctor smiled at Paul's reddening face. "Men under sixty report the highest recovery rate for potency, which we define as an erection sufficient for vaginal penetration. With help—certain positions and so on—*sufficient* is a flexible term."

"Pardon the pun."

"Exactly." Dr. Norcross marked something down. "So, no success with the Viagra yet."

"Pardon?" His sense of resignation, which had come to him easily, almost pleasantly, fell away. Paul sat frozen like a child caught red-handed in a shameful act.

"Your file from the Centre says you were prescribed Viagra—to start two days after your surgery."

"Was I?" His doctor at the Prostate Centre had given him things: pamphlets, slips of paper. Prescriptions for antibiotics, yes. He'd taken those, and followed the regimen for hygiene.

"You haven't been taking it?" Dr. Norcross said incredulously.

"I kind of—forgot," he said. Not true—he'd rejected the idea and tore up the prescription at 12th and Oak Street. That piece of paper had felt like a very cruel joke, just the possibility of needing it. After that, he'd spent the summer blanking the prescription from his mind.

The doctor frowned. "It isn't just about sexual function. Increased blood flow supplies oxygen to the area, it keeps tissues healthy. Are you married?"

"I'm with someone. But we don't need it. We don't—find intercourse necessary."

Norcross stifled an irritated laugh. "You honestly believe that? You're young, in the prime of your life. You're damn lucky."

"Lucky," Paul repeated blandly.

Now the doctor had stopped looking amused altogether. "A lot of older men require radical measures to maintain some form of sex life. Pumps, intracavernosal injections, or penile implants. Strap-ons."

"So I've heard." The images appalled him, but he also felt compelled to defend them. "Aren't those decent enough alternatives?"

"For them," the doctor said. "But at your age—no one would wish that on himself. Anyway, I highly doubt you'll need those things. Like I said, you're lucky."

He shoved the slip of paper into Paul's hand. "Here." He paused. "Sex is part of health, whatever else it means to you. Get used to being healthy, Paul. That's your future."

~

The second of January, the phone cool against his ear.

"Hello?"

"Is this Hardy Wallace?"

"That's right." The voice was scraped raw by age or lack of use but uncannily self-possessed.

"My name's Paul Rasmussen. I'm conducting a study. I understand you were once a resident of Lambert?"

"That's right."

"I've been interviewing people from the valley. Gathering their thoughts on their lives before and after the dam. Would you," Paul paused. "Would you be interested at all in such an interview? That is, would you be able to tell me about how things—changed? In your life?"

Jesus, he thought. Listen to yourself. He was so nervous, he'd even squeezed some lemon juice into a glass of water hoping the tartness would keep his mouth moist. It didn't.

"Oh." A wary chuckle, a mocking tone. "You sound like a Monashee fellow."

"I'm not from Monashee, Mr. Wallace. I'm doing research. For a university."

Hardy said nothing for a moment, though there was breathing, a slight wheeze. "I don't come into town in winter."

"At all?"

"No."

This had to be a lie, but he couldn't do much about it. "What if I came out there?"

A scratching over the line, maybe beard stubble across the receiver. "That would be fine."

He left the next morning just before nine, hoping the snow would hold off. The dam's grey concrete blended into grey sky, the spillway gushing steely water past stalactites of dull ice. A tall industrial crane, its arm brightened with Christmas lights, added colour to the horizon. The reservoir was low, the shore a vast, snowy plain marked by jutting boulders and lumps of hidden stone. He recognized landmarks, things lifted from aerial photographs and transcribed interviews: the remaining strip of Agnes Hutchinson's old property, the abandoned wharf pilings and stone trestles.

He started thinking about his visit to the doctor the other day, and his upcoming blood draw. If the test went badly—but no, he knew, as did the doctor, that the odds were in his favour. For Dr. Norcross, the real questions were of potency, masculinity. Actually, there was no question at all, only the necessity of regaining those things, as though there were only one way to live as a man—*at your age*. It was absurd to think there was some monkish middle ground, or that Paul might want to choose, as an older man might, to surrender and adapt. He was just clinging to self-pity. Stupid, and cowardly. He needed the pills.

Once he left Bishop behind, the snowbanks on either side of

the road grew higher and thicker until there was barely enough room for two vehicles to squeeze by each other. It began to snow. Mesmerized, anxious, he almost missed Hardy's place. The driveway was an icy slope, a toboggan hill with Hardy's truck blocking the bottom. If he parked up top, hopefully no one would come by. He turned the wheel and rammed the left side of the truck onto the bank, thinking the snow would have compacted and frozen into a solid-enough crust. The wheels sank almost immediately. He'd hung himself up.

He turned off the ignition and watched snowflakes relentlessly settle on the windshield. 11:45, fifteen minutes late. He climbed out the passenger side door with the daypack that contained his notebooks and recorder. He stared at the sunken front tire, then turned and negotiated the icy driveway. Halfway down he slipped and flung himself sideways into the snow to break his fall. He struggled to the bottom of the driveway, bracing himself against Hardy's blue truck to brush himself off. Then he realized the old man was standing next to the woodpile, watching him with a blank expression.

Paul inched away from the truck, testing the ground for traction. "Mr. Wallace?"

He looked much like Paul remembered. Someone who had probably been husky and imposing once, now diminished by age but still capable, fit. He wore the same fleece he'd worn that day at the fish fence, with a heavy, grey wool cardigan thrown over top. The white hair that poked out from the bottom of his toque looked like it had been roughly hacked by kitchen scissors, though the full beard made him appear oddly staid, composed.

"I'm Paul. Sorry I'm late." He pointed to the top of the driveway and was about to speak when Hardy interrupted.

"Six elk in the yard this morning." He picked up an armload of wood. "Grab a bundle."

Paul fumbled four pieces of split birch into his hands and cradled them against his chest, keeping the top piece steady with his chin. They kicked off their boots in the small mudroom and entered the kitchen.

"Air's so still out there I heard you coming the last half-hour," Hardy said over his shoulder. "I've put coffee on."

The stove sat in the middle of the living room on a bed of rough inlaid stone. The rest of the floor was dark-stained hardwood in surprisingly good shape, partially covered by mismatched rugs, a brown, threadbare sofa, a low wooden coffee table, and two old rocking chairs. Paul stacked the firewood by the stove and followed Hardy back to the kitchen, where the old man motioned for him to sit. The table rested beside two large windows that overlooked the Immitoin. The black water weaved past the mounds of snow that topped each boulder, sheets of ice like wings on the sides of stones.

As Paul shrugged off his coat and hat, Hardy rummaged through cupboards, pulling out a bag of white sugar and two mugs. It was a simple house. Everything could be seen from the kitchen except where two doors were closed—probably the bedroom and bathroom. The table was a sturdy rectangle of thick maple, stained with coffee rings and darkened. The solid, ornate bookshelves in the living room, the broad windowsills—he remembered how Agnes Hutchinson and Elsie Hubert had preserved so many relics from their old homes, but he hadn't expected the same degree of care from this man.

"So why did your father build a bunkhouse here? The mill was quite a ways up the road," Paul said.

Hardy looked mildly puzzled at Paul's question, then pleased. His large hands, scarred and leathery, slid a mug toward Paul. He pointed out the windows. "Where the deck is, that used to be two rooms full of bunk beds. Tore those down, finally, in '72."

"Mr. Wallace, would you mind if I recorded our conversation?" He placed the recorder on the table.

Hardy shrugged, scrutinizing Paul's face through the shag of his eyebrows. "You said you were writing an article for the paper?"

"No." There was no harm in keeping his reasons vague, not in this case. "Research project. More like a book, I guess."

"A book. Better, even better. Good." Hardy settled into his chair and rested his elbows on the table with a low chuckle. "Because he liked this place—the answer to your question before. He could watch the logs go past from here, and catch trout along the seam of the pool."

Paul studied him a moment. Hardy was much more focused than he'd expected.

"Mr. Wallace, do you remember me? From the weirs on Basket Creek?"

Hardy stirred his coffee, staring into it. When he looked up, the smile he gave Paul was either embarrassed or crafty. "The officer mentioned that the person minding the fence didn't require an apology."

"I suppose he doesn't."

"Well, then," Hardy said, satisfied. "Sugar?"

"As I mentioned, I've been asking people how the relocation affected them. What the big changes were, good or bad."

"You get different answers depending on who you ask, don't you?"

"Of course."

"It depends, for example, if you were fairly compensated or not."

Paul cleared his throat. This was good, already edging close to delicate territory. "Were you?"

Hardy barked a single laugh. "Well," he said. "Sometimes I think so. In strange ways."

From his experiences interviewing people—it helped that he wasn't being confronted by a Wentz—he'd learned to respect silences, not to be afraid of them. While waiting for Hardy to continue, he gazed at the salt and pepper shakers along a dusty ledge, a piece of china, or the black-and-white photo on the wall. The photo, presumably taken from the forest above Lambert, showed farmland by the river, fruit trees in their tidy rows, clusters of raspberry canes and dirt roads, countless other details he couldn't make out. On a far wall in the living room hung a map, a yellowed and wrinkled white copy of the one Elmer had shown him: Lambert overlaid with its contour lines, property boundaries, and lot numbers.

Outside, gusts of wind swept snow off the trees and the roof of the house and sent white wraiths dancing over the river. How would he get home in this? Daunted now by the passing of time, he turned back to the table and began to fire questions at Hardy.

"What year were you born?"

"I think I turn seventy-three in June."

"Your father passed away . . ."

"Three years after they started building the dam. I found him lying facedown on the path to the woodshed, middle of winter."

"Your mother . . ."

"In '63. Still believing they'd never flood the valley. Seems unfair, doesn't it, that a man as old and banged up as my father should outlive her by ten years."

"You have children?"

"Never married."

"You spent most of your life trying to get fair compensation from Monashee Power, to prove their land-grab was illegal."

Hardy blinked. "Wasted most of my life, you mean. I was always making a big stink." He laughed, a cheerful, phlegmy cackle. "I'd stand outside the Shellycoat courthouse waving a sign. I had a sandwich board I wore too. 'Monashee crooks!' 'Lies and fraud!' Doesn't get you too far."

Paul coughed uncertainly, unsure whether it was safe to laugh along with him or not.

"Here," Hardy said. He stumped off to the living room and rummaged through a small desk opposite the woodstove, setting aside stacks of papers and magazines. He returned with a bundle of manila envelopes and dumped them on the table, scattering pages of yellow foolscap.

"Thirty years of correspondence."

Paul grabbed sheets at random and skimmed through them. Letters, each one similar to the one he'd read at Gina's camp. The sheer number was remarkable.

"I'm slowing down with age. I hit my peak in the eighties. Gerry Lang was editor. I buried him in letters."

"Trying to stir the hornet's nest." Flattery was sometimes a good technique in drawing a participant out. "Did you get that from your father?"

"He was a real politician—I'm just an old shit disturber. The Fruit Growers' Association was as good as government in the valley." Hardy looked to the ceiling, licking his lips. "July 22, 1940: two thousand crates of cherries, seven thousand boxes of strawberry, cherry, and raspberry jam. Of those boxes, six thousand to the prairies, three overseas."

"Sorry?"

"Those are poor numbers, by the way. That's the industry in decline. Jam for the war effort kept Lambert going in those years."

"Did your father keep journals?" Paul asked, suddenly hopeful.

"No. I was quoting the association's records—purchases and whatnot. Read them so many times I've memorized most of the entries."

"Why do you read them?" Paul asked, disappointed. The archives held the same sets of records, and they didn't tell him anything about the relocation or Caleb Ready.

"The numbers somehow stir things up, they bring to mind days growing up around the ships and ferries, the packing sheds, our trees and garden. Mostly, they remind me of how rich the valley was before I was born. I was not born into an easy age." Hardy paused, lost in some memory. "He had real power, my father. He made himself heard."

Paul said, maybe condescendingly, "In a way you did as well, I guess. With your letters."

Hardy gave a low, disdainful hiss. "Sure, I made some real progress with Monashee and their goons. Still waiting for answers."

"And what have you done, while you've been waiting?"

Hardy shrugged. "This and that. I travelled during summers. Logged in Horsefly, cut cedar shakes near Armstrong." He challenged Paul with a look. "1987, I was a tree planter."

"Really?" Paul's voice cracked, half-amused, half-incredulous, but Hardy looked more pleased than insulted. He tried to imagine a middle-aged version of Hardy on a company like Gina's: a dour and tired man shouldering a surly pride, alone on the far side of the mess tent while scruffy college students and lanky highballers yukked it up.

"Was it bad?"

"Work is never bad. Just the constant scrounging for it. But I'm on the pension now."

Strange how Hardy and Cyril, for all their shared history, had ended up on such divergent paths. "But you always had this place to come back to."

"I cling here, yes. It's thin soil."

"Not like Lambert, you mean. You can't farm."

"I've trapped and shot animals for food. I catch trout."

He remembered watching Hardy fish, or not fish, at the Flumes. The aimless drifting of the line.

Hardy said, "I should have gone to that, that thing they held. In Castlegar, way back fifteen years or so."

"The Kootenay Symposium?" Yes, he could imagine Hardy with his list of grievances clutched in his hand, queuing up for his chance to speak, like the other farmers in the video.

"Maybe that was my chance." The old man shifted in his chair. "It's the knowing and the waiting . . . and the *not doing* that makes you a bit crazy."

~

Paul's vehicle looked like something abandoned all winter. It sat keeled over to one side and buried under snow, and when he opened the door to grab his shovel, snow slid off the roof, onto the seats, and down the back of his neck. He scooped a few shovelfuls around the front tires and knew he was overmatched. The bleak afternoon light was waning. It would take an hour, more, and then he'd have to brave the road in the dark. He'd end up stuck in the middle of nowhere, worse than now. The road was a whitewashed plain. Not a single snowplow had driven by all day. Behind him, Hardy stood with his arms at his sides.

"You picked a fine day to visit."

"What should I do?"

"Come back to the house."

A deep cold swept up from the river and stirred the falling snow into spinning figures. "Christ," Paul muttered. He tried to think, but the air nipped at his face and limbs, herding him back down the driveway. Hardy picked his way over the ice with untroubled patience, his arms still hanging loosely by his hips.

Back in the kitchen, Hardy dumped a Tupperware container full of beef stew into a pot and heated it up. In between stirs, he took a loaf of dark rye bread, cut thick slices, and buttered them. After he set down the food, he pulled out a bottle of whisky from the cupboard and poured them each a glass.

"You can ask questions while we eat, if you like."

The stew tasted homemade, bright with fresh bell peppers

and carrots, the beef and potatoes neatly cubed. The bread was speckled and scented with caraway. It all seemed too good for Hardy to have made himself. If he didn't drive into town, who brought him food? Paul eyed the whisky with some trepidation. "So what happened to the rest of the crew?"

Such poor discipline: he couldn't resist dredging the past, even though Hardy was the ideal research subject, one who perfectly illustrated the worst consequences of displacement. This could more than make up for the disastrous Wentz interview. But no, he still wanted to be led to the drowned man.

Hardy took a noisy sip from his glass and shrugged. "Some did quite well."

Here we go, Paul thought. "Do you mean the ones who worked for Caleb Ready?"

Hardy barely flinched at the mention of Ready's name. "Young bucks always want to pick the winning side. Not like the greybeards on our crew. Men from the orchards. Old farmers becoming chokermen, fallers. No money saved for retirement is why. Loyal and desperate."

Paul took a breath. "But what about men like Marcus Soules, your father's arborist? I mean, wasn't he the first to sell to Monashee?"

Hardy's face bunched up as though he'd been spit on. You picked a bad place to finally ask the tough questions, Paul thought.

"Marcus had no choice. He was in bad shape, mind and body. He didn't have much fight in him. His son, Arthur, ran their household."

"So it was Arthur who sold?"

"Never was an orchardist—no money in it. He'd worked as an engineer for the trains, up around Chase and Kamloops, out to the prairies. Spent most months gone from Lambert. He saw things different. Had a certain respect for progress. Call it that."

"He opened the door for Monashee Power."

Hardy shrugged, shot back his drink. It caught in the old man's throat, and he gargled and sighed, a long soft groan. The stove made a slight rushing noise, air down the chimney. The fire flared and snapped inside the stove.

Paul tried another angle. "Cyril Wentz—I'm sure you remember him—mentioned that your company's contracts began to dry up when Monashee began expropriations. Was that just a coincidence, you think?"

"Not at all," Hardy laughed. "It was because we said no to selling the Dalton Creek mill."

"Dalton Creek? I thought they were just after your homes."

"Oh, our homes were a foregone conclusion."

"How was the sawmill connected to land acquisition?"

Hardy irritably flapped his hand in the air, like someone hounded by black flies. "Beats the bloody hell out of me. Had nothing to do with the dam. Caleb Ready wanted us to sell the lease for the mill site. Then later he sicced his goons on the valley, the big companies from outside got Monashee's lumber and pole contracts, and we went bankrupt a few years after the flood. Sold the chutes and saws off for scrap."

Paul dared once more. "And then Caleb Ready ends up dead in the river, some forty years later."

"Yes, well." The old man wiped around his mouth, then rubbed his eyes. "Never really understood the Immitoin, that one. Thought he did. Figured since he wore the cap, the river was his to command."

"Did you recognize him when they pulled him from the water that day?"

"They look much the same when they've drowned." He grabbed the bottle and put back another shot. Paul opened his mouth and hesitated. A man at his host's mercy, without a means of leaving, wouldn't be wise to force the issue any more than he had.

Hardy chuckled suddenly, as though he'd read Paul's mind. "It's good for you to record all this. One day soon I'll succumb to old-timer's disease, and there'll be few left to tell the truth of things." He coughed whisky spittle onto his beard. "Monashee'll like that. I waited all these years for their goons to come shut me up, put me down like a dog."

"Most I've met seem nice," Paul offered.

"The new breed," he scoffed. "Polite young gentlemen apologizing about the past and doing nothing about it. Bunch of softies waffling about downstream benefits, so-called compensation— putting in a few parks and rest stops. And their goddamned garbage fish." He fluttered his hands overhead like an ardent preacher. "Protect the garbage fish. *Save* the garbage fish."

~

The bathroom was spare, the walls undecorated except for a tarnished mirror above the sink. Not even a shower curtain to pull around the clawfoot tub. A window looked out toward the forest, the panes old and warped. Like the rest of the house, though, the floors, windowframe, and door trim were dark and solid, and the heat from the woodstove warmed every corner. If this were another person's house, another time, he might have been immensely grateful to be sheltered in such a place. His reflection in the mirror was slightly warped. The whisky was going to hit him hard if he didn't slow down.

"You piss a lot," said Hardy when Paul returned to his seat at the table. "Who's the old man here?"

Paul chuckled nervously. Hardy was wearing him down, had somehow put him on the wrong track, had him asking the wrong questions.

Outside, snow gathered in drifts below the porch light, and the darkness squeezed the cabin from all sides. Drunk, Hardy began to mutter to himself, a winter's conversation with his father's house, whispering and then railing against the wooden creaks and groans that answered. The kitchen light flickered, surged, and steadied. On the counter, an oil lantern and a stack of candles stood at the ready. Hardy's eyes had lost all sense of acuity and gave way to confusion, despair. Finally Paul saw the man who had pointed a rifle at him.

"Kai," Hardy began. "No good in the bush, that one. His father had him daydreaming about university, building bridges and highways, making it big off real estate. Meanwhile, Arthur had run off and taken Marcus away to die in some city somewhere."

"Kai," interjected Paul, trying to steer the conversation.

"Kai Soules, goddamn you. I promised I'd take care of him the way his grandfather Marcus looked out for me when I was a boy. But he couldn't drop a ten-foot lodgepole without nearly killing himself. So we put him to work with a peavey, down from where the log chute met the river."

Paul's digital recorder blinked numbers—four hours, twelve minutes. At least something could keep pace with Hardy, because he was lost.

"We got back to headquarters about five o'clock. We said to my dad, He went into the rapids. He's fucking gone. We're sorry as hell. And he says to us, Did you try to save him at least? We tried, we tell him, We did everything but jump in after him. And he says, Well, bully for you cocksuckers."

The kitchen and porch lights flickered again, and Hardy wiped at his eyes and then fumbled for the oil lantern. He had it lit a few seconds before the lights finally went out. Paul grabbed a candle and looked for a holder. Hardy gestured toward a drawer and went to throw more wood in the stove. "There."

In the drawer lay an assortment of metal and clay candle-holders, dented or chipped and covered in wax. Some must have been more than fifty years old. One was a fine piece of pottery, heavy in the hand, the glaze spider-webbed from age.

Someone had painted tiny cherries around the edges. He imagined dozens of identical candleholders at the bottom of the reservoir. Within a few minutes, he and Hardy had placed candles around the house.

Hardy put his face against the window. "Look. You can see it better now."

Paul stood beside him and smelled old sweat trapped in wool. Outside, a blanket of white among shadowy tree trunks and then the dark gap where the pool swirled.

"My father, you see, had already known about Kai—the body had showed up in the pool that afternoon, then kept drifting by, he told us."

Outside, the river took shape, a negative space in the white landscape except where crests of water caught a minute source of light. Hardy was mumbling now, his eyelids drooping. "Cyril always says this pool's as good as a grave, and when you go, we'll bury you there if you like."

Paul, groggy and leaning against the cold windowpane, jolted upright. Cyril had told him he hadn't talked to Hardy since the mill had folded, decades ago. Either Hardy's sense of time had slipped, or Cyril had lied to Paul.

"I told him I might," Hardy said. "I might like that."

~

Steady, gurgling breaths came from the bedroom where Hardy had passed out. Paul opened the woodstove and rustled the coals with a poker until they flared, then added a piece of birch. The fire kept the small house warm, but he needed blankets. The shelves and windowsills were filled with books and artifacts—old belt buckles, tins, and coloured medicine bottles, an empty bottle of Mitchell's Old Heatherdew Whiskey. A rusted harmonica, a penknife, a yellowed doily beneath a scattering of wooden buttons. Leather-bound encyclopedias dating back to the 1940s or earlier.

On another shelf, a stack of dog-eared mystery novels and penny westerns, thrift-store books.

A large chest made of dark, oiled wood, girded by bands of riveted metal and two heavy brass handles, took up one corner of the living room. He set aside the jumble of old trousers and flannel work shirts piled on top and lifted the lid. Inside lay a jumble of objects: a leather caulk boot, a set of pruning shears with its wooden handles pale and cracked like driftwood, a few empty burlap sacks with "Wallace Ranch Apples" printed in bold red letters. Beneath the lettering, in faded yellows, greens, and blues, were houses, fields of apple trees and open skies, the fruit-seller's promise.

He lay down on the sofa, piling Hardy's trousers and work shirts over himself. The couch's loose springs pressed against the fraying material. Flames flickered in the woodstove's vents, the muted roar of the fire akin to the sound of the river's dark snaking beneath the ice.

~

Hardy's earthy and sour breath woke him. The old man had him by the shoulder, shaking him. "Get up now. You've slept too late."

The trees outside were faint purple shadows. Paul kicked off the pile of jackets and trousers. Hardy was pulling on his coat. "They'll be coming by soon," he growled.

"Who?"

"They plow the road themselves. Like to jump ahead of high-way maintenance."

"Maybe they'll get my truck out." Whoever they were.

Hardy grunted, his hand already on the door. "Maybe they'll make things worse."

Paul threw on his coat and backpack and followed the old man out into the cold. They waded through the fresh snow down the steps. The firs and spruces stood ghostly, bone-straight like white menhirs. Ahead of him, Hardy grabbed two shovels from the woodshed. Snow had erased all tracks and treads from the driveway, turned Hardy's truck into a humble mound.

In the bleak light, they dug out the front wheels of Paul's vehicle, their shovels meeting the resistance of the crusty bank underneath the fresh drifts. The old man attacked the snow with surprising ferocity. "Get some sand from the woodshed," he said. "There's bags. Go." Paul heard the faint sound of an engine, a metallic scrape, a few kilometres away at most. He jogged down to the shed, wondering why they were racing against whoever was clearing the road. He found the sandbags, cradled two in his arms back up the drive, the weight sinking him past his ankles. Hardy crouched in front of the grill, poking the shovel underneath the bumper, opening up space for the tires. He rolled away and back to his feet, face in a ruddy sweat.

"Crack them open," muttered Hardy, gasping and hawking phlegm. Paul gave him a questioning glance, and the old man winced as, closer now, the blade of an approaching plow struck frozen earth, ice, and steel on stone. "They won't like that you were here," Hardy said. Suddenly, Paul understood. He dropped the bags and then thrust his shovel down hard until the sand spilled. They scattered it under the tires like a hasty offering, swept the windshield free, and chipped the ice off the driver's side. He yanked the door open and flung himself inside. The engine wouldn't turn. If the cold had drained the battery—"Christ Almighty," he hissed. The motor revved into life, and he flicked the windshield wipers to see Hardy waving him on. "Ease it forward, gentle, don't gun it," the old man shouted between breaths. He sounded like a grizzled foreman—the man was like a set of bagpipes, puffed up one moment, deflated the next.

The wheels spun, the vehicle swaying and foundering on the high drift until finally the right front tire caught a pocket of grit.

The bumper lurched and dipped, and then he slid onto the solid road. Hardy shouted directions: come ahead a few feet at an angle, turn the wheel, back up, go forward then back again. The old man hopped from foot to foot impatiently. A twenty-point turn later, his rear wheels skidding and threatening to bog down in the drifts, Paul had the vehicle facing south. He leaned out the window again and could hear the other truck clearly now.

"Mr. Wallace," he said.

"Ah." Hardy looked too alert, too alive, eyebrows lifted to the edge of his toque. "*Go*, for the sweet love of fuck."

Paul gunned it and almost put himself in the bank again, his back end nearly clipping Hardy—he checked the side mirror to see him gathering the shovels and lurching down the driveway. The front wheels searched for traction as snow sprayed over the bumper, and Paul jerked the steering wheel from left to right like some manic cartoon character. He'd only just eased into a steady glide when he came to the first corner and saw fog lights cut across the road. A moment later, a black pickup pushed its yellow plow straight at him, and he swung wide and let off the gas, grazing the high drifts. The two vehicles brushed past each other, less than a metre gap between them, and there was Billy behind the wheel, cap pulled low across his forehead, with Cyril in the passenger seat. Billy's mouth dropped open as he met Paul's gaze. Then the Pathfinder hit the cleared road, the tires chewing into the sudden firmness and rocketing him forward. He pressed down slow and sure on the accelerator, rolled up his window, and let out a long, shuddering breath.

The banks on either side of the road towered above him, the trees bent into misshapen arcs. Sometimes he would hit an icy patch and fishtail. Mostly it felt like he floated above the road, lost in the vacuum-like roar of the defrost vents and the dashboard glow, the crunch of snow beneath his tires the only thing keeping him grounded.

Had the old man been worried for Paul's sake or his own? The Wentzes must have come to dig Hardy out, check on his supplies, bring him more food.

Gina had made the stew and bread.

It was bewildering. Everyone he'd talked to, all those interviews, and for what—the slightest tip of the iceberg, the faint beginnings of a truth. And Gina, connected somehow, but to what? Bloody secrets, he thought. The people in this damned valley.

The Immitoin reservoir appeared before him, a slate-coloured eye in the furrowed white brow of the world. Old cars and tree stumps, broken fence posts, the skeletons of barns, sheds, and houses—all pushing from underneath to give shape and texture to the smooth, rolling dream of snow.

RECOVERY

I

Paul pursued the old constable, trying to find a rhythm in his own huffing breath, the gentle scrape and hiss of his skis in the grooves of the set tracks. He remembered, from a handful of lessons on Cypress Mountain back in elementary school, the basic mechanics of the diagonal stride: left arm leading with the right foot sliding the slender ski forward, then a smooth transition to the opposite foot and hand. This should have resulted in something more graceful, less lumbering. Somewhere between childhood and now, he'd lost his sense of balance. Leaning too far forward, he broke into a thigh-cramping jog that faded to a shuffle after thirty metres.

The trail meandered through a patchwork of clear-cuts and sub-alpine forest. Animal tracks crisscrossed the path: moose, deer, snowshoe hare, and something smaller, a weasel or squirrel. Hoarfrost crystals clung to branches, and his skis, a pair of classics Lazeroff had lent him for the duration of winter, grated over shards of ice. He descended back into forest, where lichen-covered firs and veteran larches absorbed every sound. He stopped and unzipped his jacket, the trapped, slightly fetid smell of wool and sweat a comfort, so resonantly himself. His limbs quivered and trembled. Not a sound in the grove except his own heart beating fast, a buzz in his ears, the rasp of crisp air sucked down his throat into the warming bellows of his lungs.

He caught up to Lazeroff near a signpost that marked the

junction of two trails. The constable was leaning on his poles and flexing his legs. As Paul approached, Lazeroff gave him a cheery wave and then continued on, an effortless, steady pace at odds with his heavy build. A hundred metres farther, they arrived at a simple A-frame cabin with aluminum siding: Ziggy's Hut, named after Sig Tollefson, an outdoorsman who founded Shellycoat's first Nordic club back in the fifties. The original cabin had been built in 1944, rebuilt and repaired several times since. There were no skis on the rack outside, but smoke drifted from the chimney.

"Good," said Lazeroff. "I hate starting my own fire."

They went inside and hung their jackets, toques, and mitts on nails driven into the beams. An iron potbellied stove sat in the middle of the hut, surrounded by wooden benches and an ancient-looking church pew. Stacks of firewood lined the walls, peppered with mouse droppings and pitch-gummed clumps of old spider webs. On a simple wooden shelf, rusted tobacco tins held packs of matches and weighed down a map that marked the location of two other warming huts along the trails.

"Mark us down in the guest registry. They like to keep track of how many use the huts. Helps with government funding." Lazeroff opened the stove, stirred the fire, and added another piece of wood. From his backpack he pulled a flask of coffee and tinfoil-wrapped sandwiches that he placed on top of the stove.

"There's a skier's lunch," he said. "Want one?"

"All right." Paul flipped through the registry. "Book's filled up."

"This place was packed over the holidays." Lazeroff gestured to the empty benches. "Always is. Kids come back from college, families bring mulled wine and Christmas treats to the hut—a regular party in here."

"Figured you for a snowmobile guy." Paul sat across from him, holding his hands close to the stove.

"This is cheaper." He laughed. "Also, the doctor told me a few years back to get healthier if I wanted to enjoy my retirement."

"Good choice."

"I'll get you hooked, you'll see," he said. "Speaking of retirement, turns out Caleb Ready had a hobby in his old age—a good old-fashioned prospector."

"Come again?"

Lazeroff grinned. "Not what I pictured either. His wife somehow thought it wasn't important to tell us. I got a phone call from the storage place outside of town. He had a long-term rental on one of the big lockers, and the lease just ran out. Owner phoned, wondering if I knew the executor of Caleb's estate. Lots of stuff in there. A compressor and portable sluice machine hooked up to an ATV. Very modern. Plus the standard pans and sieves."

"Sounds like an expensive way to pass the time."

"Maybe it paid for itself," Lazeroff said. "But I doubt it. I've known some prospectors."

"Where was his claim?"

Lazeroff leaned over the stove and flipped the tinfoil packages over with adept flicks of his fingers. "Don't know yet. Even his wife didn't know. His little secret."

"Somewhere close to where his truck was parked. Maybe Basket Creek."

"We'll find out as soon as I make some calls. Stove's damned hot." Lazeroff grabbed the foil packages and tossed one to Paul. The bread was toasted golden, singed around the crust, stacked with sausage and melted cheese that burned the roof of his mouth.

"Anyhow." The constable waved his hand dismissively. "Sounds like your interview with Hardy didn't go so well."

In terms of gathering data, he supposed the interview had gone very well. Hardy hadn't made much sense at times, but the way he lived and viewed the past said something interesting about the effects of displacement. In the meantime, he was still shaken up by the meeting, its aftermath and implications. He'd blown up at Gina the night he'd returned from Hardy's.

They were in the bedroom, and as she undressed he blurted out, "Wonderful stew, by the way."

"Sorry?" He must have looked a little unbalanced, because her jaw dropped. "What are you talking about?"

"Hardy. The food he gave me—I know it was yours. The care that went into it. This was before Billy and Cyril showed up, by the way, no doubt bearing another creation from Gina's kitchen, and Hardy thinking for some reason they were going to kill me."

"I've never made anything for Hardy Wallace."

"Who then?" he asked. She said nothing. "It's none of my business if it's because of Billy. I get it. I do." He swallowed. "But why did Cyril lie about not talking to Hardy since the seventies? And why was Hardy scared shitless?"

"How would I know? I'm sure he wasn't scared. Their families go way back, almost a hundred years."

"You know who else they go way back with? Caleb Ready. The guy who turned up dead." This little theory he wouldn't be running past Lazeroff just yet. A more intelligent man wouldn't have shared it with Gina either, even if he was a bit lunatic at the time.

She held up both hands, trying to slow him down. "What are you saying, exactly?"

"I wonder how well you really know Billy—what he might be capable of. You need to stay away from him. You and Shane."

"You're not serious."

"Think—why would they need to lie to me about Hardy?"

"I don't know." She gave him a weary, sad look, as if to say, I sure know how to pick 'em. "Maybe they felt they didn't owe an outsider the truth."

Which stung, even if she wasn't wrong. "What truth? That they murdered Caleb Ready?"

By this point, she was already pulling on her clothes, laughing incredulously. "This is too fucked up for me, Paul. I have enough to deal with." She angrily wrestled her shirt over her head, then closed the bedroom door behind her, firmly enough to make the frame moan. She slept on the couch beside her son. Twice that night, Paul had to creep to the bathroom knowing she was still awake, holding her breath in the dark as he tiptoed past. She left before he woke.

He and Lazeroff finished their lunch and stoked the wood-stove for the next group of skiers. Outside the hut, Paul squinted in the bright glare. "I can't nail that glide."

"Think of reggae music."

"Reggae?"

"'Jammin'.' 'Three Little Birds.' Get that rhythm into your head. And then transfer your weight from hip to hip." The constable did a comical stutter-step from side to side, humming under his breath. "That's the glide."

Paul laughed. "A Doukhobor cop and Bob Marley, there's a match. Your wife teach you that?"

Lazeroff coughed, embarrassed. "We learn a lot from women."

"Not quickly enough, in my case. Thanks, by the way. For telling me about Caleb."

"Who else?" Lazeroff said. "Trust me, no one at the station gives a shit. Hip to hip. Or you'll keep shuffling along like an old man."

~

Elsie Hubert came down with a nasty stomach flu and needed taking care of. The timing was good: Gina could take the time and space to cool off. She phoned in the afternoons and they would talk—mostly he would apologize, retract his accusations, and she would sigh and change the subject to Elsie and Shane. At least she was still speaking to him, and didn't seem to think he was completely insane.

He'd hit a lull in his research. The remaining participants on his list couldn't be tracked down, tucked like voles in tunnels beneath the snow, leaving him to blink vacantly from his owl's post. Since his strange night at Hardy's, he'd become obsessed with Donald Wallace and the Soules family. He immersed himself in the archives, this time in the oldest records. Now that he knew where to look, there were new discoveries. Donald Wallace had returned home from the Great War with a serious leg injury—that must have been what Hardy was referring to when he said "banged up." It might also explain why Donald and his wife, Belinda, didn't have Hardy until many years later. Marcus Soules, meanwhile, had been blind in one eye from a childhood accident and had not gone overseas. Instead, he plied his trade up and down the Arrow Lakes and the Immitoin Valley, managing orchards and helping the families whose sons and husbands had left to fight and often die.

He and Elmer found a photo of Donald Wallace from the 1920s. Proud, at least the upper half of him: rigid military posture, shoulders pulled back, chin thrust out and slightly upward, thick greying moustache. Then below the belt: hips askew, all the weight on one leg, the other leg at a slightly derelict angle, with his walking stick partially concealed from the camera, his trousers stained from work, the material drooping around the crotch. Behind him, Marcus stood awkwardly in his starched shirt and suspenders, forcing his lean body straight and still, ironing out the back and shoulders that naturally curled toward work and motion.

Kai Soules was a much more obscure figure than his father, Arthur. A small paragraph in the Shellycoat paper, dated 1965, reported his death on the river. A brief mention of how he'd been battered by rapids and boulders, pierced by sweeping branches. The writer didn't seem to recognize Kai's last name, a sign, perhaps, of how removed Shellycoat had become from Lambert and the history of the Immitoin Valley.

Each night, he waited for Billy to show up. What kept him away? Sometimes, late at night, he heard the guttural engine noises of a truck coasting slowly down the street, and once there was a clumsy shifting of gears, the clutch being ridden—the sounds of a very young, very old, or very drunk driver. Cyril? Billy? Hardy? But nothing ever happened.

Maybe Gina was sneaking over to Billy's while pretending to be at her mom's. The idea didn't make him jealous—well, it did, but so what? He'd never been convinced she could shake herself free of Billy so easily. And did Paul really offer enough to keep her from returning to her ex now and then? Even the word *sneaking* presumed too much. He couldn't force things. But he still wondered how dangerous Billy might be, or how much Gina actually knew.

2

A snowboard company from California threw a sponsorship deal at Jory—film roles, the face of their clothing line, endless free swag. To celebrate, he launched from a ten-metre cliff over the ski hill road while two cars passed underneath. His friends filmed it, posted it on the Internet.

"You're a bit of a rock star now," Paul told him, and Jory didn't deny it. There was the extra attention he received from company reps, from his friends and peers, and girls who came into the store or spotted him at the bar. The more attention he received, the more volatile he became, and the more Sonya hung back from the scene, avoiding the shop and coming home early from the all-night parties and raves.

In February, three snowmobilers died in the backcountry. There were more than two dozen men in Fiddler's Bowl at the time, a mix of locals and sledders from Revelstoke, Kelowna, and Calgary. They'd spent the day high-marking, gunning their sleds up a steep slope, cresting the hill and racing back down. When the last rider dropped in, the slope above him broke in a perfect slab, loud as a thunderclap. The avalanche gained momentum, turned into a white cloud, house-sized chunks of snow that snapped trees in half. Seven riders were hit by debris, thrown from their sleds and then buried. The four buried at the fringes of the avalanche were quickly dug out. The other bodies were recovered two days later by the Search and Rescue team.

The tragedy became fodder for the coffee shops and pubs. But the town had seen this before: people died every winter in their mountains. They were not shocked, though people used the word. Paul would have described it as a deep, communal uneasiness, as though the avalanche had swept past Shellycoat itself and only missed by inches. The deaths even put a chill into Jory and his crew. They scoffed and cracked dark jokes but quietly swore off the backcountry until the snow profile changed. At the same time, a cold snap arrived and the ski resort's slopes turned icy and unpleasant. The season looked set to end on a dismal note, and Jory took to working longer shifts at the shop and then partying all night.

One morning, Paul intercepted him on the porch and invited him in for a coffee. At the kitchen table, Jory held up a bruised hand and turned his head to show a cut near the temple. "Banned for two weeks from the bar," he said. He confessed to growing some pot upstairs, using lights in their bedroom closet. "Don't worry, it won't get you in trouble," he said quickly. "It's no big deal." He wanted to give Sonya hours at the store just so he could keep an eye on her, he said. She was acting different, and he didn't trust these mood swings of hers. Jory glanced upward at the sound of footsteps above them and rubbed his temples. "Shit's not so good right now."

Paul considered how difficult it was to maintain the balance between the domestic life and the life of risk. Relationships complicated your identity, nullifying and remoulding. The narcissism of risk, on the other hand, was so pleasantly streamlined: every time you conquered the impossible, you became more yourself than you were before.

Late one afternoon, another fight upstairs. When Jory shouted, his voice had heft and musculature, and when he pleaded and begged, it broke into high-pitched fragments of sound. In everything he did, Jory wobbled between boy and man.

"You're always talking to the same guy—ten people in the room but always the same fucking guy."

"Maybe it's because he's your only friend who doesn't talk to me like I'm your brainless little snowboard bunny."

"Yeah, well, I'll pound that so-called friend of mine if he keeps that shit up."

This time Paul hadn't wanted to eavesdrop. He retreated to his bedroom, where their argument was reduced to a muffled din. After that, he rarely went upstairs to visit. He decided to transcribe his interview with Hardy himself and had no other work for Sonya. He abandoned her to the bleak winter.

~

Gina answered Elsie's phone, as he'd hoped. Her mother's flu was still pretty bad, and Gina didn't want to leave the house. The television blared in the background, the unmistakable swelling strings and wooden dialogue of daytime soaps. The noise faded as she walked the phone into the kitchen.

"I've been running the puke bowl all day," she said in a strained voice. "And in between that, she complains."

"About you?"

"About everything."

"Need me to pick up Shane?"

"That's all right."

"Seriously. I could bring him back here."

"Better if he's here."

He swung by Elsie's anyway and convinced Gina to lend him the car seat. Stubborn. Maybe she was wary of him trying too hard to be the surrogate father. He'd honestly never considered it until now, but being with a single mother might be his only real shot at becoming a dad. Maybe she anticipated being put off by his desperation, unless he'd done that already when he called her ex-husband a murderer. He stopped at the pizza place, bought two mediums. Would this also be considered too eager, an act of bribery?

At the school parking lot, he stood outside and watched the kids throw snowballs at one another. He saw Shane through the crowd of snowsuits and mittens and waved to him. The boy ran over, then hesitated, wondering where his mother was, a little shy. "There's pizza," Paul told him, and Shane scrambled into the back of the vehicle. He buckled him into his car seat and handed him a slice. "That's using your noodle," the boy said with the practised air of someone who'd repeated the arcane phrase a hundred times that day.

"Hey." The voice froze Paul. He closed the door carefully and turned. Billy marched toward him, his ears a bright pink beneath his ball cap. He was hunched over slightly, his jacket collar up.

"He's coming with me," Billy said.

Paul shivered under his jacket. "It's Gina's night. Until the weekend. That's the agreement."

"Who the fuck asked you?" Billy took another step forward, and Paul stumbled back against the passenger door. He heard a rubbing sound on the window, and he and Billy stopped to look. Shane, blank-faced, was wiping the fog from the glass, tomato paste smeared in an arc.

Paul said, "You're going to beat me up in front of your son?"

A loud, cowboy's guffaw, a friendly clap on Paul's shoulder calculated to trigger an explosion. He had to bear that without flinching, not give him a reason. Billy squeezed his shoulder again, condescending, trying to set him off. Paul gave him nothing—he was just as tall as Billy, he realized, but probably a hell of a lot weaker.

"I should," Billy breathed. "Show him how bullshit you are."

Paul risked a glance back. Shane was looking down at his lap, his mouth and chin buried in his jacket. Billy backed off a step and waggled his fingers at his son and forced a thin smile.

He said, "This isn't right. Gina's supposed to be picking him up. What if I hadn't come by and he was left alone?"

"Elsie's sick. I'm helping out."

Billy stomped his feet in a quick jig of frustration, comical in his shin-high snow boots and tight blue jeans. "Mind your own fucking business. Stay out of everyone's lives."

"You mean Gina's life, or Hardy's?" Paul, angry enough to dare, pushed himself away from the car.

Billy shook his head slowly, eyebrows raised in astonishment. "You're in real need of a serious ass kicking, bud."

"Do you wonder what Hardy told me? What he said?"

Parents had stopped dragging their kids toward their cars and were staring. Billy backed away. "He didn't tell you shit," he hissed, then turned and jogged, head down, to his truck. He tore out of the parking lot and down the road. Paul slowly opened his door and climbed into the driver's seat.

"So, like, I'm freezing now." Shane liked to imitate the snooty tone of the teenagers on *Glee*.

"Sorry." He turned the ignition and cranked the heat.

"That's okay," the boy said. Shane grabbed another slice of pizza and devoured the rest of his piece as they drove. "Dad says you're a goof," he told Paul in a kind and conspiratorial tone.

"Your dad's probably right." Paul tried to smile.

Encouraged, the boy added, "Says you're a home renter."

"A home renter?" He studied Shane's face in the rear-view mirror, the shape of his jaw beneath the baby fat. The boy was like a translucent shell, the Wentz blood clearly running underneath.

The entrance to Elsie's place smelled musty, like clothes dampened by sweat, and Gina urged him not to stay long or even cross the threshold of the apartment. "I don't want you to get sick," she said, although she didn't seem worried about Shane.

He handed her the pizza boxes as the boy kicked off his boots and raced into the living room. No point telling her about Billy.

She looked completely rundown. "I'm sorry about things," he said. "I was just frightened that day. Hardy freaked me out. The way he acted."

She smiled wearily. "Quit apologizing, goddamn it."

"You sure you don't need help?"

She kissed him on the cheek, dismissing him. She had fallen into things too quickly with Billy and wouldn't make the same mistake again. Or maybe she found it easy to keep her bearings with Paul, not get swept up in things or leave herself vulnerable. He inspired a careful apportioning of passion, rational doses of lust.

~

He woke up from a dream of a chaotic brawl—things clattered and fell. An uncontrolled, mindless noise from upstairs. Something knocked hard and steady against a wall—a bed frame, a kitchen table. With each percussive slam came male grunts and curses, a girl's explosive, staccato sobs.

He was awake and not awake, lucid and mindless as a sleepwalker, still gummed up in the residue of a dream. The sound of her crying out made him rise from the bed, his body tingling. He stood, and his cock pulsed and swayed, solid and heavy in his hand. There was a door hidden in a wall somewhere. He was certain, in an instinctive, animal way, that the door he wanted was in the living room where the wall was blank and white. He pawed and scraped at the wall looking for hinges, cracks. Nothing. Someone had superimposed a new house over the old house, and the bedroom door—but whose bedroom?—was gone. No echo of hollow space behind the wall. His mouth filled with a thick, salty saliva, and he emptied the spit into his hand and rubbed it over his erection. The noise upstairs had faded, but now someone was crying, a muffled sound. Sonya upstairs, or the woman in the room he couldn't find. He needed to be in that room, but the house's foundation had been turned in some direction to confuse him. The unfindable room in the centre of the house. He went into the bathroom and flicked on the light, saliva still draining into his mouth as though from a wound, and came. The orgasm buckled his knees, not from pleasure but from a sharp throb of pain—and the surreal absence of ejaculate.

He thrust a hand against the mirror to keep upright and stared at his clean, empty hand, the pristine rim of the sink. There was no proof, other than the fading pain in his groin, that he'd come at all. This was like a dream in which you flew without wings, were cut but did not bleed, shouted but did not make a sound.

He slumped to the cold tile floor, fully awake now. The crying upstairs had stopped, or had never been. There was no bedroom hidden behind the wall, his apartment was bare and plain. The memory, the eerily tangible presence of the old house, was gone. He'd never lived in such a place.

3

Sex was not a route on which he could travel backward. It had propelled him forward, inexorably and mercilessly, from that first dizzying, alien spasm at adolescence, onto whatever so-called sex life he was granted, for as long a time as it was granted. Could he pass through the damp crucible of incontinence and impotence and come out the same old Paul?

In the morning, he soaped and palmed his groin while in the shower and achieved nothing. As the day went on, he tried to focus on sex, as though a type of mental discipline were required. His body remained mulishly indifferent, refusing to be pulled and tugged toward arousal. Truthfully, he didn't even feel like thinking about it. By lunch, he was convinced that last night's events hadn't taken place, or had been a strange fluke, an accidental jolt of nerve endings.

Gina came by in the late afternoon to tell him Elsie was getting better, but she'd stay at her mother's for a few more nights to make sure. She'd just dropped Shane off at Billy's.

"Was he angry?" Paul asked.

"About you picking up my kid? Shane told me about that right after you left."

"I didn't want to add to your worries."

"Billy said it was a misunderstanding. No big deal."

He didn't believe her—such diplomatic words didn't feature in Billy's vocabulary. "Well, never mind then."

She had a few hours of spare time and wanted to spend them in bed with him. When her questing hand crept between his legs, he pinned it against the bed with his arm and moved his mouth and free hand over her aggressively. He was afraid of her ministrations, her patient hands and the soft nest of her mouth. What if she coaxed just enough of a twitch, a surge of blood, to fill both of them with false hope? Before last night there had been no possibility of performing, and therefore no real sense of failure. It had been easier to have nothing—now he risked a deeper humiliation.

A relief when she finally fell back, satisfied, and her hands stopped struggling to reach him. A reprieve. "You're all right?" she asked, as she always did. How could she not be bored of him already?

"Perfect." His body was silently reconfiguring itself, remapping channels and pathways. Last night may have been an aberration—or maybe his capillaries, nerve endings, and drive were conspiring against him. Better to tell her nothing.

Hi Paul:

Your dad saw an interesting news clip he wanted to tell you about, but I figure I'll go ahead and spoil it for you because he'll never get around to calling. He's decided to renovate the basement, did I tell you? Anyway, the story was about this river on the Olympic Peninsula off Washington State—the Elwha. Apparently they're tearing down the dam, a full restoration of the river, which of course he found quite fascinating. Turns out it was a Canadian, Thomas Aldwell, who built the dam in 1910. It put an end to a very large salmon run, destroyed clam beds along the delta, and drowned the site of the Klallam people's sacred creation legend (I didn't quite get what the legend was, and I'm pretty sure your father didn't either). After that, someone built a lumber mill on top of their ancestral village.

There are volunteers growing native plants in local greenhouses, ready to replant the old river-banks after the dam's foundations are blown up and the reservoir has been drained. I love that idea, but your dad's a bit skeptical. He figures they'll be planting in a hundred years' worth of sediment filled with mercury and methane. The way he sees it, the river won't be restored so much as it'll become something entirely different.

A biologist said there are still salmon genetically programmed to return to the river—some continue to make the trip each year, poor lonely stragglers, and then sit at the base of the dam poking around for decent gravel until they die. I wonder what they'll think when they find the river navigable for the first time in more than a century. Well, I guess they won't think anything at all, they'll just starting heading upstream, right? What with the job you had counting trout, you're probably more optimistic than your dad about trying to turn back time.

Watched the weather channel today—don't go driving around in the snow too much, there's sup-posedly more on the way. I do hope you're feeling more like your old self.
Love,
Mom

A group portrait beneath the flumes, the patriarchs Donald Wallace and Frederic Wentz, gnarled and stern, at the centre of a group of farm punks and weathered toughs. A young Cyril like an aristocratic version of Billy, leaning against a massive circular saw, all pride and mud. A row of smirking, scowling teenagers—the wildest and biggest of them would soon jump ship for good-paying jobs on Caleb's crew. Easy work as land agents, maybe a future in engineering like the boss himself.

He was sifting again through the archives' photo collection, happening upon familiar names. Frederic Wentz, Billy's grandfather, in his prime: an image captured while he leaned on his axe, a quick breather while clearing the new homestead at the turn of the twentieth century.

"So many interesting lives," Paul said. "Surprised more people haven't written about them."

Elmer looked up from a series of old soil type distribution maps he was sorting and gestured to the crowded bookshelves around them, confused.

"No, like a real book. I mean—sorry." He laughed at the archivist's half-offended, half-amused expression, his wiry eyebrows comically rising up his bald pate. "A novel or something."

"I'm not a big fan of most historical fiction, to be honest," Elmer said. "All that guessing what a real person from a hundred years ago might have thought or felt. Too much speculation."

"Sounds more fun than what I'm doing. Guesswork isn't a viable option in my profession."

"Those stories get too convenient. Just give me the documented facts and I'll fill in the gaps myself, thank you very much."

Paul laughed. Elmer had to be bullshitting him—his desk was littered with crime novels set in ancient Scotland or Greece, pages bent and powdered with cookie crumbs.

Finally, near the bottom of the stack, Kai Soules, a beaming, slightly paler version of his grandfather. Sixteen years old in 1964, a year away from death. The photo was black and white, faded, the men all drenched in the same mix of sawdust and oil—it tricked the mind into seeing resemblances.

"Kai could be his kid brother, don't you think?" Paul asked.

"Whose?"

"Hardy's."

Elmer squinted at the photo, then shrugged.

"Kinda has the same mouth and jaw," Paul said. "Do you have a photo of the whole Soules family?"

"No, oddly," Elmer said. "Granted, they lived in the shadow of the Wallaces, but I've never run across anything—no photos, diaries, mementos."

"Probably all disappeared when Arthur moved Marcus away from the valley." Too bad. If he had enough decent photos, he might spot family resemblances that had skipped a generation. "No chance you carry old medical records or anything like that?"

"Now you're really reaching. We're not a spy agency." Elmer was bent close to his stack of maps, jotting down dates and numbers and mumbling to himself.

"Or maybe some anecdote from a person who knew the extent of Donald's injury."

Elmer finally looked up. "Sorry, but what are you getting at, exactly?"

"Never mind."

~

Eavesdropping on Sonya and Jory was dark, effective medicine. It was necessary to stray into this taboo territory, to brush against the fringes of what he found acceptable. He'd succeeded in getting himself hard two or three times now while listening to the two of them—or not exactly *hard*, just solid enough to feel good. The erections didn't last long, nothing to make him any braver with Gina, which, he reminded himself, was the real point of this exercise—not Sonya, not the idea of her. Part of him wanted desperately to see her—the part of him that lurked under the stairs—but he knew this was shaky ground.

Lately he heard more arguments or silence than sex, and Gina and Shane became a constant presence again with Elsie's recovery. He was, for the most part, relieved that his evenings under the stairs were coming to an end.

One night, Gina took him in her mouth and suddenly there came the small, unmistakable throb he'd dreaded, a small rush of pleasure followed by a cold swell of panic in his chest. Gina made a muffled, surprised noise and worked her mouth faster. The bobbing of her head revolted him, the ridiculous sucking sounds, her apparent desperation. He pulled away, and she looked up, surprised. He slumped against the wall, knees against his chest.

"I spotted your pills," Gina said. "On your desk." He'd hidden them behind a stack of papers, but the papers were always sliding onto the floor. Her face collapsed in sympathy. "They're not working, are they?"

"I haven't taken any."

"Oh, sweetheart."

"I don't know why. I really don't."

"Wait," she said. "You haven't taken any? Not even one?"

"Is it that important?" he asked. "That I, you know, be *inside* you or whatever?"

She shrugged, defensive. "It would be nice," she admitted in a low voice.

"Jesus, I must bore you. I'd be bored—we're stagnating."

"No." There was a bit of steel in her voice. "We're not. Everything's getting better. We are. Sex is just one thing."

"Don't know why I feel this way." He rested his forehead on his knees and spoke into the hollow between his head and groin.

Her hand slid over his foot. "It's fine."

"Oh, bullshit." Childish and defiant, snuffling.

"We don't need the stupid pills. We'll take our time."

"We've taken our time. All fucking winter."

So why not the pills? Two years ago, healthy and potent, he

might have taken them recreationally, just for the hell of it. But now he had this fucked-up notion that the pills would undo who he was becoming: either they'd work so well they'd inspire a hunger that devoured all his time, or they'd fail and he'd be utterly devastated, knocked back to square zero. None of it made sense, and it was impossible to explain it to her. But that's how he felt. The pill was an unfeeling thing. It offered amoral erections, a prick-centric view of a man's existence. It said he deserved sexual function, a hard-on, regardless of what he really did deserve. It obligated him. The pill was not an instrument of grace. And why was he in need of grace, except that, up until very recently, he might have been guilty of wasting his adult life?

They had been silent a long time when she suddenly sniffed and crinkled her nose. "Do you smell pot?"

"They're growing it upstairs," he said. "In their closet."

She nodded. "I'm pretty sure Billy was growing last summer with his buddies."

"He wouldn't tell you?"

"Afraid of losing Shane. Doesn't want to give me leverage."

"You never noticed anything inside his house?"

"It would have been an outdoor show, somewhere in the hills." She shivered and they both slipped under the covers. "Or were you talking about Caleb Ready?"

"No. No, not right now." He checked to see if she was annoyed, but her eyes were half-closed as she shifted against his chest. "Ready's death never bothered you that much," he said after a moment.

"I didn't know him. Despite what he did all those years ago, or how angry I can get about the past—he's a piece of history, nothing more."

"I like that you can't make yourself hate him."

"Sure, but then I feel guilty, because of Mom, because I can't quite hold on to her resentment."

"You shouldn't have to. What good would that do?"

"I just feel, when she's gone, that part of our family's story will be too. But it won't make things right."

How many people, he wondered, harboured Gina's anxiety that time was running out? For decades, Caleb had spent his summers in Bishop, the derelict ghost town he helped create. Paul tried to imagine how he must have felt. Smug? Repentant? Maybe indifferent to people and their changed lives, the way a prospector might be oblivious to his surroundings, his thoughts immersed in the glittering creekbeds. And then along comes a man, or men, dreaming of an action that could answer the past, no matter how many years later.

Paul,

You are right to say there are some interesting parallels between what your subjects have described and what can be found in other parts of the world. In fact, I've found a rather dizzying number of coincidences. For example, Mr. Pilcher's trappers, a marginalized community who were not properly informed and did not know what they were witnessing, experienced something very similar to what the Tsay-Keh Dene hunters did when the W.A.C. Bennett Dam was built on the Peace. They too returned home along a ridge and were mystified by the rising waters. One also thinks of the Senecas' forced relocation from their reservation along the Allegheny River (did you get around to reading that book?), or the fifty-thousand Gwembe Tonga relocated to make way for the Kariba Dam, among dozens of other examples.

Likewise, doesn't the loss of the Immitoin Valley's orchards echo the orange groves drowning beneath the Yangtze River, or the cherry trees along the Arrow Lakes long ago? Or the ranches and settlements along the Peace River—not just what was lost in the late sixties, but the land now threatened by the most recent dam proposals?

Still on the subject of the Peace River and Arrow Lakes, I've found reports—mostly unsubstantiated—of suicides similar to those of Frederic Wentz, and even the presence of a villain (unnamed, a sort of bogeyman) who bullied people out of their homes by using, of course, fire. And, finally, the mercury-poisoned fish of the Immitoin can also be found in Kinbasket Lake—and in the vast reservoirs of Africa, where hungry villagers eat them by the bucketful.

Don't be alarmed by all my snooping around— you can't blame me for a little mistrust, all things considered. And, unlike other supervisors I know, I won't steal your ideas for my own work. I wouldn't have the time. Christine and I are planning another conference, "Identity, Family, and the Sporting Body," to which you're welcome to submit a paper. But I imagine all your old projects must feel very far away by now.

Disoriented (but not displaced),

Dr. Elias Tamba

4

They'd worked up a good sweat on their afternoon ski, and after shucking off their wet socks and wool long underwear in the bedroom, Gina jumped in the shower, leaving Paul to gather up his digital recorder and notebooks to prepare for the evening.

It had been spectacular out there, the trees shaking off their loads of snow, sending shimmering flakes like lace curtains gliding across the blue sky. He'd kept pace with Gina as she sped along ahead of him, her skis slapping the groomed corduroy runs, and toward the end he'd finally gotten a feel for the glide and had felt near weightlessness out there, performing levitation over the frozen bogs, his momentum addictive and heady. The leg cramps came after, in the car, but he'd had his victory.

The phone rang while Paul was stripping off his thermal underwear. "It's Cliff. You busy?"

"Just got back from a ski. What's going on?"

"We were right about Ready's claim. Kind of."

Paul, distracted and hungry, wandered naked through the kitchen looking through cupboards. "Basket Creek?"

"Farther up. Starts at the mouth of Dalton Creek."

Paul was pulling out a bag of wagon wheel pasta from the cupboard. He stopped. "Above the Flumes, you mean."

"The Flumes?"

"A set of rapids. Jory and his friends launch kayaks there."

"Is that the old mill site? Didn't know it had a name."

"Frederic Wentz and Donald Wallace built the mill. Ready's claim would be right beside it." Paul went back to the bedroom and pulled a sweater and jeans out of his closet. "How recent was the claim?"

"Don't know yet. I'm getting copies of the mineral rights sent up from Victoria."

"So what do we do next?"

"Right now? Not much, unfortunately. We could snowmobile there, but I don't see how that'll help."

"Help who with what?"

"Us. You and me. Find some kind of clue, for Christ's sake. We'll have to wait until spring, though, so don't hold your breath."

~

The Spry Creek town meeting was held in the local theatre. Representatives from Monashee Power were on stage right. A young man scrambled to set up a laptop and white screen, while a middle-aged woman and two stocky bald men sat ramrod-straight in their chairs, leafing through notes. Gina pointed out the mayor and council on stage left. Between the two groups stood a lone microphone, and in the centre aisle, down among the theatre seats, someone had set up another microphone and lectern facing the stage. Near the front row, Elsie Hubert bustled about with a handful of men and women—the Friends of Spry Creek, ready to hand out their pamphlets. With five minutes to go before the meeting, the theatre was nearly packed. In the crowd, he picked out Molly and Joseph Kruse, and a few biologists and technicians, including Daryl and Tanner, who sat inconspicuously at the rear of the theatre.

Paper rustled, and there were pockets of low muttering among the audience as the mayor stood at the microphone at centre stage. He thanked everyone for coming out and introduced those on stage. "This meeting," he said slowly, assessing the room, "is to announce the application for an official environmental assessment review of the proposed Spry Creek Hydroelectric Project."

More rustling, renewed murmuring. He pressed on, a short speech about the potential economic benefits of the project and the province's need for clean energy, and then turned over the mic to the woman. She echoed his promises of high revenues and local employment and emphasized the dam's minimal impact on the creek. No water would be retained, only diverted to run through turbines before returning to its original course to the Immitoin. There would be some new road built, yes, but not much, since the Spry Creek logging road provided access. The transmission line corridor would be as unobtrusive as possible. The audience shifted restlessly. Paul, thinking of academic conferences and difficult lectures, found himself sweating on behalf of the people on stage.

While the representative spoke, images appeared on the screen behind her: charts and graphs, photos of turbines and cables, improbably clean-cut men in hardhats, knee-deep in rubble. There were also picturesque riparian scenes, untouched wildernesses, colourful pebbles under clear running water, alders hanging over dappled pools. He had to admire the rep—she managed to drum up a few pockets of applause with the promise of jobs, at least. When she was done, the mayor invited members of the audience to ask questions. He did not say, "Begin protesting," but judging by his tone, that was what he anticipated.

The people who stepped up to the microphone were not always whom Paul had expected. A slender woman in her early fifties asked about sufficient water levels and the need to dredge and disturb the main channel, the ramifications of glaciers receding in the future. A teenager with dyed blue hair, reading from notes, raised the issue of grizzly bear habitat, while a slouching, articulate man Paul's age angrily pointed out the number of new transmission line corridors needed and the spread of invasive plants. A paunchy fishing guide, followed by a paunchier fisherman, wondered about the cutthroat and bull trout. A woman the spitting image of Paul's grandmother said the provincial government had been handing out water licences like candy. Who would be accountable if anything happened? A scar-handed mill worker liked the sound of new jobs, but asked if this would be like last time—short-term gain for long-term pain.

That was the first time someone had alluded to the flooding of the valley, but Paul sensed an underlying, old anxiety in each speaker—remembering, maybe, their own helplessness, or their parents' impotent protests at the town hall meeting in Lambert forty-five years ago. They had adapted, over time, to one vast change, and now they were being asked to adapt to another. Were they wondering how much ground they would ultimately have to give, how much change before everything changed, until all that remained of the original valley was stacked in Elmer's archives?

He thought about why he'd agreed to come to the town meeting, other than wanting to be polite to Elsie. Maybe it was symptomatic of being trapped in a dark valley the entire winter, but the work he'd done, the scribbled notes, the recorded and transcribed interviews, had started weighing on him. Would it really mean anything to anyone who didn't live here? Outsiders like him could only relate to the valley's flood and people's displacement in the most abstract way, and that was partly because they'd heard this type of story so many times, they'd become desensitized to it. Tamba had already pointed out a disheartening number of similar events, and he'd barely scratched the surface.

He'd always taken pride in finding unusual material for his ethnographies: international students using parkour to adjust to their surroundings, or the complex tensions within a peloton of high-strung middle managers. Stuff that had a pop culture appeal. Now he worried he'd been digging himself into a hole by monkeying around with the overused, tired theme of displacement. It was a subject that might come off as quaint and old-fashioned not only to most academics but to general readers as well—more history, more memories and sorrows, all the old clichés. Another study dabbling poetically and inconsequentially in the past. And located somewhere too regional: remote but not exotic. As good as he felt about the effort he'd made, the amount of data he'd gathered, in the end, it would all end up lying inert on the page.

But the meeting was making him realize a small truth. The participants in his previous ethnographies had always chosen their quirks and obsessions. For them, the stakes weren't high— broken bones, wounded pride, minor jealousies. They were interesting enough as subjects, but they'd risked little. Some people here tonight had lost a great deal and were afraid they'd lose even more. The palpable anxiety in the room was urgent, collective, and modern. How could he properly bottle the faint note of fear he heard, connect it to his ethnography, and make it resonate with anyone who read his research? He looked around for reporters, video cameras. If tonight made the news—not just the local papers, but the *Vancouver Sun*, maybe a quick spot on CBC—that would help give his research some weight, some relevance.

A husky man with a robust grey beard and cowboy hat stepped up to the lectern. "I live in Grand Forks now," he said. "In the sixties, my family gave up our farm to make way for what's now called Lake Koocanusa, so I understand why people are protective about their rivers." He paused to clear his throat.

"Thing is," the man continued, "creeks like Spry have to do all the compensating—habitat-wise, wetlands, spawning beds—for what was lost to the mega-dams. And in some ways they compensate for what people have lost as well. Something to consider." He shrugged and stepped aside.

Elsie Hubert finally approached the lectern and introduced herself as a representative of the Friends of Spry Creek, which got the cheers going again, the placards raised and waving.

"Someone earlier mentioned short-term gains. Speaking of which, if your run-of-river dam can't store power, then how does it address the problem of capturing energy when we need it the most?" Her voice wavered, but with that first question out of the way she seemed to shake off her nerves. "Where is this power really going? Who really benefits? The local economy? Or a foreign company shipping our power and resources elsewhere?" It was a clever question—talking about money and ownership might bring the loggers onside with the environmentalists, and she had a certain drawl that made her sound down to earth, trustworthy.

"You just heard someone talk about how his family was relocated to make way for a dam. Today, in the Immitoin Valley, we have someone conducting an ongoing study on our own displaced citizens. Paul? Could you stand up?"

His pen, which he'd been using to take notes, slipped from his grasp, and he watched it roll out of reach beneath a seat. *Oh, Christ.* He rose slowly, and his eyes locked on Elsie, trying to shut out the stares of an entire theatre. Gut it out, he told himself. Think of the classroom, the lecture hall. He'd been a solid, though not naturally gifted, lecturer at university. Coherent and energetic, with the requisite amount of arrogance for a doctoral student. Apparently that arrogance too had been cut out and scraped away.

Elsie was reading from her notes. "His research is a story of the way we were taken advantage of back then, and I think it also speaks to how we're not going to let that happen today. Paul, could you maybe add to that?"

"Well. Sure," he said, blinking sweat from his eyes. He hated the way she'd appropriated and twisted his work, but he couldn't risk humiliating Elsie or coming off like a cheerleader for the dam. She'd left him without much to say.

"It's tough, putting these interviews, these narratives, together. Someone said to me last week, 'It's a myth, you know, the story of that man who set fires for Monashee Power. It's a myth that's told in every place where something like this has happened.' Maybe that's true. But why does that myth carry on? What gives the story its power?" He paused, and promptly lost his train of thought.

"Everyone makes the best of a bad situation. They adapt. But it doesn't mean, um, doesn't mean." He shook his head, tongue-tied. "You have to be careful," he said to the company reps and politicians sitting on the stage staring at him in uncomfortable confusion. They looked the way he felt, clammy and dying in their sweat-crinkled button-ups. "You have to be careful with people."

He sat down heavily. Elsie reclaimed the lectern and was speaking again. Gina patted him on the leg, leaned into his shoulder and gently bit his sweater—to suppress her laughter, he supposed.

Elsie brought her speech to a close. "To Monashee Power, all I can say is, I'm sorry for all the dollars you've spent on this proposal so far. I would urge you not to waste more money. Because there's no way in hell we'll let you build this dam!"

More applause, and the people nearest him stood with their placards and posters. Someone a few rows back started a chant that others took up and continued after the councillor adjourned the meeting. Paul and Gina made their way over to Elsie, who looked dazed from the buzz of the crowd. People drifted by to congratulate her—way to give 'em hell, you got 'em on the run. Others, like the man from Lake Koocanusa, wanted to speak with Paul. Some had grown up on farms along the Immitoin before the dam. Others had families who'd been similarly displaced from other places, like Arrowhead and Burton. He traded numbers, e-mail addresses, and business cards, and forgot his earlier embarrassment.

"Tonight should make the news," he said. "Elsie? Don't you think? Anyone from the news talk to you?"

She was watching the crowd as they filed out. "Hardy didn't make it," she said to no one in particular, her brow furrowed. "It's very odd."

"You invited him?" he asked, confused, but then thought, yes, of course: the lost opportunity Hardy had spoken of, the Kootenay Symposium. Tonight had been his chance to make up for that, to do—what, exactly? Rant into a microphone? Finally face someone with real power and look them in the eye?

"Why didn't he show up?" Elsie said. And Paul, now wondering the same thing, stared around at the emptying theatre, scanning for both television cameras and the old man, thinking that Elsie had stood at that lectern not just for the Friends, but for people like Hardy and Cyril, neither of whom was here. She'd spoken herself into a different place and time and was coming back from it almost completely alone.

5

Winter began to wind down, and there were rumours the mill would reopen in late April. The valley warmed, the sidewalks in Shellycoat turning brown and grey with slush. When he skied, the snow was slick, dull, and wet, and the forest smelled of soil and crushed fir and spruce needles. Rivulets trickled beneath the snow, a crystalline sound. He skied out to the huts with Lazeroff to eat lunch by the woodstove one last time and went home melancholy.

One morning, he and Gina took Shane down to the park along the water, where the snow remained only in isolated clumps beneath the trees. Gina had enrolled in a government-sponsored workshop on starting and operating a small business, and a few days into the workshop some other women in the class had approached her about running a catering company or maybe a small café together. She taped charts and graphs to the bedroom wall opposite Paul's chaotic workspace, and after Shane was asleep she spread her night's homework across the kitchen table: graphs, charts, and application forms, booklets on business loans. While Paul fussed and ruminated over his interviews and notes, her hands turned pages and rearranged papers with quiet efficiency. He knew that underneath her calm, solid grace, she was panicking about the future and the probability of disappointment, just as he was.

She told Paul that with the mill reopening, Billy wanted to spend more time with his son, knowing he'd be pulling long days in the woods to make up for lost income. "You'll be at your dad's a lot for the next few weeks, big guy," she said to Shane. He was kicking pebbles free from the still-frozen sand and throwing them into the clear water.

"That's okay," the boy said. "That's a good thing, right?"

"Very good. Your dad's looking forward to it."

"Must be relieved to have his job back," Paul said.

Gina shrugged. "Ungrateful. Guess he'll always be that way."

At home that afternoon, he got a call from Elmer. "I think I may have found someone you'll want to talk to. A woman named Raina Thorstenson. You'll have to drive to Grand Forks, though. She's in a seniors home there, she's about ninety-one."

"Elmer, that's brilliant. How'd you find her?"

"Because of you, actually. A fellow was in here the other day asking about your research, mentioned his grandmother had lived in Lambert. Don't think he quite understood what you're studying."

"How so?"

"She'd already left the valley a long time before the flood, just after the Second World War."

"Doesn't really fit the research then," Paul said, disappointed. "Still tempting, but . . ."

"Well, once I had her maiden name, I dug around and found a couple of references. Her father was a foreman at the packing sheds—you know, loading the crates onto the steamship and so on. So they probably knew Donald Wallace quite well. Here's the clincher: her mother was a nurse."

"You've lost me."

"A nurse—you remember you wanted someone with the scoop on Donald's war wounds?"

"Sure. I'm surprised *you* remembered."

Elmer laughed. "Oh, I've got a knack for sleuthing—it's all that reservoir noir."

~

Grand Forks had a wide open sky compared with Shellycoat. Around the town, a large expanse of fields—not quite green, but no longer dormant—hovered on the verge of spring. The air was warm and smelled of soil and rain. All this made the Twin Willows Assisted Living Village seem like a lively place. Residents took themselves downtown using their walkers or electric scooters or congregated at picnic tables and benches along the lawns and sidewalks. At the far end of the Village, a sign on a set of metal gates designated the enclosed building as a "neighbourhood for the memory-impaired." He double-checked to make sure Raina lived on the right side of the gate.

She was a short woman with a slight tremble, alert and talkative. Her room was tidy, decorated with framed watercolours and wooden spoons hanging on the walls. She still took a long walk each day, she told him, and was quite independent— she cleaned her own apartment and cooked her own meals, eschewing the nursing staff and communal dining area as much as possible. She only had a bit of time to talk—there was a senior's yoga class at eleven and a crib tournament with friends after lunch.

Her memories of Lambert were vivid and elegiac: cherry trees flowering in the spring, the crates of apples loaded on the *Westminster*—Winesaps, Golden Russets, autumn-red Gravensteins. And pears—Anjoulems, Flemish Beauties. Recollections of swimming and rowboat expeditions along the lake, fishing and looking for petroglyphs on rockfaces. They spent nearly an hour steeped in nostalgia before Paul got to the real questions.

"Your mother—a nurse, yes?—she must have known everyone," Paul said.

"Everyone knew everyone."

"Saw a lot of births?"

"And deaths."

"Obviously, you must remember Donald and Belinda Wallace," Paul said. "Did your mother help deliver their son, Hardy?"

"Oh, yes," she said without hesitation.

"You're certain?"

"Absolutely," Raina said, sounding slightly annoyed that a stranger was questioning her memory. "We were close family friends."

"So Mr. Wallace knew he could trust your parents, your mother especially," Paul said.

She looked confused. "With what—Hardy's delivery, do you mean?"

"With other things. I know Donald had been badly wounded in the war."

She chuckled suddenly at a thought. "He couldn't bend or kneel down properly. So he never did anything that would draw attention to it—he was an absurdly proud man. It meant a lot of standing and pointing and ordering people about."

"Did you ever hear anyone say—did Donald or Belinda ever tell your mother—that because of that injury he was unable to have children of his own?"

She squinted cautiously at Paul and smacked her lips once, false teeth slipping and wedging back into place. The question had either surprised her so much she'd forgotten to be indignant for Wallace's sake or else she was weighing her words carefully.

"No one would ever have asked, or brought it up in public. It's like talking about the Queen's underwear." Raina paused, clouded eyes wandering. "It was unexpected when Mrs. Wallace became pregnant, that was all. Everyone just assumed there would be no children."

"Did you know Marcus Soules?"

"Mr. Soules once showed me how to graft a Cox's Pippin branch onto a crabapple tree. I was probably there to play with Arthur at the time, we were close to the same age."

"Do you think Donald would have told Marcus? About the nature of his injury?"

"Maybe . . . yes, him, if anybody." Her eyes brightened with interest—she saw where Paul was going. "If it *was* true about Donald, not sure how he could keep that kind of thing from Marcus."

"And of course, Marcus already had a son," Paul said. "I wonder if that was hard for Donald to take, being so proud."

She nodded, giving him a shrewd look. When is a secret ever really a secret, he thought, and not just a mutual agreement to look the other way?

Paul pictured Donald Wallace at the peak of the Great Depression. The markets for his fruit were disappearing, he had land and moderate wealth but no sons or daughters. A future without orchards wouldn't have seemed likely—everyone in Lambert probably assumed this was a temporary dip in fortune, that there would be new markets, better rail service for shipping. Despite the decline of the fruit industry, and without foreseeing the inevitability of the dam, Donald would have believed he was still key to Lambert's survival. But not to have an heir, to know his name would last only as long as his uncertain health—that must have been truly unthinkable.

Here was the kind of conjecture Elmer hated: that Donald talked Marcus into it as a business deal, a simple matter of propagation, of progeny. No different than grafting scion to rootstock. The Wallaces probably had money set aside for a nest egg, an inheritance. A portion of it could be given over to Marcus, a payment to give the Wallace orchards—and the Wallace name—a future, whatever that future might be. There must have been a strong friendship between the two men or, at the very least, the sense of a shared life, shared dreams, and shared risks.

So they took another gamble—Donald Wallace staked the last of his pride on the future—and from that came Hardy. A son for the Wallaces. The risk must have felt worth it at the time.

Perhaps Marcus had his own hidden motives—all those years tending the orchards with Belinda while Donald was overseas at war or away on association business. Perhaps, by making Marcus his instrument, Wallace took away the man's agency, rendered any secret feelings Marcus had for his wife moot, useless.

And how had Belinda felt about all this? Paul had a hunch that nothing of Belinda survived the burning of Lambert or the floodwaters, save the odd trinket and photo that Hardy kept (and probably hid from Donald, who would have been very old when they relocated). Unlike in Elmer's novels, no secret diaries would suddenly appear to magically and romantically resurrect her. No voice from the past would rescue Paul from speculation. And what was the point of all this speculating? He wasn't sure—it didn't seem to answer anything, except to show how some people in the valley, Donald Wallace in particular, were caught in a spiral of helplessness, of impotence in every sense.

Raina interrupted his thoughts. "Marcus's son, Arthur—he was a handsome boy but bookish. Very different from people like the Wallaces or the Wentzes."

"He had a son, Kai, who died."

"Oh, yes, dreadful. There was hardly anything in the paper, but I'd known because we kept in touch with the Souleses. His wife wrote the Christmas letter each year."

"Arthur had already moved away from Lambert when that happened."

"Yes, he worked with—" She stopped, straining to remember. "Well, he did something for the railroads in Kamloops. Anyway, it was all a terrible shame. Arthur was very proud of Kai because he'd taken a job with the hydroelectric company in the valley."

"I thought Kai worked at the Dalton Creek mill? With Hardy Wallace and the Wentzes."

"Arthur was hoping Monashee Power would point Kai toward an engineering degree or a government job on the coast—anything that wasn't farming or logging."

"Strange, when you think of it," Paul said. "By the time Hardy was born, it was already too late for him to become the person Donald wanted him to be—someone to take over the orchards, run the packing sheds and jam factory. There must have been a lot of shared disappointment between them."

Raina nodded. "That's why Arthur wanted to get Kai away. That valley was no place for young people." She thought for a moment. "It still isn't—don't tell me you haven't had a rough go of things there."

He smiled, taken aback. "Things are starting to look promising."

"Sounds like you're past the worst of it, then," she said.

6

He and Gina left Shane with Billy for the week and drove south past Grand Forks and then east. At Castlegar, they left the main highway and followed the road through town to the Hugh Keenleyside Dam on the Columbia River. There was a narrow lane across the dam's crest where they could drive over the navigation lock to the other side and a viewpoint overlooking the generating station and powerhouse and the man-made wetlands behind the dam. They circled back through the benchland communities of Robson and Brilliant and returned to the highway at the rest stop overlooking the Brilliant Dam on the Kootenay River. The spillway below them thundered, early spring runoff churning in a polished granite mortar, funnelled into a canyon and passing beneath the old Doukhobor suspension bridge.

They continued driving up a long valley where the river ran unencumbered, and the road wound through dark forests that would suddenly open onto fields and farms, gas stations and roadside coffee shops. There was a pristine and rustic quality here, a sense of something preserved. The river was braided and meandering, the banks weedy and wild. This place was, in essence, what the Immitoin Valley might have been without the dam.

Paul recognized the valley from coffee table books and travel magazines. He tried to imagine a new hydro project drowning this highway and farmland. The outrage, the mass protests, would be enough to bring down a government—it simply wouldn't happen in the present day. But then again, there was Site C on the Peace, as Tamba had mentioned. He'd also read about a recent American proposal to flood nine thousand acres of grasslands, sloughs, and a First Nations reserve in the Similkameen Valley. He remembered that place too—he'd driven through part of it last summer on his way to Shellycoat and stopped by the side of the road to suffer through his incontinence.

They'd booked a cabin at a resort with hot springs set among the trees. He and Gina soaked in the hottest of the two pools, immersed to their necks and wreathed in steam. It was early afternoon on a Monday, and the pools were nearly deserted. Snow fell briefly and froze in their damp hair, then turned to a light rain. Gina drifted away, eyes closed, limp body nudged by jets.

Overheated, Paul lifted himself onto the concrete edge and dangled his legs in the water. Rain fell on his head and back, steam billowing off his flushed skin. Weeks of skiing had brought changes—his frame smaller, slimmer, his limbs more fit and toned—refining and completing, in a way, the transformation that the cancer and surgery had begun. He closed his eyes and sucked in a deep breath of cool air. A raven called from a tree overhead. Wing beats, water sluicing off someone rising from the pool. An age passed. Gina returned, silently, and touched his leg with her hand.

When they returned to their simple one-room cabin, Paul showered to wash off the spring's sulphur smell. When he got out, Gina had pulled the curtains shut and waited for him on the bed, naked and reclining on pillows she'd stacked against the headboard. "Take off your towel," she said. "Sit across from me." He did as he was told.

"I think you put too much pressure on yourself. Maybe I do too," she said. No, he began to say, but she stopped him. "Not on purpose, but you're quick to give up, take yourself out of the equation. Then you put all the attention on me, to compensate."

He shifted cautiously. "I'm not sure what you're suggesting here."

"To relax." From under the covers, she brought out a curved, silicon phallus, pastel red with strange, floral ridges and folds. Her smile was both mischievous and embarrassed. She pressed the bottom of the toy, and it hummed to life. "Is this too weird?" she asked.

"Did you just buy that?" he asked, stunned.

"An old friend. Is it too weird?" she asked again. "Or threatening?"

He tried for a joke. "Not as threatening as Billy."

Sadness flickered briefly across her face. "Don't ever feel threatened by him."

"All right."

"I thought, even if things have to be different—they can also be normal."

"This isn't normal," he reminded her.

She shrugged and parted her legs. "We can take all day. Maybe you could just watch me. Or do whatever you want."

She closed her eyes, put her hand between her legs, and began, but he couldn't follow suit. She was too obviously per-forming. Her eyes would flicker open and closed as if she were checking on him. He remembered how comfortable he and Christine had been in front of each other—or not comfortable, just possessed of an arrogance that was necessary and self-preserving, because they did not really love, did not connect.

She stopped and opened her eyes. "Promise me you won't think about time."

"I'll try."

"Did you want me to turn over? So I can't see you?"

Paul thought a moment, nodded. She flipped onto her knees,

arching her back and burying her face into the blankets, and began again. She went quiet, except the working of her wrist, said nothing, did not signal. He took a deep, shaking breath. He felt, for too long, disembodied, distanced from everything except the tightness in his chest, as though he were watching the absurd, arousing scene from the far corner of the room. As time went by and she made sounds to herself into the pillow, he began to feel, mercifully, like she'd forgotten about him. She would keep going if he left the room. He sank into his being a ghost, hovering silently behind her. Waiting for something to break through, to fill cell after cell.

After, they both lay on their stomachs. She ran her hand over her lower back in search of his ejaculate, the mess couples made intimate jokes about. "Oh. But I thought I heard you . . ."

"I did. I know." He stroked the back of her neck, the first time he'd let himself touch her. "Extreme case of shooting blanks."

"It must feel so bizarre."

"Very." Bizarre enough to be disheartening if he let it. What was that all about, anyway, a man's emotional attachment to semen—his most cherished icon of physical release, that crude, ecstatic signifier of being purged, emptied? Was it an act of marking someone and laying claim to them, a symbolic transfer of one's essence to another? "Lacking the stuff of life," he said.

"Trust me, that life soon becomes someone else's. Shane is very much his own little man," she said. "How do you feel?" Something in her tone said she wouldn't brook self-pity—and fair enough. After all, she'd risked as much here as he had, they were both equally exposed and vulnerable.

"Chafed, thanks," he said. At least there hadn't been pain this time. "It's a step closer, I guess."

"Closer to what?"

"Real sex."

"That was real sex," she said. "I had fun."

"Maybe next time we'll try—anyway, you were right, you know. It's all in my mind. Or mostly." He looked at the clock. "Took some effort." She'd granted him time enough for his body to slowly work its response. It felt like an act of forgiveness.

They lay in silence for a while. "It was your mother who gave that food to Cyril Wentz, wasn't it?" he asked. "And then he delivered it to Hardy."

"Yes." Her brow furrowed. "I should have figured that out the night we argued, but I was too angry." She went to rinse the toy in the bathroom sink.

"I wonder how long they've done that for him." He sat at the edge of the bed, stretching his legs.

"Years, I'll bet."

"I didn't think they were all friends."

She returned, placed the toy on the bedside table, and stood in front of him. "They're not. Mom doesn't like either Cyril or Hardy. Who does? But they're all bound together like unhappy, distant relatives."

He lay his cheek against her bare flank. "Let's have another soak before dinner."

"We're becoming amphibious," she said happily. "A real pair of newts."

~

The reopening of the mill made the front page of the local paper, and though the article warned that operations might not last through the summer, that the hours and the number of positions had been reduced, Shellycoat hummed with a quiet relief as loggers and mill workers returned to work. From the porch, Paul could see a steady column of smoke from the burners. Trucks and crew cabs filled the parking spaces outside the coffee shops in the early morning and then disappeared until evening.

Tanner had phoned earlier to pass along some news: the environmental assessment for the Spry Creek Hydroelectric Project had been given the go-ahead, which meant the run-of-river dam was one step closer to becoming reality. Once the public learned of the assessment, the protests would begin. Tanner had offered to be the spokesman for the local Streamkeepers Association. "Not going to tie myself to a fucking tree or anything," he told Paul. "But we'll have some input."

The five members of the house—Jory and Sonya, Paul, Gina, and Shane—shared a late breakfast of pancakes, waffles, and bacon on the back porch to celebrate Paul's new research grant. He had funding now to live, very cheaply, for several months. They toasted his grant with mimosas—Sonya, unexpectedly, had been the one who bought the champagne.

She'd shed the last vestiges of punk, was plain and unadorned and somehow lovelier. Paul told her he'd have some new interviews for her to transcribe soon, but she didn't hear. Gina was telling her about the new business, the long slog through paperwork and grant applications, collaborating with two other women to buy a van with a deep fryer and grill, a smaller version of what Gina used at tree-planting camps, something they could take to summer festivals and farmers' markets.

"Sounds fun," Sonya said pensively. She was helping Shane cut his waffle into tattered, sticky pieces and seemed about to say something more when Jory jumped down from the railing where he'd been perched, ignoring everyone.

"Yo, check these out." He passed around his phone, where he'd stored photos of his latest backcountry expedition. His nose and cheeks were sunburned and raw, giving him a wild-eyed raccoon look. He was a train wreck these days, irresponsible and inconsiderate, but still sweet-natured beneath it all. He'd scrounged up a pair of skis for Paul from the cluttered backroom of his store—"you know, if you stick around for next winter"—and a kid-sized snowboard for Shane. But he no longer draped himself over Sonya, and never shared in her conversations except to argue.

As for Paul, any fantasies involving Sonya were derailed by the prospect of humiliation. Try as he might, he couldn't imagine patience or mercy from someone her age. No, his tenuous recovery, his fragile happiness, was wrapped up in Gina. Sonya, as an object of desire, was too much of a stretch, overmatched by his complicated reality. Poor Jory. They were both losing her.

The results of his blood sample had come back clean, his PSA levels decently low—a reason for his own secret celebration. Only now did he realize how tightly he'd held on to his apprehension all winter. Don't dwell on each individual test, the doctor advised, pay attention to how the antigen levels trend over time. So, a six-month respite until his next PSA test, when his anxiety would grow again, in the same creeping manner as cancer cells. Time, for him, was a snow cave, carefully cleared to house an unknown amount of future, in constant danger of collapse.

7

"I'm told the road's clear of snow past Dalton Creek," Lazeroff said. It was the first weekend of May, and the hills above Shellycoat were still in the last throes of winter.

"We'll need to bring Jory along," Paul said. "He knows that part of the river; I'm hoping he can show us some trails if we're going to explore around the Flumes."

"Sure. Wear good boots."

They stopped to gas the truck outside of town. Jory slouched quietly in the back. The fight upstairs last night had been especially loud and nasty, and his young friend had spent the morning brooding in Paul's apartment. He hadn't been all that keen to come along, and wasn't curious about why they were driving to Dalton Creek. Paul and Lazeroff both spied on him in the rear-view mirror. He had his headphones on, eyes squeezed shut, lips moving silently, and he softly tapped the side of his head against the window. Not in rhythm to the scratchy, frantic music, which Paul could faintly hear, but in quick bursts of three, as though he were imagining or practising doing the same thing much harder. Teeing up for the big hit. Lazeroff, who'd raised melodramatic teenagers, gave Paul an irritated, grimly amused look.

In the silence, Paul thought about last night. He and Gina had finally, successfully, made love—sort of. There were awkward pauses and positions, and they had to go slowly and start again several times. Stuffable, indeed. Before his cancer, last night would have been completely devastating. You could get used to anything, it seemed.

Near Bishop, a solitary man was burning a small pile of dead brush on his lawn, and in another yard a dirtbike and ATV were freshly spattered with dark mud. As they left the reservoir behind and the river appeared, Jory suddenly perked up. "Freshet's on. Look at that. It'll top the banks."

The Immitoin had already flooded in some places, leaving puddles that spanned the width of the road. The current ran grey and brown with sediment and heaped logs and debris against boulders. The turnoff to the Spry Creek logging road was marked with ribbons, and a large signboard—*Ruin of the River*—was a soggy mess.

"Classic stretch," Jory said. "Launch from the mouth of Spry Creek and ride it out until Bishop. Beautiful."

"Not right now," Lazeroff said. "That'd be crazy."

"Insane," Jory said cheerfully.

Dark smoke rose thickly from the chimney of Hardy's cabin, the driveway a soup of mud and broken spruce and fir branches. "Talked to him lately?" Lazeroff asked. "No letters in the paper this spring. Strange for him."

Paul shrugged uneasily. They continued on, tires skidding on the road's slick clay, past Basket Creek—an unexpected pang of anguish at the sight of it—and climbed until they reached the pullout above the old mill site.

"Let's walk down from here," Lazeroff said. The air smelled of lingering snow, and the ground beneath them was matted with dead leaves. Snow press had flattened the dead grass on the bench of land, exposing the rusted scraps and springs of metal. Jory headed straight for the edge of the embankment.

"The Flumes!" he shouted back with pride. "Fucking mael-strom." Paul caught up to him. The boulders where he'd seen Jory play were under constant assault from torrents of muddy water. The rapids of September, with their neat spiral shapes and subtle undertows and currents, had been replaced by an incomprehensible raging.

"Patterns are sure different," Paul said.

"There is no pattern." Jory took a step forward, his eyes never leaving the river.

Paul turned back to the constable. "So what are we looking for?"

"You tell me," Lazeroff said.

"Me?"

"You're the one who looks at all the maps and stuff."

Jory was in a trance, muttering to himself. Paul clapped him on the shoulder, startling him. "We'll drive up this summer. Maybe I can film you sessioning the Flumes." Jory's lip curled sharply in contempt. It was a stupid offer, Paul conceded, totally condescending, and he immediately felt old and lame. They returned to the field. He gestured toward the forest beside them. "Okay. So there's Dalton Creek. Caleb Ready's claim."

"His father's, actually. Purchased it in 1933," Lazeroff said. He'd obviously done his homework and was testing him for a bit of fun. But Paul was prepared.

"Caleb's father was killed at the end of the Second World War," he said. "Do I get a prize?"

"Nope. The Ready claim runs from the bottom of Dalton Creek over there"—Lazeroff pointed—"up past the road. And extends less than fifty metres to either side."

"Caleb made several offers for the mill site. Both the Wallace and Wentz families refused, of course."

"Why'd he want it so bad?" Jory asked. He stood on a corroded oil drum, balancing on one foot.

Lazeroff shrugged. "Dunno. Would have been a good place for a little cabin, you know, right beside his father's old claim. Maybe that was all."

"Maybe," Paul said. "Whatever the reason, he was furious when they said no. Stole half the crew and bullied their neighbours into selling their homes for half their worth."

"Probably wasn't the only reason he did what he did," Lazeroff said. "Even so, sentiment can be a pretty powerful motive."

"Why didn't he just buy the place after the mill shut down?" Jory asked.

"Actually," Lazeroff said, giving Paul a sly look, "there is one thing I haven't told you."

Paul thought a moment. "Hardy and Cyril still own the mill site. Damn. I'd always assumed this place reverted back to Crown land after the company went under."

"No—I tracked down a copy of the deed." The two men grinned at each other. They were like children dumping their bags of Halloween loot into a single pile on the floor. Paul regretted not bringing Elmer, who enjoyed more than they the way history could open up the world, renew and deepen it.

"Let's get to the creek." Lazeroff started off but was halted by the old Adanac stove. "I remember these. What a beaut." Paul brushed off the top and pried at a compartment for him.

"Jesus," Jory said. "This ain't the fuckin' *Antiques Roadshow*." He charged ahead into the woods. The forest was cold and damp, the thick canopy of second-growth cedar and hemlock starving the spongy, matted floor of sunlight. Black leaves littered pools of meltwater. The Immitoin became a hushed roar in the background, a susurration in the gloom.

Dalton Creek was not wide, no more than two metres across here on the bench of land, and narrower as it descended steeply through the trees, a series of falls and small pools. They were standing in black sand at the edge of the water, the same dark substrate among the pebbles, the banks craggy with exposed rock. This was where Caleb's father, and then Caleb, had worked this streambed, sifting through the black magnetite, deeply hypnotized by the symphonic voice of the creek. Each with his different hopes and expectations, his stubbornness and wilful impracticality.

Lazeroff grunted. "Maybe we're starting too low. I assumed Caleb accessed the creek from the mill site, but why not from the road above?"

"He'd cut through the mill site to spite Hardy," Paul said.

"Sure, but what about his ATV? And that compressor? He didn't take them through here. I'll bet he had access somewhere farther up. A skid trail off the main road, maybe."

"But we're also getting farther from wherever he fell in," Paul said. Lazeroff agreed, but they continued upstream.

Jory had crossed the creek above them, hopping from stone to stone. "There's something there," he called, pointing. "Like a barrel."

They found a semicircle of old staves jammed into the creek bottom. "A catch-basin," Lazeroff said. He brushed leaves from the surface. "It's lined with plastic. Look." Black PVC piping snaked from the basin and through the forest. The young man laughed and then patted the constable on the back jokingly. "Looks like you missed one last year," he said.

"Missed what?" Paul said.

"A grow op," Lazeroff grunted. The piping led them through a pale copse of snags and deadfall until they reached the bottom corner of a regenerating clear-cut that sloped gradually uphill, ringed by thick stands of juvenile pine and larch. A stack of plastic buckets was hidden beneath a yew, and nothing but empty holes and a crude system of pipes remained where marijuana plants had grown in rows.

"Someone had to work the valves, check the lines," Lazeroff said.

"Plus fertilize, pest control." Jory grinned as the constable glared at him. "C'mon, everyone knows how this shit works."

"Some more than others, apparently." Lazeroff looked around. "Pretty good harvest."

Jory shrugged. "Maybe eighty grand worth."

"That's about right," Lazeroff agreed. "Certainly not the biggest I've seen. Doesn't tell us anything about Caleb, though, unless you think he was the one growing."

"Definitely not him," Paul said, and Lazeroff nodded in agreement. "But what if it's not a coincidence? Maybe someone planted their crop here as a type of joke, an irony. A kind of, I don't know, poetic justice," he argued. "Why grow pot this far up the Immitoin, where the season's short and the soil bad—except to draw water and make a profit on Caleb's claim? Or maybe scare him off, or bait him into a fight."

Jory interrupted. "That's a pretty crappy revenge tactic."

"Not revenge," said Lazeroff. "A territorial thing. A principle. I can guess who you're thinking of," he said to Paul.

"Gina told me she thought Billy had a grow op in the woods. She didn't know where."

Jory was still shaking his head, lips pursed in ridicule. "How about the simple answer, boys? This Caleb dude—assuming *he's* not the grower—follows the pipeline, stumbles on some biker gang tending their patch, and they turf him in the river."

"Okay. But why bother taking his car to Basket Creek?" asked Lazeroff.

"Beats the piss out of me." Jory yawned irritably. "Same reason Billy Wentz would?"

Leaving the two of them to banter, Paul wandered through the plantation. Cyril and Billy, Hardy and Caleb: four men trying to hang on to their part of the valley's history. Even Caleb, who helped destroy much of that history. Growing pot, logging, fishing, prospecting—each was a means of staying connected to their fathers' different legacies, no different from the customs and habits Elsie and his other participants cultivated to maintain their roots in the land below the reservoir. The bit of money they pulled from the water and soil hardly mattered, was simply a way to keep score, to lend flesh to the ritual of memory.

~

They were above the mouth of Dalton Creek, where it tumbled from a shelf of rock down sheer granite banks treacherous with spray and mist. Jory explored along the Immitoin, working his way downstream. Paul and Lazeroff searched the pools, nooks, and quieter spots where Caleb might have rested or stashed a tool.

"I found something," Lazeroff said uncertainly. "By the stump here." He handed Paul a dented pan stained green. "Probably not his. Too old."

Paul turned it in his hands. "His father's, maybe."

"Maybe. Check out that conk," Lazeroff said. The orange fungus extended like an autumn-coloured clamshell from the trunk of a fallen tree. He made a half-hearted attempt to pry it loose with a jackknife.

"Let's say that was Billy and Cyril's grow op up above," Paul said. "Do you think they would drive here every few days?"

"They'd have to."

"Unless they had help. Someone to look after things."

"Hardy, you mean."

"Exactly."

"*If* the grow op belonged to the Wentzes," Lazeroff said. "You think Hardy ran into Caleb at the plantation or walking through the mill site. Or here. And something happened."

"Yes. Except—why phone the police about the body?" Paul said.

"Trying to look innocent. Guilty people make that mistake all the time." Lazeroff gave up on the conk, put his knife away. "Mind you, when we fished Caleb out—he did not enjoy seeing that, I'll tell you. Didn't strike me as a performance."

"Hey!" The shout was manic and alarming. Jory stood at the

beach where'd he'd launched his kayak last fall, where the grey boulders stacked together across the width of the Immitoin to create the Flumes. He was pointing urgently at the largest stone in the middle of the river.

"What?" Lazeroff boomed impatiently.

"Marks! Words!" Jory's voice was faint because he'd already leaped from the shore onto the first rock, his feet sliding a bit before gripping. Paul hadn't noticed before how lousy Jory's shoes were, a ratty pair of sneakers. A small hesitation, then Jory jumped onto the next boulder, then the one after that.

"What the good goddamn," Lazeroff said.

Paul would never know if Jory really believed he'd seen something on the rock. He would remember only smooth granite faces polished by centuries of water and scoured by sand, maybe a few divots and ledges that could possibly be mistaken as petroglyphs or engraved intials. More likely Jory had needed an excuse to appear useful, in order to do something that had no reason or purpose, a thrill. Tramping around in the woods had been a bad idea: the boredom and quiet just amplified Jory's bleak thoughts.

Maybe another reason: Jory loved the Flumes. Paul remembered the day he first met him, when the young man had hidden his fear, entered the rapids, and become inseparable from them.

When he saw one of Jory's feet slip, Paul had already crossed Dalton Creek and was running. A fallen tree blocked his path and, still in motion, without thought, Paul placed his hands and vaulted over the deadfall, his legs tucked close to his body. He bungled the vault and crashed full-speed onto the forest floor, but then tumbled forward and used the momentum to regain his feet and stop his slide toward the river below—hours of practice not quite forgotten. His feet lightly touched fallen trees, found the sturdy mounds of earth between the jumbles of slash and brush. A springy-looking piece of deadfall bent under his weight and snapped as it catapulted him forward. He fell again, felt the crisp brightness of a grazed forehead, and kept sprinting. Fired with adrenalin, he was stupidly exhilarated.

Paul reached the edge of the Flumes, and from the corner of his eye saw Lazeroff labouring through the woods behind him. Jory had fallen between two boulders and was trying to use his back and legs to brace himself. Without hesitation, Paul jumped onto the first rock, landed on all fours, and then sprang onto the next.

He slid, hugged the top, and steadied his feet. The river exploded into sound—he'd only heard his own breath before—a smashing of water against rock, against itself. Hissing, slapping spray, deep, gurgling notes of the undertow beneath. The world around him was violently reduced to the stone against his face, the water a quicksilver turmoil at the periphery of his vision. The river churned in disorienting, vertiginous patterns of light and shadow, and all that parkour stuff—his instinct and training, the altruism and courage supposedly at the root of the sport—abandoned him. He couldn't budge or he would be swept away.

His very first climb at the gym with Christine, he'd nearly reached the top. Then, mid-stretch, he couldn't find the next hold. All his weight rested on the toes of his shaking left foot and a desperately clenched fist. Just breathe, Christine had called up to him. Relax your muscles. He was perfectly safe, held by his harness, the rope, and belaying devices. She had him. And still, terror had pinned him to the wall until his leg muscles trembled and seized and finally gave out. Christine lowered him and he'd descended into embarrassment, the harness tugging and bunching at his crotch.

His lips brushing the granite, he sobbed out a laugh. What a fucking completely unhelpful memory.

Lazeroff called from the riverbank, a hundred miles away.

Another voice, higher pitched, cut through the roar and hiss ahead of him, once, and then again. Paul shouted back, a word-less yell, and slowly, as though he were trying to pull himself out of a dark, sucking vacuum, inched onto the top of the boulder. His cheek against the cold rock, he blindly stretched a leg out over the torrent in the narrow channel between stones. Nothing but moist air, too wet, water cascading over his boot. The inside of his thigh strained and stretched as he lifted his leg higher. Finally the side of his foot hit a ledge and held.

He raised himself up—the trees and river lurched back into focus, the nauseating expanse of the sky threatened to topple him—and pivoted his other foot until he faced the other boulder in a split-legged crouch, suspended over the river. He transferred his weight to the leading leg and pushed off with the other. Both knees smacked against rock as he landed face and chest first. He gripped the side of the boulder with his thighs, blood in his mouth. Water surged against his boots as he scooted along the boulder's ridge, dizzy and trembling.

On the downstream side of the rock, a tiny eddy curled away from the rage of the main current and calmed, until each pebble beneath the surface was clear and vivid. His eyes clung to that one strangely tranquil spot as he forced himself onward. A shallow, limpid, yet mysterious place—it hid its essence in plain sight.

He reached the edge and blindly swung his arm where he'd seen Jory slip between the rocks. His hand grabbed at air. He raised himself up and peered over. Only endless water funnelling darkly through the breach. Nothing in the rapids downstream, nothing in the logs and sticks piled against the upstream side. It had all been a trick, a joke played out of boredom and anger, revenge for every time he'd listened under the stairs—there was no way Jory had really been here.

8

The two of them returned to the Immitoin the next morning. Gina was staying with Sonya. Jory's father was somewhere along the river with the Search and Rescue team, while his mother waited in Bishop, where police and volunteers coordinated the search effort from the old fire hall. A helicopter thudded overhead as he and Lazeroff drove.

"You sleep any?" Lazeroff asked. Travel mugs rattled in the plastic holders, the fire hall coffee half finished and forgotten.

Paul took a while answering. "No." Their faces mirrored each other, sallow and bruised. A chill had dogged him all night. Everything outside the vehicle floated, a cold, sickly sort of beauty. They drove a police suv—this time, the logging trucks pulled over for them. Cars and trucks were parked along the side of the road, volunteers combing the river. Someone radioed: "Cliff, we're here. You want us to wait?"

Lazeroff slowly picked up the receiver. "Go ahead and start. We're right behind you."

At the top of Hardy's driveway were two police cars, a Search and Rescue truck, and a gathering of men. The odds of finding Jory there were good, but with the river so high and wild right now, not a sure thing. The body could still be tumbling in the Flumes, or caught on a sweeper near Basket Creek. Maybe he'd drifted past already.

A muffled crack came from outside. Three volunteers hid

behind one of the cars. A cop ran up the driveway, head low. Lazeroff jerked the vehicle halfway into the ditch and jumped out. Paul followed, staggering as the road's soft shoulder crumbled under his feet. The cop—it was the young guy from last autumn, Davis—had his gun drawn.

"He's shooting at us," he said, astonished.

"Sure it wasn't for himself?" Lazeroff asked.

"The ricochet whistled past me."

"He's frightened."

"Barry's behind the woodshed."

"Tell him not to fire." They ducked and loped to where the volunteers were huddled.

"He was yelling before he shot," one of the men said eagerly. "Couldn't make it out."

Another added, "Kai. That's what he said."

"What the hell does that mean," Lazeroff muttered.

"Yelled it a bunch of times. Sounded like a crow."

"I'm going down there." Lazeroff stood. His hands were empty, his gun holstered. Paul sat on the ground, his head near the wheel well, breathing in the smell of dried mud and warm rubber. "Hardy," he heard Lazeroff call. The men were silent, straining to listen. He rubbed his eyes. Thrushes called their single, reedy note back and forth and wrens grated and buzzed in the underbrush. Someone next to him lit a cigarette, the sharp flick of the lighter close to Paul's ear. Wisps of acrid smoke, a raven calling from across the river.

"We're good," Davis was saying. Paul struggled to his feet, leaning against the car door. He heard boots scuffling on gravel, a struggle. Lazeroff and the third cop had Hardy in cuffs and were dragging him by his arms while he pulled and strained toward his house. He threw his head back and howled, snuffled for breath, and howled again. The old man was shockingly thin and dirty, his eyes lost within dark sockets, a filthy beard. He saw Paul and suddenly pulled toward him. The cops yanked him back, and he howled one final time as they shoved him in the back of Davis's cruiser.

Lazeroff was covered in sweat as he turned to the crowd of volunteers. "Okay. Sounds like the body was here. Early this morning." Lazeroff hesitated. "Hardy pushed it back into the current."

A collective gasp—the sound grated on Paul's nerves. He felt suddenly and irrationally protective of Hardy. "Why the hell would he do that?" a volunteer asked indignantly.

Lazeroff rubbed his forehead angrily. "How would I know? Might as well radio up to the Flumes, tell them to call it off. Everyone get down to Spry Creek or Bishop."

Davis and the third cop went to drive Hardy into town. "Get him fed," Lazeroff told them. He walked with Paul down the driveway. "The place looks like hell inside," he said quietly. "Not a crumb to eat."

They checked his truck and found the battery dead and a flat tire that had been chewed by rodents or porcupines, probably during that last cold snap before spring.

"He's never had trouble getting through the winter before," Lazeroff said.

No more food packages from the Wentzes. Elsie probably believed her bread and soups and roasted chickens were still being delivered. She would have said something to Gina otherwise. Maybe Hardy had lost his mind just enough that he didn't phone anyone for help, was rotting away in dementia. Paul remembered the old man's fear that morning, Billy's face when they passed each other on the road. Maybe they'd punished Hardy for speaking to Paul. Because Paul wouldn't stay out of people's lives, as Billy had warned him to do.

"He thought we were coming to arrest him. Kai—he was shouting that at me too." Lazeroff stopped at the front door and rubbed at his eyes. "Makes no sense."

Through the window, Paul could see old newspapers strewn on the kitchen table, a torn-open bag of millet or birdseed on the counter. Paul's stomach lurched, and he wrapped his arms tightly across his chest, shivering. It was like the sun couldn't reach him. "Kai's a name. I know who that is."

Lazeroff studied him for a moment, then shook his head. "Later," he said. "Tell me later. You look done for the day."

~

Two days later, they gave up on the river and lowered the reservoir. The simple act of opening the McCulloch Dam's floodgates was a massive exercise in engineering, hydrology, communication, and cooperation. It required the coordinated efforts of governments, scientists, and hydroelectric corporations from the Immitoin, Kettle, Columbia, and Kootenay Rivers, all the way down to Roosevelt Lake and the Grand Coulee Dam in the States. The Waneta, Hugh Keenleyside, Revelstoke, and Mica Dams closed most of their gates and let their reservoirs fill, as did the Duncan, Brilliant, and both Bonnington Falls Dams on the Kootenay River. Below these dams, biologists and their technicians salvaged rainbow trout eggs from redds suddenly left high and dry. They filled plastic laundry baskets with gravel and buried the eggs inside, then lowered the surrogate nests into deeper waters. All of this done to maintain the balance of the Columbia River system and its floodplains, while the Immitoin poured itself through the McCulloch Dam.

The drawdown lasted two days. Finally, a search team found Jory among the old wharf pilings near Bishop. Paul and Lazeroff were flying over the reservoir at the time, covering the opposite side. Lazeroff made the pilot take them over Lambert—a gift to Paul, who wouldn't have thought to ask, his mind in a bleak, swirling fog. The pilot tilted the helicopter to give him the best possible view as they hovered over a handful of summer cottages built on high ground. Below the high water mark, preserved in a skeletal state and exposed now by the drawdown, lay the crumbled foundations of houses, the traces of concrete walls where the packing sheds had stood, rusted scraps of tin roofing, the black stubs of old fence posts and cut trees. Near the cottages, scattered and abandoned among stands of fir and pine, stood the collapsed remnants of split-rail fencing, overgrown garden plots, and hay sheds, and scattered rows of what were unmistakably fruit trees, ancient and mossy and being swallowed by the natural forest.

Paul, because of the effort being made on his behalf, tried desperately to take in the sight of the drowned village, as if he could grasp all that the remains of Lambert signified in a brief glance. Finally, Lazeroff tapped the pilot on the shoulder and they banked north. A moment later someone radioed to say Jory's body had been recovered. The static in the headphones was bad—for a moment, he thought they'd said "restored."

~

There was a multitude of polite requests and suggestions as to where Jory's ashes should be scattered. His parents, both stunned and touched by Shellycoat's apparent affection for their son, acquiesced to the snowboarders, the kayakers, and the co-owners of Jory's shop. His father went to his potter's wheel and kiln, fired a series of small clay urns, and divided the ashes. The managers of the ski hill reserved an urn for a memorial at the lodge, while his friends planned trips to his favourite backcountry runs, the ridges and peaks where he'd gained his small piece of fame. The remaining urns were for Jory's family and Sonya.

Paul and Gina had been taking care of her, as had Jory's parents, bringing food and staying with her in the apartment. She was flying out east to stay with her own parents for a while. The morning before she left, Paul went upstairs and found her sitting on the couch, a map of the Immitoin Valley spread on the coffee table. "When will you be back?" Paul asked.

"A month or so." She didn't look up from the map, and her dull hair hung in front of her eyes. "I got accepted," she mumbled. "University of Toronto."

"Well. Congrats." He hadn't known she'd applied for university. Had she told Jory?

"But I'll be here for most of the summer," she added.

"I'm glad."

She rubbed at her face with her sleeve. "We were going to break up."

"I know." A clay urn, he suddenly noticed, was in her lap, and despite all the help friends and family had given her, the apartment was a mess of dirty dishes and towels heaped on counters. "Can I help with anything? Can you make rent?"

She didn't need money, but there was a place she wanted to go in July when she came back. She pointed to the map. You followed the Immitoin way past Basket Creek and the Flumes to where the logging road ended. A trail led to alpine meadows and a series of small lakes. "He took me hiking there—it was like our first date." She asked if Paul and Gina would take her there to scatter her portion of the ashes.

She was bent into herself, crying now. He awkwardly stretched his arm over the coffee table and squeezed her shoulder, thinking the right thing would be to go sit next to her, offer comfort, but his memories of the winter held him back. It was strange to think, but he'd needed to need her. Despite it being pointless and disturbing and just plain misguided, desire had been a way of riding out his past until it smoothed into the present. They'd come together, he and Jory and Sonya, at a temporary but necessary place where Paul could live his wrong-headedness for a while and enjoy these unlikely friendships before they drifted apart. In two or three years, he and Sonya would hardly know each other, and that was the way of things.

~

The fuggy, fried-egg smell in the A&W was strangely comforting. Elmer was stirring a packet of cane sugar into his tea, managing not to look out of place, while Lazeroff dutifully picked away at his breakfast sandwich. The constable had no particular love for the food, Paul realized. It was a prairie sort of loyalty (he didn't know why the prairies came to mind) to an atmosphere that had changed little since the seventies, that resisted contemporary gestures toward luxury and leisure, the foaminess of coffee shops, their vanilla and hazelnut frills. A loyalty to the old men in their denim jackets, their baseball caps advertising excavation services and chainsaws.

"You talk to any of these guys yet?" Lazeroff gestured at the other tables.

"I'll get to it," Paul said. "Our list is pretty big." Jory's death and the earlier town hall meeting had pushed his research into the public consciousness. Life had become busy, scarcely giving him time to think or grieve except in the quietest hours of the night. Strangers phoned to talk about the past, and Monashee Power had proposed that Paul, with Elmer's help, create a comprehensive website about the reservoir: the history of the communities and the dam, rare photos, video interviews with the displaced. If the funding came together, the contract could easily run a year or two in tandem with Paul's dissertation.

"They want me to interview Hardy again," he said. As far as he knew, the old man wasn't leaving the psych ward in Trail anytime soon.

"Who does?"

"Monashee."

"Jesus," Lazeroff said. "He's in no shape for that. Most days he still thinks it's 1965."

"Did Jory look anything like Kai Soules?" Elmer asked dubiously. "Same age, I suppose."

"There was enough resemblance, I think, to bring back

Hardy's shock at seeing Kai in the pool all those years ago," Lazeroff said.

"But he didn't see him," Paul said. "His father did—that's what he told me. I'd say it's the shock of killing Kai Soules."

That was how he figured it. He imagined Kai alone on the riverbank, downstream from the flumes, completely out of his element, timidly prodding each passing log as though it were a sleeping beast. Some of his friends have already gone over to Caleb Ready and Monashee Power, and the only reason he hasn't left yet is because he's scared to tell the Wallaces. He lives with them in Lambert, and at the bunkhouse downstream from the mill, and he's been under Hardy's wing the whole summer. Now that his parents have left for Kamloops, the Wallaces are the closest thing to family he has. So when Hardy charges over, rips the peavey from his hand, he figures it's nothing, he's just doing a lousy job again. All the foremen have rotten tempers, but they get over it quick. And then Hardy shoves him, hard. Kai topples backward off the bank into the water between logs.

Hardy thrusts the peavey like a man spearing a fish, metal striking bone. He forces Kai under, and pins him there until a cluster of felled timber sweeps over and takes the boy with the current. Maybe Cyril has been watching the whole time, and this will bind the two men even more strongly than the memory of Lambert and everything else they will lose.

Suppose it was true that Hardy was Marcus's son. Which was the greater tragedy, that Hardy knew, or that he didn't? Did he unwittingly murder his nephew out of frustration, a self-righteous rage at Kai and Arthur's betrayal? Or was it simply too terrible a wound for his mind to handle, to be abandoned by his own blood?

"Considering all the accidents that happened in those logging camps," Elmer said, "I doubt we'll ever know the absolute truth."

"Someone knows," Paul said. "Half the Dalton Creek crew could have witnessed his death. Maybe if we ask around at the Barber Chair."

"You've been in there," Elmer said. "Did you honestly get the sense those men would give up that kind of secret?"

"Or any secret, for that matter," he admitted. "Doesn't bode well for our project, does it?"

"Not to be a pessimist," said Lazeroff, "but even if you got to the bottom of the Kai mess, would it change anything for Hardy? I doubt it."

"He'll be home eventually, right?" Paul asked.

Lazeroff shrugged grimly.

Elmer changed the subject. "So what do you need us to bring?" he asked the constable.

"To the party, you mean?" Lazeroff's wife had made the invitation cards by hand, thick, soft paper with dried flowers and stamped with pastoral scenes and fish in faded blue ink. Very confusing, or maybe she had a strange sense of humour. "Depends if you're willing to eat *pyrahi, golupsti*—oh, and steak. Mostly it's steak and cake," Lazeroff said. "Bring more beer, how about."

"No retirement gifts?"

"Accepted in the form of fishing lures." Lazeroff smiled and, inexplicably, patted his belly. "Otherwise, please don't."

"And what happens after you ride into the sunset?" Paul asked.

"I'm going fishing, obviously. All goddamn summer."

"What about the grow op?"

"Someone will keep an eye on it, see if anyone returns. But it still won't prove any connection to Ready's death."

"They won't come back," Paul said. "The mill's open again, Billy doesn't need to take that risk."

Lazeroff's eyebrows raised, though his face remained tellingly blank.

"You know it was them."

"I don't *know*, otherwise—well, that's how these things go. They can drag out for years, so buckle up for the long ride or forget about it." Lazeroff paused to wipe his hands on a napkin and emphatically tossed it on the table. "And live your life in the meantime."

Two evenings ago, Paul had bumped into Billy in the grocery store. Billy's jacket was stained with chain oil, the cuffs of his jeans blackened by mud, and he swaggered as he pushed a cart filled with jugs of milk, white bread, and deli meat. He wore his layer of sawdust the way other men wore expensive watches. He glared at Paul with heavy eyelids, his jumpy rage tempered by fatigue and restored pride. Cocky too—Hardy was institutionalized, and he was still a free man. As he passed Paul, he said over his shoulder, "Hey, thanks for gettin' Shane to that dentist appointment."

Paul stopped, thinking for a moment he sounded genuine.

"Tell him his dad can't always be there because he has a real job. You know, unlike his mother and her deadbeat boyfriend."

"He's a smart kid," Paul said. "I think he gets it."

"Go fuck yourself." Billy grinned sourly and sauntered on. When he pushed Caleb into the river, Paul wanted to ask, did he do it for his father or himself? He could ask Hardy the same question about Kai. And he could have both stories dead wrong.

He stared at Lazeroff across the table. How could a person come this far, gain nothing, and then just carry on?

"You thought about Basket Creek?" the constable asked. "Tagging those trout?"

"Not for me this summer," Paul said. "Too busy."

His friend looked disappointed. "It's such a great set-up."

"It is," Paul said. "And I did get you a retirement gift, of sorts." He took out Tanner's business card and handed it to Lazeroff. "I told him you're the perfect man for the job. Apparently, you're allowed to bring your wife. Improved working conditions, he calls it."

9

After the Canada Day weekend, the Yellow Pine Creek campground was still three-quarters full. The celebrations in Shellycoat had fetched enough income for Gina to take time off before driving the catering truck to a music festival outside Nakusp, so they'd reserved a site in the shady inner loop of the campground, a short walk to the beach and playground. Paul and Gina had a tent to themselves and made beds for Shane and Elsie inside Gina's camper. Elsie set the propane grill on the picnic table and unpacked the ice coolers. The sound of children echoed through the woods, while RVs slowly circled the loop looking for empty sites.

On their way down to the beach, Shane pointed at the saskatoons that towered over the path. "See? Toiletberries." But he'd already outgrown his own joke. Paul reached up and plucked a few ripe ones, gave some to the boy, and ate the rest. A grainy texture, the sun's warmth trapped in the juice. They went past the playground, where the grassy meadow— a minefield of groundhog holes—sloped down to the water. The beach was a narrow strip of gravel and sandy patches. The water was brutally cold—Paul tested it with his toe and retreated back to his lawn chair—but Shane waded up to his hips while he worked a pair of goggles over his face. He dipped his head under, looking for minnows, shyly edging their way toward the other children.

Motorboats crisscrossed the reservoir, towing teenagers on inner tubes and wakeboards. Closer to shore, a few people in canoes and sea kayaks slipped past, looking for solitary beaches. "What time is Sonya coming tomorrow?" Elsie asked.

"Around nine." A line of sweat trickled down Paul's belly.

"Will you be all right with Shane, Mom?" Gina asked.

"Of course."

Shane emerged from the water, shivering and looking wistfully at the swings and spiral slides. Gina wrapped a towel around him and walked him to the playground, leaving Paul and Elsie to sunbathe in their chairs. Paul twisted around to look at the field. There were clues to what this place had once been: by the playground where Shane now dangled upside down on the monkey bars, a lone hawthorn stood near a very old apple tree, spaced evenly between two others that had died long ago. They were inconspicuous, their grey bark fading into the field, overshadowed by the pines and tangled hedges of wild rose and thimbleberry.

A difficult task, to imagine the soil that would have covered this loose, lacustrine stone, to mentally restack the layers of dark, chernozemic dirt, replant the bunchgrasses and the plowed earth. To superimpose fences, fallow pastures, horse paddocks over the glassy water, or replace the flat field with rows of *Robinia pseudocacia* that the tree farmers grew to burn in the steamships. Or the bulrushes and willows and muskrat dens, the smell of an evening on a verdant shore. Most difficult of all, to resurrect a farmer, or a war widow, or a family. Difficult to do so without presumption, without romanticizing sorrow and loss, without burying the present under a dredged-up past. There was no denying the solidity of what was before him now, the families on the beach, the children in the playground. No denying the goodness in these ill-gotten things.

Elise would remember this place, a farm not too far from her childhood home. Instead he asked, "Was it true—that you didn't know Caleb had died until I told you?"

She was sipping a beer, seemingly fixated on the hills across the reservoir. Hardy's descent into squalor and madness had devastated her, he knew, and the discovery of his relation to the Soules must have been equally disorienting. When she spoke, it was with an almost cheerful finality. "When I heard that he'd washed up at Hardy's, I just assumed—well, I thought it best to say nothing."

Paul's back peeled wetly from the chair as he stood. How naive he'd been. Everyone he'd interviewed had known. It was like a signal had gone out the moment Caleb's waterlogged corpse was hauled onto shore. He stepped into the water, shuddering, forced himself deeper until his shorts were wet to the hips, then dove. It was clear enough underwater that he could open his eyes and see tufts of sedges stretching away into a green, impressionist haze. The bull trout would be preparing now to travel up the Immitoin, gathering at the head of the lake, where Jory's body had come to rest.

The thought sent him kicking to the surface. He spat, stood rubbing the water from his eyes, lifted his face to the sun. When he was warm enough, he hesitated a moment, then dove again. He gave up his game of re-envisioning the vanished farm, the drowned valley, and, for the afternoon at least, surrendered to his own ignorance, his outsiderness. Today, the reservoir was just a lake, and this was just a beach, just water.

~

Night in their tent. The sound of sparks popping from neighbouring campfires, the muffled slam of an RV door. The air had cooled, still warm enough to throw open their sleeping bags and spread them across the width of the foam mats. Gina's hips were propped up with pillows—a more accommodating angle, the doctor's suggestion—and he moved slowly and quietly inside her while their feet scrabbled for grip against the nylon bags.

Sex would never feel the way it once had. It would not overwhelm or promise transcendence, only a brief, awkward flight, a blunted orgasm. Maybe that was true for all men as they aged—every pleasure yielded a slight aftertaste of mortality. He had to stop being angry about it, that was all. He had to give way to humility, to accept that he was stripped down to nothing and had no high-wire act, only a flawed performance to offer. His body was a living ledger of successes and failures that would never balance but keep him staggering along with a knocked-about sense of what was normal.

He woke at the first faint light to a strange sound outside, a single *voom*, then another one. It took a few moments to puzzle it out: a nighthawk diving to declare its territory. An owl called, then the dawn chorus began, a swelling of robin song, sparrow chatter. Gina breathed softly beside him, radiating warmth.

He'd dreamt that he was wading down the middle of the Immitoin with his rubber chest waders, scanning beneath the surface with Jory's homemade fish scope. Immense schools of bull trout fought their way upstream, brushing past his legs, ramming their toothy maws against the scope. Through the gaps between shimmering, haloed flesh, he glimpsed the body of a faceless young man tumbling downstream, ragdolling off boulders—he realized he'd been chasing after this body. But he would lift his gaze from the scope, and the dream would change, the riverbanks replaced by Granville Street shops or a narrow brick alley in Skinnskatteberg or, completely different, his living room, a bed, a small café full of noise and people and wooden chairs. And as he wandered through each new scene—talking with a friend, studying, or lovemaking—he could still feel the loneliness of the pursuit continuing. Eventually he would remember to look through the scope and he'd be beneath the surface again, to see a flash of jeans and sneakers slip into the river's darkness.

Sonya would soon wake in Shellycoat, in her lonely apartment. She would bring Jory's ashes to the park, and then Gina, Paul, and Sonya would drive upriver, past Bishop, past Hardy's cabin and the camp at Basket Creek, until they were beyond all the landmarks he knew. They would go, ascending, until the Immitoin fractured into smaller, steeper tributaries and impassable waterfalls, unbraided itself into creeks and rivulets that coursed through the alpine meadows, spilled from small glacial lakes or seeped out of the earth and between stones. To where the river both disappeared and began.

Acknowledgments

First, thanks to Ruth Linka and the rest of the Brindle & Glass family for taking a chance on the book, and for their collaborative spirit. And to John Gould, who took on the task of editing my manuscript with his unflagging cheer, kind advice, and keen eye.

Funding support from the Social Sciences and Humanities Research Council of Canada allowed me to undertake the necessary research, and gave me the time to draft the first half of the novel.

Small portions of Part One have been modified from the original version of "Valerian Tea," published in the *Malahat Review* (Issue #152, 2005). On that note, a warm thanks to everyone at the *Malahat Review*—particularly John Barton, Rhonda Batchelor, Susan Sanford Blades, and the editorial board—for the chance to be immersed in fine Canadian writing.

Though many of the events involving hydro dams and displacement mentioned in the novel are real, I've often taken liberties with the facts, as well as the geography of certain places. Any errors or inaccuracies are mine alone. The Arrow Lakes Historical Society provided literature—such as J.W. Wilson's remarkable *People in the Way*—air photos and archival interviews that lent perspective on the voice and landscape of displacement. The Columbia Basin Trust and the librarians at Selkirk College pointed me toward some useful literature and films on the subject of relocation.

Among the dozens of articles and papers I read while researching prostate cancer, I was especially struck by Denise Ryan's 2010 article on prostate removal surgery and sex, which included remarkably brave and candid conversations with cancer survivors and their wives. The previous winter, Stephen Hume wrote an intimate and honest account of his own experience with prostate surgery.

Walter Volovsek shared advice and his extensive historical knowledge. He also hired my friends and me to help build hiking trails along the Kootenay River many years ago, an experience that profoundly influenced my writing. Jack Hodgins provided advice and wisdom during the early stages of the book. John Gould, Brian Hendricks, Tim Lilburn, David Leach, Lynne van Luven, Lorna Jackson, and Bill Gaston offered mentorship, inspiration, and acts of friendship during the last several years.

Finally, undying love and gratitude to my wife, Alana, who has given me a rich life outside of writing and whose patience, faith, and sense of humour keep me going even in the leanest of times. And to our friends and families for their support and love.

AARON SHEPARD has written award-winning short fiction and has been published in a number of Canadian literary journals, including the *Fiddlehead* and *PRISM International*. His personal essay "Edge of the Herd" appears in the anthology *Nobody's Father: Life Without Kids*. He is a graduate of the University of Victoria's MFA in Creative Writing program, and has served on the *Malahat Review*'s fiction board. He is an avid outdoorsman, enjoying hiking, camping, birdwatching, and cross-country skiing in his spare time. *When is a Man* is his debut novel. Visit aaronshepard.ca.